BROKEN BEAST

CRYSTAL KASWELL

Copyright

Chapter One

ADAM

"I'm sorry, Mr. Pierce. I dug into every pocket of this asshole's life. And there's nothing I can use. Not officially."

"Unofficially?"

"He has a vulnerability. A woman." He shows off an image on his cell.

A woman holding a sheer sheet to her chest.

Not one of Neil's grainy, long angle photos.

The work of an artist.

Black and white.

Soft lighting.

Beautiful composition.

He scrolls to the next.

The same woman, standing at the window, in the glow of the morning sun.

Her hair swept over her shoulder.

Her head falling to one side.

Her bare back on display.

"She's hot, huh?" He chuckles, pleased with himself. "And even better from the front."

My stomach churns. I'm overcome with the urge to protect her. It's not like me.

After what happened with Bash, I gave up on protecting anyone.

"She goes by Beauty," he continues. "Broken Beauty, technically. There's plenty available publicly, but I can dig if you want more." He raises a brow. "You like her, huh?"

"She's talented."

"I'll say." He chuckles. "She must have a hundred self-portraits on her site. More on social media. She's got the followers to match too. A few hundred thousand on Instagram. Two, three times that on her site."

I pull up her website.

There it is, a picture of her standing in front of a mirror, bathed in soft white light.

The image is well-composed.

The lighting is perfect.

And she's gorgeous.

An unfamiliar sensation overtakes me—desire.

I want her.

I haven't wanted anyone in months, but I want her so badly I can taste it.

"How does she know Fitzgerald?" Is he a fan? Or is there more?

"He's obsessed with her. Shows up at the gallery where she works once a week to buy a new piece. Just to talk to her. Doesn't let on that he's seen her naked."

Mostly naked, but what's the difference?

"He hasn't crossed the line, but it's only a matter of time. I can put eyes on him. Set up a honey trap. Who knows? Maybe she's game to participate for the right price."

"No." It's not enough to put a dent in his marriage, career, image. I need to do better. "I have another idea."

A divorce will destroy his finances.
But a marriage?
That will destroy *him*.

Chapter Two

DANIELLE

People say money doesn't buy happiness, but that's bullshit.

Rich people get whatever they want.

The second they hear no, they add another zero to their offer, and voila: the world is their oyster.

Here I am, sitting in the back of a black town car, two hours into a drive to a secluded mansion, babysitting a framed photograph.

It's not even an original painting.

It's a print.

But no, Adam Pierce can't stop by the gallery himself. He can't send an assistant (and a guy with this kind of cash is bound to have at least one assistant).

He asked the gallery to hand deliver the photo.

And since the owner can't be bothered with such a trivial task, he sent me.

His pretty, underpaid assistant.

Emphasis on pretty.

Wear a short skirt, Danielle. Guys like girls with gams like yours.

Okay, maybe my boss didn't say gams. Maybe I added

that. Maybe, in my head, my asshole boss sounds like an old-timey journalist.

Or one of those film noir detectives who loses everything to a dangerous woman with a great pair of gams.

Those movies are gorgeous. The black-and-white photography, the lingering close-ups, the cunning woman who destroys the man who underestimates her.

If only.

I close my eyes. Rest my head against the cool glass.

I'm a born and bred New Yorker. I'm not used to long drives. Especially long drives in luxurious automobiles.

Courtesy of Adam Pierce. Not that I'm complaining. As much as I want to find fault with the reclusive billionaire, he paid handsomely.

A thousand dollars for home delivery.

And all to the courier.

He insisted.

Did he know a pretty girl in a short skirt would accompany his new art?

Or is he the kind of guy who takes care of the help?

The car turns onto a quiet street. For a mile, we're surrounded by woods, then a clearing, a rocky beach, a winding driveway.

A mansion straight out of an old movie.

Three stories, stone walls, gargoyles perched on the edge of the steep roof.

Hidden behind overgrown evergreens and a wrought iron gate.

An actual gate made of actual iron.

Did I fall asleep and wake up in a fairy tale?

What the hell?

After we park in the massive driveway, the driver helps me out of the car, opens the trunk, smiles as I remove the framed photograph.

We walk through the equally grand backyard—outdoor pool, enclosed pool, solarium, and all cliffside—then through the French doors, into the ballroom.

An actual ballroom, with a hardwood floor, high ceilings, crystal chandeliers. I have to stop myself from staring. I'm not here to contemplate the eccentricities of the rich.

I'm here to hang this photo and collect my commission.

I hold the frame carefully as we walk up the winding staircase and down the long hallway. All the way to a massive oak door.

The driver knocks. "Mr. Pierce. Your photograph is here."

Mr. Pierce grumbles. Annoyed by the interruption, no doubt. Rich men are used to the world revolving around them.

"The woman from the gallery came a long way," the driver says.

He pauses for a moment, then he calls, "Send her in."

The driver opens the door.

I take a deep breath and step into the office.

It's huge. Bigger than my apartment. Hardwood floors. Bookshelves filled with old paperbacks.

Dark curtains. They block the bright white sky. Cast a tall man in shadow.

He pulls his hands from his pockets and steps forward.

Light falls over his short, dark hair.

His deep blue eyes.

The scars on his forehead, cheeks, chin.

Jagged red lines covering the left side of his face. Marring his Disney Prince looks, but beautiful in their imperfection.

And I'm staring.

I shouldn't be staring.

"I'm Danielle Bellamy." I hold up the frame in lieu of offering my hand. "You must be Mr. Pierce."

His deep blue eyes fix on me.

I swallow hard. Force an awkward smile. "Would you like me to hang the photo?" There isn't enough free wall space in the office, but we can make do if we push the bookshelves apart. "Or I can leave it and you can hang it later. It's my favorite. I'd love to give her a good home."

"Do you say that to all the collectors?"

Is he a collector? The walls in the house are bare. "Only when I mean it."

"Where would you put it? If it was yours?"

My stomach flutters. Usually, I have no trouble discussing art. Even exceptionally erotic art. Even with men who do nothing to hide their carnal interests.

Adam Pierce is different.

Intense.

Overwhelming.

Extremely attractive.

Even with the scars. Or maybe because of them. My fingers itch to trace every line.

I want to know exactly what happened. Where he got them. How he feels about them.

Can I take your picture? Please.

Shit. I'm still staring.

And he's staring back with a perfect poker face, his deep blue eyes boring into my soul.

What are we talking about?

The photo.

I take a deep breath. Let out a slow exhale. "In my apartment? Or in this house?"

"Here."

"I haven't seen the house. Is this your office?"

He nods.

"If it were mine, right here." I motion to the wall behind me. "I'd open the curtains, let light fall over her, stare all day." I unwrap the frame and hold it high.

There she is, *The Voyeur.*

A woman, standing in front of a window, bathed in soft light, completely naked.

Her long, slim body on display.

Only she's turned to the camera with a coy expression, as if she's watching back.

Is she the voyeur? Or is it the photographer?

The viewer?

Society?

The dichotomies are fascinating.

"Would you get anything done?" he asks.

"That's a small price to pay."

His eyes flit to the photo. "If I keep the curtains down?"

"Then somewhere with natural light. A bedroom maybe."

"A bedroom?" He steps out from behind the desk. He moves closer. Closer. Until he's three feet away. "What do you think I'm going to do as I stare?"

My blush deepens. "You wouldn't be the first."

"No?"

"No." Did I just give him permission to fuck himself to the photo? My boss is going to kill me.

"Would you?"

My cheeks flush. "Art is supposed to inspire."

"True." He half-smiles.

I think. It's hard to read him. "And the photographer was intentional. Have you seen the others in the set?"

"No."

"They're more explicit. I can show you, but—" I tap the frame.

He nods *of course* and leads me down a hallway, to a room at the front of the house.

It's a beautiful bedroom. Clean white walls, hardwood floors, sheer curtains, silk sheets.

Everything cast in the light of the bleak winter sky.

There. The wall perpendicular to the windows. Enough light to show off the photo. Not enough to fade. "Here." I point to the spot in the middle of the wall.

"Are you sure?"

"Positive. But only if someone stays regularly. It would be a shame to hide her."

His eyes meet mine. "It would."

"And there's room for the rest too." I pull the pamphlet from my purse and offer it to Adam.

His eyes flit to the portraits on display. The one in my hands. Then the two on the handout.

The Exhibitionist, the same model leaning against the window, her head thrown back, her hand between her legs.

And *The Act*. The woman, her hand between her legs, her eyes on her reflection.

"Why is *The Voyeur* your favorite?" he asks.

"The photographer turns our expectations around. The model isn't just a pretty figure. She's looking back at us."

"And getting off on it." His eyes fix on the photo of *The Act*. He's interested.

As a collector?

As a man?

As a guy who wants to fuck the pretty girl with gorgeous gams?

I can't read Adam the way I can read most customers. Usually, I know if I need to flirt or fawn or focus on composition.

I have no idea what he wants.

10

So I tell him the truth. "At a glance, *The Voyeur* is another photo of a naked woman. But the model isn't there for the viewer. She's there for her own pleasure."

"She's fucking herself."

My blush deepens. "Simulating it."

"You'd hang this on your wall?"

"If I could afford it." They go for more than I make in six months. "I'd put them in my bedroom. So they were mine."

He studies me carefully. He's looking for something. I don't know what it is, but he must find it, because he nods. "My handyman could use your help in positioning this, but I imagine you have to get back to the city."

"Yes." I'm tempted to stay, to see her in action, but I promised Remy we'd watch his favorite show, and I'm already going to be late. "My brother is waiting."

"Louis can drop you at home."

I consider saying no, so this strange man doesn't know my address, but the offer is too tempting. "That's generous. Thank you."

"I can send you a photo." He motions to the wall. "Once I settle on a placement."

He's asking to contact me again.

If it was anyone else, I'd say yes, but I'm already picturing Adam ordering me out of my clothes.

Backing me into the wall.

Sliding his hand between my legs and growling dirty demands.

I can't fuck a customer.

I certainly can't fuck a strange man who lives in a Gothic castle of a mansion.

But I can't turn down the chance to see my favorite photo in action either.

"I'd appreciate that." I pull a business card from my purse.

His fingers brush mine as he takes it. "Thank you, Danielle."

"My pleasure."

He walks me downstairs, to the company of the driver, then he disappears. Back to his office. Or maybe to the bedroom to fuck himself to the photo.

I use the bathroom next to the kitchen. Find coffee, bottled water, and a wrapped bag of snacks waiting on the counter. Fancy snacks. A ten-dollar bar of chocolate. A bag of artisan kettle corn. Salted hazelnuts.

It's good coffee and better chocolate. I don't question. I follow the driver to the town car, don my headphones, escape with my favorite seventies singer-songwriter.

It doesn't hit me until I'm four blocks from my apartment.

I know Adam.

Not personally. But I know of him.

The tech mogul was in the news last year. He and his brother Sebastian were in an accident.

His brother died. He walked away with scars and a broken arm.

It was gossip for weeks.

Everyone tossed around theories.

But only one really stuck: The accident was foul play.

And Adam was the prime suspect.

Chapter Three

DANIELLE

After three hours in the back of a luxury car, I'm ready to move.

I drop my bag on my desk, change into a sports bra and leggings, find a workout to stream on my laptop.

I feel a little silly, high kicking and grape-vining across the living room, but I need the sweat.

After Mom died, I fell apart. I barely managed to drag myself to my job serving overpriced whiskey. And I failed to bring enough energy to charm rich guys.

My boss gave me an ultimatum: show up in a short dress and a smile or don't show up at all.

A week off—he insisted—did nothing to alleviate the ache in my heart or the emptiness in my gut.

But what choice did I have?

I donned my shortest dress and my hottest boots, plastered on a smile, struggled through my eight-hour shifts.

It took all my energy. Mental, physical, emotional. I needed another way to cope.

I gave into bad habits until Remy caught on.

I promised him I'd stop.

For a while, I did. I switched to aerobics. Really cheesy, peppy, eighties style aerobics.

Between the high-energy music and the endorphin boosting sweat, I survived. I didn't thrive. But I kept Remy in school and I kept food on the table.

It was hard. It's still hard. No matter what I do, there's never enough money.

After I finish my workout, I shower, dress, find a message from Adam on my cell.

A picture of *The Voyeur* on his wall.

Adam: Do you approve?

The grayscale photo looks perfect against the white wall. There's even space for the other portraits.

Danielle: You left room for her.

Adam: You're right. It's a shame to break a set.

Danielle: It is.

Adam: You truly believe that.

Danielle: Yes, but I don't blame you for doubting me.

Adam: Will you deliver them?

Danielle: Whatever you like.

My cheeks flush at the implication.

Adam: I'll pay double the asking price if I get them tomorrow.

That's a lot. Way too much to turn down. Especially for a simple task.

Danielle: Of course. I'll email the paperwork.

The front door opens. My brother steps inside. Brandishes a takeout bag from the Thai restaurant down the street. "Extra spicy and extra greasy." He motions to the coffee table. "Just how you like it."

"How did you make that sound dirty?"

"It's a skill." His eyes go to my cell. "Are you talking to a guy?"

"A customer."

"A customer you want to fuck."

Way too much.

I can't explain it. He's handsome, yes. Tall, broad, strong. With incredibly blue eyes and extremely kissable lips.

And this intense stare.

Like he's already picturing me naked.

Like he's going to watch me strip out of my clothes and fuck myself for his viewing pleasure.

"I'm closing a sale," I say.

"Is that what you call it now?" Remy chuckles. "I closed a great sale over the weekend. The guy was *fiiiine*."

"I am!"

"Uh-huh. I can put your food in the fridge if you need more time for your sale."

My cheeks flush. I want Adam way too much. It scares me. "Give me a minute."

"Just one?"

"Just one."

"Sixty seconds and I'm starting the show."

"Go for it."

I turn my attention to my cell.

Adam: I'll send a car tomorrow. And the delivery fee. All yours.

A thousand dollars on top of the commission.

I can't turn that down.

Yes, I want Adam, but I'm an adult. I can control myself.

Danielle: Make it noon. I want to sleep in.

Adam: Done.

Remy sets up dinner on the coffee table and pulls up our current binge watch. *Blood Borne: Legends of the Vampire Clan.*

It's trashy in the best possible way—a lot of vampire on

human combat and even more sex, with ridiculous twists, great acting, and gorgeous cinematography.

Something he likes—hot vampire dudes, including some who like other dudes.

Something I like—wonderfully composed images.

Well, I don't exactly mind the forbidden romance and the attractive men.

The star kind of looks like Adam, actually. Only not as tall or broad or imposing.

I'm here, having dinner with my brother.

I'm not picturing Adam naked.

Remy shakes his head. "Is he that hot?"

"Huh?"

"The guy on the phone?" Remy asks. "Is he that hot?"

"He's handsome, yes." I taste my red curry. Mmm. Coconut milk, curry paste, fresh vegetables, mounds of white rice. Yum.

Remy's gaze goes to the screen. He sighs *if only* as the vampire king rips off his shirt.

The woman across from him gasps. Then she moves closer.

Puts her hand on his chest.

"I thought she was a vampire," I say.

"Danny, keep up. She drank the potion that turned her back into a human."

"But if she has sex with him, won't she become a vampire?"

"Duh."

"I didn't realize it's so obvious."

"It's the only rule the show follows," he says.

"Silly me. Working instead of memorizing the details of *Blood Borne, Legends of the Vampire Clan*."

"Working? Or thinking about the handsome customer?"

Uh…

"Oh my god! I knew it. You like him."

"He's just a customer."

"No way. You'd totally go vampire for him."

My head fills with images of Adam. His arm around my waist. His hand on my wrist. His hard, strong body against mine. "No." I don't have the conviction I expect.

I want him. Badly.

I take another bite. Chew. Swallow. I'm starving and this is good, and eating means not having to ask myself why I want Adam so badly.

I try to find distraction in the show, but it's wall-to-wall sex. The vampire/human (soon to be vampire/vampire) couple is writhing in bed, naked, groaning like there's no tomorrow.

For a few seconds, I contemplate the framing.

Then the image shifts.

And it's me and Adam, in the clean white bedroom, on the soft sheets.

"Holy fuck, Danny. I know that expression. You fucked him." Remy shakes his head *I can't believe it*.

"What?"

"The guy on the phone. You fucked him."

My cheeks flame. "No."

"Not the student who asked you on a walk in the park."

"What's wrong with a walk in the park?" I ask.

"Oh my god. Did you go to his dorm room? Did it smell like beer?"

"You're twenty-one." And I'm not so old at twenty-three, but, hey, it's older than twenty-one. "And you're a student."

"Ew. No wonder you wouldn't turn vampire for sex. College boys don't know how to fuck."

"Please do not tell me how you got this information."

"Straight boys."

"How… how would you know what straight boys are… no. Don't tell me." I try to focus on my food, but my head goes back to Adam.

The quiet office.

Him, bending me over the oak desk, pushing my panties to my ankles, driving into me again and again.

"Ew… Danny, you're seriously replaying your sad dorm room fuck, right now?" Remy shakes his head.

"I didn't have sex in a dorm room."

His expression twists with distaste. "Not a college party."

"I didn't have sex with anyone."

He looks at me curiously. "Really?"

"Really."

"Then why are you flushed?"

I take another bite. Buy myself a moment to think. But I only think of Adam. His intense eyes, his deep voice, his strong hands. "The customer today. He was handsome. But that's it."

"Is he a straight man?"

"Yeah."

"You're a total babe. He wants to fuck you."

"How do you figure?"

"Men aren't complicated. They see someone hot. They want to fuck them."

Maybe. But that doesn't sound like Adam. And even if he does want to fuck me, I don't have time for trysts with strange men.

"Yeah, he would. I can tell from your look," he says.

"How can you tell if he'd fuck me from my look?"

"You know he would."

"I really don't," I say.

"Uh-huh…" His eyes flit to the screen. He shakes his

head, deeming the show less entertaining than my life, and looks to me. "Let's say, for the sake of argument, that he would."

"Okay."

"You want to fuck him?"

"He's attractive."

"What's the holdup?"

"It's too complicated."

"No. It's not. You fuck him. You say goodbye. You fall asleep satisfied. The end."

"It's different for me. I'll get attached."

"Why can't you get attached?"

"He's a customer."

"So then he's hot and rich. Sounds like a win-win."

That's true.

"Do you have a picture?" Remy asks.

"Why?"

"I want to get a vibe."

"No. You'll say something weird."

"Like what?"

"Like when you said my prom date looked like he had a small dick."

"Did he not?"

I clear my throat.

"I can tell. It's a sixth sense."

"A dick sense? Really?"

"Really," he says.

"I'd rather be surprised."

"What if it's a micro-penis?" he asks.

My laugh gets louder. "Oh no, a micro-penis."

"Have you even seen a micro-penis?" He shakes his head *it's sad, truly sad.*

"Women don't care about dick size."

"Women. Or you?"

"Both."

He stares me down. "Really? If Mr. Suit had a micro-penis, you'd still want to fuck him?"

"I don't care how big his dick is. I'm not fucking him."

Remy looks at me incredulously. "There's something you're not telling me." He studies me, looking for cracks in my story. "Did you blow him in his limo?"

"No."

"The backroom? Next to Mr. Davey's office? Risky. That's what makes it hot."

"Gross. And no."

Remy shakes his head. "But you did fuck him."

"Can we talk about something else?"

"Is it your technique, Danny? Are you worried you don't know what to do?"

"Oh my god, please stop now."

"I can show you with a cucumber. It doesn't have to be weird."

"That's the definition of weird."

"A link to some instructive videos."

"I'd think about you the entire time!"

"And channel my skill," he says.

"You're disturbed." My laugh breaks the tension in my shoulders.

My little brother is disturbed.

But there's a method to his madness.

Adam is handsome, rich, in control.

Why not indulge in a few fantasies, when I'm alone, by myself?

I'm a grown woman. I can see Adam Pierce without melting into a puddle of desire.

No problem.

———

For the first time in ages, I sleep late. Wake to the smell of coffee.

Mmm. I put my steel-cut oats on the stove, pour a mug of drip, add plenty of almond milk and honey.

Not syrupy, not bitter, not too bright and not too creamy.

Balanced. Like a perfectly composed photograph.

I eat a quiet breakfast, don my nicest dress and a pair of riding boots, fix my hair and makeup, find a gift on my stoop.

A long-stemmed rose on top of a folded envelope.

Lush red petals. Sharp green thorns.

And the letter sealed with red wax.

All straight out of a fairy tale.

Adam.

Who else could it be?

I break the seal, open the handwritten card.

Danielle,

Please join me for dinner tonight.

I have an offer for you.

One I'd rather not put on paper.

Sincerely,

Adam Pierce

So he does want something from me. Something besides advice on where to hang his art.

There's no way he's this formal about sex.

It must be something else.

But what?

What the hell does a billionaire tech mogul want with me?

Chapter Four

DANIELLE

"**I** should officially introduce myself." Adam's driver smiles as he pulls the door open for me. "Louis Diaz. Everyone calls me Lou."

"Danielle Bellamy. My brother calls me Danny. Everyone else calls me Danielle."

"It's a beautiful name."

"Thank you." I slip the envelope into my purse.

Louis notices, but he doesn't mention it. He helps me into the car without a word on the rose, the invitation, the man who employs him. "Do you have everything you need?"

"Do I need something special?"

"It's a long drive. I can stop for coffee first."

"I never turn down coffee."

He smiles and slides into the car.

For a few minutes, we talk caffeine options. He's used to Adam's standards and Mr. Pierce is exacting. Only single-origin beans or premium blends.

We compromise on a hipster coffee joint down the

street. Then we pick up the photos at the gallery and settle in for a long drive.

For a little while, I make conversation with Louis. His family moved here from Puerto Rico when he was a kid. He's the oldest, with three younger sisters, each more difficult than the last.

My family is from Trinidad, but we only visited once before Mom let her strained relationship with Grandma fracture. I remember their arguing—over my father, who bailed after Remy was born—more than I remember the beer-cap covered beaches.

Mom wore her home on her sleeve. She drank a lot of Sorrel and played too much bad reggae music, but she was a New Yorker too. She loved every inch of the city, from the tip of the Empire State Building to the basement dive bar around the corner.

She was vibrant and alive, the same way the city is.

And then she was gone.

And I still don't know how to survive without her.

But I can't tell Louis that. I can't even tell Remy. So I mention something about my heritage—we're Indo-Caribbean, but most people assume I'm from India—then I claim a need to take a nap, don my headphones, watch the city whiz by the windows.

By the time we arrive at the mansion, the sky is a soft shade of blue. It casts the mansion in an ethereal glow. It's every bit as imposing and grand as a storybook castle.

Inside, the space is the same. Beautiful and untouchable, just like the billionaire who inhabits the space.

Louis leads me straight to the bedroom.

There she is, *The Voyeur* in the middle of the wall, stunning in the twilight. Breath leaves my lungs.

It's not the beauty of the model, though she is beautiful, or the composition of the photo even.

It's the questions it asks.

Good art challenges the viewer. Sometimes, so shrewdly the viewer doesn't notice.

If this was my wall, my room, my art?

I'd never stop staring.

The handyman interrupts me, takes my advice on hanging the photos, leaves me alone with the set.

The photos bring the still room to life. Charges it with erotic energy.

There's no other way to say it.

These photos are sexual.

A lot of art is—it's made by men, for men, and straight men like looking at naked women, especially if they can call it art.

A lot of our clients are in it for the T&A. They aren't as obvious as men at a bar, but they never manage to hide their true colors.

Is that what Adam wants?

Did he invite me here to fuck me?

My fingers curl into my thighs. I want to fuck him. If things were different, I'd say yes. Spend the night in his bed. Wake to coffee and breakfast and a long drive into the city.

But things aren't different.

My life is complicated.

And he's dangerous.

I practice a soft no.

I'm flattered, but I'm not for sale.

I don't do casual.

I can't handle how I'll feel in the morning.

Fuck. I'm getting ahead of myself. Adam hasn't made an offer. I shouldn't assume it's sex for money.

The scent of fresh tomatoes pulls me downstairs, through the foyer, into the kitchen.

An older woman, in an apron and comfortable shoes, her gray hair pulled into a bun, stops stirring sauce to look at me. "You must be Ms. Bellamy."

"Danielle." I offer my hand.

She shakes. "Patricia, but you can call me Trish. I run the Pierce house. It used to be quite the job, when all four brothers were living here."

"Oh?"

"Yes. You know boys. Even the well-mannered ones are rascals."

"They are."

"Oh?" Her eyes perk. She wants to hear about the boys in my life.

"My little brother, Remy. He's more of a nerd. A video game designer. But he gets into his own kind of trouble."

"A handsome young man?"

I can't help but laugh. "He is."

"I imagine. You're a beautiful young woman."

"Thank you."

"Do you get into the same kind of trouble?"

Is she making conversation or spying for Adam? Either way, the answer is the same. "I don't really have time to date."

"Men can be demanding."

"They can."

She smiles, intrigued. "Is there anything you don't eat, Danielle?"

"No. Whatever is fine."

"And you drink wine?"

Not usually. I can't afford good wine. I can't afford good anything. "When in Rome."

"Mr. Pierce is expecting you in the dining room. He's already opened a bottle."

"Sure."

"I'll take your coat."

Right. I'm still wearing my coat. Not good manners. And this is a place where that matters. I nod a thank you and cross the foyer to the dining room.

It's a big space with high ceilings, wide windows, candles on the long oak table.

And Adam is sitting there, ready to make an offer he doesn't want to put on paper.

Deep breath.

Slow exhale.

Here goes nothing.

I step inside.

He stands from his spot at the end of the long table. "Danielle." He says my name like it's familiar. Like he's been testing the weight on his tongue.

"Mr. Pierce. It's nice to see you again."

He pulls out a chair for me. "You too."

I sit.

He picks up the bottle of wine. Pours a glass. "Do you drink wine?"

"I drink anything."

"Would you prefer something else?"

"If I would?"

"Trish will fix whatever you like."

"Really? What if I want a four-hundred-dollar bottle of brandy?"

"I'm not sure we have anything that cheap."

Is that a joke? I think it is, but I can't really read him. "I'll make do with, what, an eight-hundred-dollar bottle?"

"A noble sacrifice."

"Thanks."

He almost smiles. "What do you want?"

"Anything, really?"

Almost. "Trish is particular."

"Oh?"

He nods. "She won't allow an unsuitable pairing."

"So no gin and ginger beer?"

"Revolting."

It does sound revolting. "How about a grapefruit martini?"

"I'll call her."

Citrus and gin. Yum. But I don't want to ask her for more. "Wine is good. Thanks."

He pours.

"What would you do, if you wanted something Trish wouldn't allow?"

"She still works for me."

"So you overrule her?"

"If it comes to that." He takes a long sip. "But I pay her because I trust her judgment. If she tells me no, I listen."

"Really?"

"You don't believe me?" His voice stays strong, even, impossible to read.

"I don't meet many men who take no for an answer. Especially not the wealthy ones."

He's quiet for a moment, studying me. "What do they ask?"

"Bottles we don't offer, late closing, women who aren't for sale."

"You?"

"No."

"Never?"

"Never directly." I swallow a sip. It's good wine. Rich and fruity with a hint of sweetness. My head is already fuzzy, but it's not the alcohol.

It's him.

He's intense. Intriguing. Handsome.

I'm sure there are women who don't think so, who think the scars ruined his good looks, but they're wrong.

I checked for photos of him before the accident. He was handsome, yes, but in a plain way.

Now, he's fascinating.

"I don't believe you," he says.

"Why not?"

"You know you're beautiful." Somehow, he makes it a compliment and an accusation at the same time.

"How do you figure?"

"The way you dress." His eyes rake over my body. "The way you hold yourself."

"Mr. Davey insists I wear a short skirt. Says guys like gams."

"He says gams, really?"

"Close enough."

He half-smiles. "You disagree?"

"No. It works. Guys like pretty girls in tight clothes."

He raises a brow *see.*

Okay, maybe I know I'm conventionally attractive, but — "Beauty is all perception. If I dyed my hair green and wore baggy sweats, men wouldn't have the same reaction."

"Who's stopping you?"

No one. He's right. "It's not me."

"Is this?" He motions to my dark, wavy hair. My tight sweater dress.

I nod. "Mostly." I take another sip. "Would you still invite me here if I dyed my hair green?"

"It wouldn't suit you."

"You're a style expert now?"

He motions to his suit jacket and tie. "You disagree?"

"No. You're well-dressed. But I'd bet good money you paid someone to put your look together."

"How much? I could use some spending cash."

A laugh spills from his lips.

He is teasing me.

He's funny.

A reclusive rich man with a sense of humor. That's a rare combination.

"I don't have much on me," I say. "If I win, you get whatever's in my wallet. If I win, I get the photos."

"That doesn't sound fair."

"No. But you know the truth. You can agree and make —" I check the wallet in my purse. "Forty bucks and a Starbucks gift card."

"How much is on that?"

"I can't remember. I can't bring myself to go into Starbucks when I'm in the city."

"Not up to your standards?"

"It's for tourists."

"Why not admit it?"

I don't know. I guess I don't feel like I deserve them. "I can't always afford to be choosy."

He nods and takes a long sip of his wine. "It must be strange, working with men who can afford to throw money at their problems."

"Women too."

"Yes, but I imagine women aren't the ones who offer to buy you."

"They're entitled in different ways."

"Am I entitled?"

"I haven't decided." I swallow another sip. Then another. I need to be careful. To go slow. But I'm nervous, and this might be my only chance to savor good pinot noir. "Is that why I'm here? Are you trying to buy me?"

His eyes bore into mine. He examines me, deciding how I'll react to his offer. "Not the way you mean."

"What do I mean?"

"I want you, Danielle, but I don't pay for sex."

"No?"

"No." He takes a long sip. "I didn't invite you here to fuck you. I'm after something else."

"What?"

His eyes fix on mine. "I want to marry you."

Chapter Five

ADAM

Danielle's dark eyes go wide.

Her wine lips part.

She starts to speak, but nothing comes.

She's surprised.

Is she offended too?

Since the accident, I don't know what to expect from people. Women who used to beg for my attention stare with horror.

Others barely notice the scars.

Some find them fascinating.

I'm not sure which is worse, someone obsessed with the physical markings of the accident or someone who barely sees them.

Maybe someone who sees the way it changed me.

That was what happened when my father died. I was fifteen. I looked normal to people who didn't know, but those who did—

They could see it, somehow, this curse overtaking me.

I'm not the man I was before the accident. It isn't just the physical changes that make me a monster.

Losing Bash destroyed me.

"Did you just say…" Danielle sucks a breath through her nose. "You want to marry me?"

"Yes."

She blinks, confused. Overwhelmed, maybe. "Why?"

My eyes trace a line down her body. Long wavy hair, light brown skin, lush curves.

That black dress cutting a line between her perfect tits.

Every inch of her soft skin begging for my hands.

I'm a monster now, but I'm still part man.

She's gorgeous.

I dodge the question. "Do my intentions matter?"

Her eyes fill with surprise.

"You need money. I have money."

"There are other ways of making money."

"Not what I'm willing to pay."

"How much is that?"

"A million dollars."

"But…" She sucks in a shallow breath. "You barely know me."

"I know enough."

"How?" She studies me carefully. Not the way other women do. Not looking for the man I used to be or horrified by the monster I've become.

With curiosity.

Need.

Desire.

"Mr. Pierce?" her voice softens. "Adam?"

"If that isn't enough, name your price."

She sits back in her chair, stiff, frustrated.

I'm another rich asshole who thinks I can buy her.

It's not true, but it's not wrong either.

"I want to know why," she says.

She wants to know I have good intentions, but I don't.

My motives aren't pure. If anything, they're despicable.

"Family." It's not the whole story, but it's the truth.

"Family?"

I nod. "My siblings." Vengeance for Bash. And the fringe benefits. "They worry." They want me to move on, meet people, leave the fucking house. "I'd like them to stop worrying."

"And they will if I marry you?"

"If we convince them we're in love."

"Oh." She softens. "That's kind of sweet."

I don't correct her.

"What does that entail?"

I can barely get past leaving the house. But I have to. I have to convince everyone—my family, our friends, our colleagues, the man who destroyed my brother—we're in love. "Dinners with friends. An engagement party. Mingling."

"A party, really?"

I nod.

"I can't imagine you at a party."

"A small party."

"An art show maybe."

"Exactly. We show up, stare into each other's eyes, laugh at each other's jokes, convince people we're happy."

She nods. "For how long?"

"A million dollars for the first year. At the end of the year, we can walk away or renew the contract."

"And we really get married?"

"Yes." The paperwork needs to be there. Or someone will discover the truth.

She picks up her wineglass. Traces the stem with her index finger. "What about... consummating the marriage?"

"It's not a part of the arrangement."

Her eyes fill with doubt.

"I'll put it in the contract. I won't touch you unless you ask me to."

Already, my blood is rushing south.

My body is threatening to take over.

No more negotiation, no more terms, no more bullshit.

Her, naked on this table, spread wide, coming on my face.

"If I don't? Will you find someone else?" she asks.

"We're going to marry."

Her eyes meet mine. "And a married man has never cheated."

"Vows mean something to me."

"You'd give up sex?"

"I have a hand."

Her laugh is nervous. "And a wall of erotic art." Her eyes go to her wineglass. "It's not the same."

She's not asking me if I'm capable.

She's asking herself.

"I do want you, Danielle. I want to take you right now." I press my palms into my slacks so I don't touch her. "But that's got nothing to do with my offer."

"If I say no, you'll still ask me to spend the night?"

"No."

"No?"

"I'm not that easy."

Her laugh softens the tension in her jaw. She half-smiles, still nervous, but no longer terrified.

She wants to say yes.

She will. It's only a matter of time.

"Take a few days. Call me when you decide." I have to leave or I will invite her to spend the night.

Trish will berate me for abandoning dinner, for abandoning a woman at dinner, but it's better than the alternative.

I stand and offer my hand.

She looks at me funny, but she still stands and shakes.

———

AFTER THE ACCIDENT, I SPENT WEEKS IN A DRUG-INDUCED haze. Doctor's orders. To control the pain. Keep me from hurting myself.

The drugs were supposed to keep me sedated, so I wouldn't fight my restraints, stall the healing in my bones.

But I needed the numb in my heart too.

I didn't know how to live without Bash.

I didn't know how to live with guilt.

It would have been better if he'd been the one who survived.

He could light up every fucking room in the house.

Damn, this place is as guarded as your heart, huh, Adam?

Then he'd laugh at his own joke. Like he was the funniest asshole who ever lived.

It doesn't get easier.

I miss him more every day.

I feel emptier every day.

After I was healed, physically, doctors weaned me off painkillers. My body ached for weeks. A punishment I deserved, but not enough to lessen the agony in my heart.

I didn't sleep, I barely ate, I thought only of the loss, and how I could make it right.

Only one thing brought me peace—revenge.

Against the man who paid a mechanic to sabotage my car.

Cole Fitzgerald. Another old money asshole. I thought

it had to be that, a competitor who wanted to secure his spot as number one, but it wasn't business.

It was personal.

And so I'm hurting that asshole the way he hurt me. By taking something he wants.

It's not right, treating Danielle like a pawn.

But it's the only way I can survive.

If I didn't have this purpose, I would have already joined Bash.

He wouldn't forgive me, but maybe he would understand.

All night, I toss and turn.

When I rise, I follow my routine, the structure that keeps me grounded.

Two laps around the grounds. An hour in the gym. A cold shower. Breakfast in the dining room.

A full cup of black coffee.

Another in my office.

Most days, I work until I'm too tired to think. It's the only way I get a hint of sleep.

I break for lunch and dinner, and sometimes even afternoon tea—Trish insists—but I rarely notice anything except the white sky.

As usual, Trish buzzes me at one.

I consider saying no, asking her to bring lunch into my office, but I know how that conversation goes.

I went to all this effort, Adam. You can leave your office for thirty minutes. A gentleman sits at the table. He doesn't eat at his desk.

What would your father say?

Most days, I curse her for playing that card. Today, I wonder.

My father was a merciless man. He would have done anything to protect us.

But vengeance never entered the equation.

Would he approve of my plan?

Would he insist I take it further, kill the asshole myself?

Or would he beg me to let go, move on, get out of the fucking house the way my brothers do?

I don't know anymore. It's been too long. His memory is too faded.

The buzz of my cell pulls me from my thoughts.

I know it's Danielle before I check the message.

Still, I move down the stairs, through the massive ballroom, to the quiet backyard.

Whipping wind, crashing waves, bleak white sky.

In winter, the beach is freezing.

Cold, brutal, totally unwelcome. Just like you, Adam.

You should start writing poetry.

I'm so moody.

Also broody.

This poem's shoddy.

I need more coffee.

That's a slant rhyme.

It's more artistic that way.

The memory of my brother's laugh warms my heart.

Then I see the accident and my body goes cold.

This is supposed to be simple.

I marry her. I show her off until Fitzgerald is consumed with jealousy.

I savor his pain.

I don't fall for her. I don't fuck her. I don't worry I'm going to hurt her.

Danielle: I have a few terms.

Warmth spreads through my chest. My stomach flutters. My limbs buzz.

The cold disappears.

Replaced by a strange mix of affection and desire.

Wanting to fuck her is one thing. But liking her?

That's a complication I can't afford.

Adam: Name them.

Danielle: My brother gets a scholarship, one he'll believe he earned.

Her brother is a programmer. A game designer. He shows promise, but it's a competitive field. Not a lot of room for scholarships. Even with his background.

Adam: I'll ask a friend to offer him a scholarship. A competitor.

Danielle: Now?

In two minutes, I arrange the details. And it's done.

Danielle's brother doesn't have to worry about his tuition.

Adam: Now.

Danielle: And the mortgage. I want that paid.

Adam: Done.

Danielle: It could be another million dollars.

Adam: Send me the information and it's done.

Danielle: Like that?

Adam: Like that.

Danielle: I haven't said yes yet.

Adam: You will.

Danielle: It's that easy?

Adam: Unless you have another term.

Danielle: We'll have to kiss in public.

My body buzzes. The promise of a kiss is nothing, but it overwhelms me.

I want her too badly.

Adam: Only in public.

Danielle: We'll have to practice.

Adam: We will?

Danielle: If we want to sell it. That's how you develop a skill. You practice.

Adam: Then we'll practice.

Danielle: Only kissing?

Adam: Only kissing.
Danielle: When do I sign?
Adam: Tomorrow. I'll send a car for you.
Danielle: Then?
Adam: Then you're mine.

Chapter Six

DANIELLE

R emy invites me to join him at his favorite Williamsburg bar, but I'm not in the mood to drink overpriced beer with hipsters.

My head is too full.

A million dollars to marry Adam Pierce.

To pose as his wife for a year.

To ease his brothers' doubts. And maybe other people's too.

I look for answers in old photos of the Pierce family. Adam wouldn't have his brother killed—he looks so happy in all these pictures with Sebastian—but there's something he isn't saying.

Adam appears in hundreds of images with his brothers. With all three but especially with Sebastian (Bash to his friends).

Business events.

Social occasions.

Vacations even.

They complement each other.

The matter-of-fact older brother. The trouble-making younger brother.

The two of them irresistible to every woman in a six-block radius.

I'm not sure who was more handsome.

Adam had the Disney Prince thing going before the accident. But Sebastian had this devil-may-care smile. His eyes were the same deep blue, but they were bright with joy.

Even when he was smiling—and he was, in a lot of these photos—Adam always looked serious.

After I finish dinner, clean up, and check on Remy, I do what I always do when I need to clear my head; I take pictures.

Since I have the apartment to myself, I take over the main room. Once I push the coffee table out of the way, hang a white sheet, and set up my lights, I have a perfect studio.

All white background and soft light.

Small, yes, but mine.

I close my eyes, let images fill my mind.

A woman at the window, looking back at the camera, like *The Voyeur*.

Only I don't see her slight curves or her light skin.

I see my wavy hair, my round hips, my dark eyes fixed on the space just past the camera.

On Adam.

He's not there to photograph.

He's there to watch.

And he's standing there, with that firm posture and intense focus, ordering me out of my clothes.

Ordering me against the wall.

Ordering me to fuck myself.

I set up the camera. Perfect the light.

The soft glow of morning, heaven, bliss.

Images fill my head.

Adam behind the camera.

His voice in my ears.

His hands on my thighs.

His lips on my neck.

Curves of flesh and cloth.

Dark and light.

Soft and hard.

Exposed and hidden.

Fuck, I'm flushed everywhere. I stop fighting it. I grab the remote for my camera and I snap a photo.

The long line of my back.

The curve of my neck.

My messy ends of my hair.

I turn my face to the camera, like the woman in the photograph.

Then all of me.

A full body shot. I've taken plenty, but I've never posted one publicly.

Never with my face.

Click, click.

My chest flames as I take a photo. Then another. Another.

It's dangerous. Illicit. Thrilling.

I close my eyes. Let my thoughts drift to Adam.

Does he know about my website? Is that why he hired me? It shouldn't thrill me, but the thought of him fucking himself to one of my pictures sets me on fire.

I slip my hand between my legs.

Like he's here, on the other side of the camera, watching me with those intense blue eyes.

I come fast.

Too fast.

I'm dizzy.

And I'm standing here, naked, my camera filled with proof I fucked myself in my living room.

What would Adam say if he saw this photo?

Would he break, admit he knows my alter ego?

Or would he stand strong and silent?

Something tells me it's the latter.

I started posting self-portraits on Instagram a few years ago. At first they were camera phone selfies. Clothed, but moody and artistic.

Then I found the money for a camera, lights, reflectors, tripods. I was at home one day, trying to recreate one of Dana Delaney's photos. An artistic nude.

I was trying to figure out how to make the light fall over my torso just so, but it didn't look right with my shirt in the way.

And it didn't work with my bra either.

So I tried it. Lost the clothes. Took the photo.

Just to see if I could nail the composition.

I did.

I was so proud I had to show it off.

My social media was connected to my name, my face, my job at the gallery. So I made a new account.

Broken Beauty.

I posted a PG-13 crop. Woke to dozens of likes and comments.

Then I did it again.

Again.

I couldn't afford a model, so I kept shooting self-portraits.

After a dozen photos, I was ready to show more. Full-size. Explicit.

So I bought a domain, started posting a few photos a week.

My audience grew, bit by bit.

I haven't tried to sell anything. Not yet.

I'm not ready to let go of anonymity. There's something about revealing myself without revealing my face.

My art, my body, my work, on display for anyone who wants to see.

Only I'm completely in control.

This is the only place I feel in control.

I can't give that up. Not for Adam. Not for money. Not even for Remy.

I need the outlet. I won't survive without my pictures. This is the only place where I get to make noise and take up space.

It's mine.

This is risky. Stupid maybe.

But I always follow my instincts here. And they're screaming *yes*.

I crop the photo. Add a caption.

Is it better to stay strangers?

Or show our scars?

A little obvious, I know, but I want a reaction.

If this is why Adam chose me, I want to know.

———

I FALL ASLEEP BEFORE REMY GETS HOME. DREAM OF THICK wool coats, creamy lattes, overflowing glasses of wine.

All the space and time to perfect my photography.

Money to hire models.

Adam, agreeing to pose for me. Doing away with his suit jacket. Then his tie. Shirt. Slacks.

I wake up flushed and nervous.

And... hearing my brother talking to someone?

Someone familiar.

"She works hard, but she sleeps like a rock. It might be another hour," Remy says. "Are you sure you want to wait here?"

"If it isn't a problem," the familiar voice says. "I have the car."

"You could bring more coffee."

"One wasn't enough?"

"Enough coffee?"

The voice laughs.

No. Not a voice. Louis.

Shit.

I throw on a dress and move into the main room. Find my brother chatting with Louis.

No. Not chatting. Flirting.

"Danny." He brandishes a takeout coffee cup. "You didn't tell me you had a boyfriend."

Is that a plausible explanation? "Hey, Louis."

He nods hello.

Remy smiles. "Already friends with Louis. You've been busy."

"Yes. Busy working."

"Uh-huh." Remy smiles. "Doing some very *hard* jobs I imagine."

Oh god.

"What kind of car did you say you drive?" Remy asks Louis.

"Not one with that much privacy," Louis says.

"Really?" Remy deflates. "Never? 'Cause it would be pretty hot to engage in that kind of action. Or is that weird for you?"

"I used to drive a limo," Louis says. "I'm used to it."

Remy motions *see*.

"Oh my god, please ignore my brother. He's a depraved pervert," I say.

He motions *oh stop*.

"Thank you for the coffee." I take it from Remy.

He raises his brows *oh my god, you better explain.*

Mmm. It's good. Sweet and creamy. Just the right mix of espresso, almond milk, and honey.

"Is Mr. Bellamy accompanying us today?" Louis asks.

"Today?" I ask.

"Yes. We have to sign the papers for your... agreement," he says.

Remy's eyes go wide.

"Mr. Pierce asked me to help you pick out a few things. Since you'll need to feel comfortable," he says.

"Yes, Mr. Bellamy will be joining. Thanks Louis. Can I call you Louie?" Remy asks.

"I hope you do." He smiles at Remy, but I can't tell if it's flirting or friendliness.

Remy takes it as flirting, of course. "As long as you call me Remy. And not Mr. Bellamy."

"Mr. Bellamy has a nice ring to it," Louis says. "But whatever you'd like, Remy."

Yes, flirting.

Definitely flirting.

Is my brother getting more sex out of this than I am?

"Can you tell me about this mysterious agreement?" Remy asks.

"I'm afraid I've signed an NDA," Louis says.

"If I ask nicely?"

Louis shakes his head.

"What if I get on my knees and beg," Remy says.

"Then you're uninvited," I say.

"She's so mean. Can you believe that?" Remy teases. "Keeping her mysterious rich boyfriend a secret. Then she turns it around on me. Do you have a sister?"

"Three," Louis says.

"So you know the pain," Remy says.

"They can be difficult. But they mean well." He looks to me. "And I know the three of them would do anything to protect me."

"Damn, he's just like you, Danny. Makes everything sentimental." Remy shakes his head *what a shame.* "Do you need a minute? I can entertain my new friend."

"How will you do that?" he flirts back.

"Five minutes. Be good. Please," I say.

He smiles *maybe I will, maybe I won't.*

He really does live to torture me.

I pee, wash my hands, brush my teeth, find a suitable pair of socks and boots. My hair is a little messy, but it's not a total travesty. And I suppose makeup free is the best for trying on clothes. I don't want to accidentally stain a several-thousand-dollar gown.

There.

I meet Remy at the door, grab my coat and purse, follow Louis down the stairs.

Louis keeps my brother engaged as we climb into the back seat, drive to midtown, stop in front of a skyscraper.

He insists Remy stay in the car with him. "We'll grab another cup of coffee. Talk about your sister's taste in art."

Remy jumps at the opportunity to flirt, but he still hugs me goodbye and whispers, "Are you sure you'll be okay alone?"

"Yes." I leave before he can ask questions I can't answer with confidence.

I don't know if I'm making the smart choice. I don't know who Adam is or what he wants.

I take the elevator to the office myself. Spend half an hour with my lawyer. One from a different firm. To look after my interests.

She explains the details of the contract.

My year at Adam Pierce's beck and call starts the minute I sign. For three hundred sixty-five days, I do what he asks, whether it's staying in the mansion, in my private bedroom, traveling halfway across the world, or donning a tight dress and charming rich assholes.

In public, we present as a loving couple. He'll never ask me to do more than kiss him. Not as part of our ruse.

In exchange, I earn seven-figures, plus Remy's scholar-ship and the rest of the mortgage.

A year of my life for a million dollars.

A year of my life to secure my brother's and my future.

There's no question.

This is the right choice.

I sign on the dotted line.

Chapter Seven

DANIELLE

The department store is all glass walls, wide aisles, expensive clothes.

A place for stylish rich people.

"Oh, let me pick something!" Remy squeals as he takes in the display of women's clothes on our right. Three mannequins, in fabulous suits: simple black, bright pink, subtle metallic leaf print.

"You're not dressing me." I scan the massive space for something more my style. Professional, yes, but more artist than CEO.

"I dress with more intention than you do." He motions to his jeans. His chunky grey sweater. His long bangs.

Yes, Remy's hair is more well-managed than mine.

But he dresses like a hipster artist. He's a Brooklyn-based game designer. It works for him.

For my new role as Mrs. Adam Pierce?

Not so much.

He turns to Louis for support. "What do you think? Who dresses better?"

Louis smiles, somehow charming both of us. "I'm

afraid I'm not the stylish type." He motions to his simple black suit. "I wear the same thing every day."

"I'm an actual artist," I say.

"Maybe behind the camera." Remy takes in my outfit with his now critical eye. He examines my faded wool coat and shakes his head.

Louis nods. "Let me take that for you, Ms. Bellamy."

"Thanks."

He helps me out of my coat. "And you too, Mr. Bellamy?"

"I'm good." Remy smiles.

Louis drapes my coat over his arm and turns toward a tall brunette in a sharp pantsuit and expensive heels.

"Mr. Diaz." She smiles and holds out her hand. "How lovely to see you. How is Mr. Pierce?"

He shakes. "Not that Mr. Pierce."

"Oh?" She arches a brow.

"Adam," he says.

"I didn't realize he was attending social occasions." She turns to Remy and me. "He needs help with his… friends."

"Only Ms. Bellamy," Louis says. "She's going to be accompanying him."

"Really?" Her eyes perk. "That's lovely. He's had such a difficult time since his brother passed. I'm glad he found someone."

Remy shoots me a *you better explain* look.

I wave him away. Later. When I find a way to articulate this. Something that isn't *I agreed to marry a reclusive billionaire. In theory, because he offered me a million dollars. But is that really why I said yes? Or is it because I want to fuck him?*

"I'm Bree. It's nice to meet you, Ms. Bellamy." She offers her hand.

"Danielle." I shake.

"Remy. Her brother." He waves hello.

"And your brother will be accompanying you on our shopping?" She tries to hide her frustration, but she doesn't get there. *Difficult rich people.*

I appreciate Remy's moral support, but I have to agree, this will get weird fast. "He'll leave once we start trying things on."

She smiles with relief. "Perfect. I have a few questions, then you and your brother can talk while I pull outfits."

"Sure," I say.

"What do you do, Danielle?" she asks.

"I work at an art gallery." Well, I did. I can't exactly work there and live in Adam's secluded mansion at the same time.

"She's a photographer," Remy says.

Bree makes that *hmm, interesting* noise. "An artist?"

"You could say that."

"Is that how you want people to see you, as an artist?"

Is this really about how I want people to see me? Or about how Adam wants people to see me?

I understand. If I show up to dinner in a Zara dress, his friends and family will either wonder why I'm clueless or why he isn't taking care of me.

Rich men have certain expectations. That includes dressing the part.

If that means a wardrobe of fancy clothes for me, well, I can't exactly complain.

I close my eyes. Try to conjure an outfit that defines me.

Instead, I see the image I posted last night.

Me, naked, covered only in my wavy hair.

No layers, no pretenses, no costumes.

When I'm behind the camera, in control of what I present, I can reveal myself.

I'm powerful, in both my vulnerability and my shield.

How do I explain that to Bree? Maybe artist is enough.

"An artist, yes, but the femme fatale version. Wielding my beauty and my skills as power," I say.

"Yes, the boots, the short dress, the stare." She nods. Starts drifting into her head. "Do you prefer any type of clothes?"

"Dresses and skirts," I say.

"She never wears pants," Remy agrees.

Bree smiles. "Men prefer skirts."

Remy nods. "We think with our dicks."

I clear my throat.

"What? It's true." He chuckles. "See, you need me here. She's difficult."

"Even so. We'll need privacy to do our best work." She shuts him down with a polite smile. "Take twenty. Go to the cafe if you'd like. Or my assistant can bring something here."

"I'll take a macchiato," Remy says.

"We can go to the cafe," I say.

"Enjoy being rich for the day," he whispers.

"No. We'll go to the cafe. Thanks," I say.

"I'll call when I'm ready," she says.

"Sure." I take Remy's hand. Lead him in the direction of the escalator.

He shoots me a *you better explain* look, but he waits until we're sitting at the cafe to ask.

Remy sips his macchiato. "When did you get a rich boyfriend?"

I taste my almond milk latte. It's sweet, creamy perfection. Just like the drink I had this morning. "Recently."

"And he's dressing you?"

What can I say that's true? I'm not allowed to reveal the nature of our relationship, but I don't want to lie to my brother. "I didn't realize it until today."

"Why turn down free designer clothes?" He nods *of course*. "Is it the hot customer?"

"Huh?"

"The one who was making you all flushed during *Blood Borne*?"

"I was flushed from the vampires."

"Uh-huh." He shakes his head *lies, lies, lies*. "But this is the guy you were texting?"

"It is."

"Adam Pierce. Why is that name familiar?"

"He's a customer," I say.

Remy shoots me a *really* look. "You think I keep up with the art world? It's either a blue canvas or a naked chick. Boring."

"You're an artist."

"Fun art, Danny. Not drab paintings of flowers."

"Our art isn't drab." It's not ours anymore. I no longer work at the gallery. But I still feel a need to defend it. "It was great. We worked with amazing photographers. I was lucky to have the job." Yes, it meant smiling at rich assholes all day, but there were a lot of other girls who would have happily taken my place.

"So you quit?"

Shit.

"For this guy. Adam." Remy taps his chin. "'Cause he's loaded."

"I'm going to stay with him."

Remy's eyes go wide. "It's a sex thing." He play-swats me. "And you didn't tell me. Fuck you, Danny."

"It's not a sex thing."

"God, that's so hot. He wants you so bad he's paying for it. Especially since he has a big dick."

"I didn't say that."

"You didn't have to."

"I haven't—" I can't say I haven't seen Adam's dick. He's supposedly my boyfriend. "That's none of your business."

"Did you blow him in the backroom?"

"That is so not hot. Stop asking."

"Fine, Danny. Did you blow him somewhere hot?"

"Where would that be?" I ask.

"I don't know. Apparently, you're very picky."

"Yes, god forbid I don't want to drop to my knees in front of my boss's office. On the cold, hard concrete."

"I know. Very picky."

I can't help but laugh. Remy is… Remy. He's not afraid to make noise or take up space.

"Was it some boring normal place? A bed? Ugh, I hate when guys lie down for it. The least they could do is stand up."

"These are too many details."

"You're no fun, but fine." He drops the teasing tone. "Is it a sex thing?"

"No."

"But he is paying you?"

"Yes."

"I know you're an artist, but last time I checked, you can do math."

I motion *get to the point*.

"Two plus two makes four."

"He's helping out," I say. "That's all."

"'Cause he likes fucking you."

"Because he likes me." That is what Adam said. He's paying me because he likes me. Because he doesn't want his family to worry.

Remy is right. It doesn't add up.

Something is missing.

But what? I've seen his moody mansion. I have no doubt his brothers worry.

He's a man with money.

I'm an attractive young woman who needs money.

Maybe it's that simple.

"Because he likes me and wants more time with me," I say. "He's a little bit reclusive."

Remy's eyebrows raise.

"His brother died a year ago," I say. "And he... he hasn't been ready to face people yet."

"When did you meet him?"

"Through work."

"When?" he asks.

"Recently."

"You recently met a rich dude, and he's paying you to live at his house, but it's not a sex thing."

"It's not."

"Do you think I'm stupid? Or just gullible?"

"It wouldn't bother you if it was true?"

"You doing this *Pretty Woman* thing? Nah." He shrugs. "As long as it's for you. And he has a big dick."

"Oh my god."

"Danny, no. No micro-penises!"

My laugh gets louder.

"You're going to have to send me a picture now."

"Not that kind of picture."

"But you have one?"

"No."

He reaches for my purse.

I grab it just in time.

He shakes his head *fine* and pulls his phone from his pocket instead.

Remy taps *Adam Pierce* into a search engine.

And, in that one instant, everything changes.

Recognition floods his expression. "The rich guy who killed his brother?"

"He didn't kill his brother."

"How do you know?"

"Look at the pictures of them together," I say. "They're happy."

"Danny." The humor drops from his expression.

"He didn't."

"But he… he could be dangerous."

Of course. But that's a given. Men are always dangerous.

They're bigger, stronger, more powerful.

Adam would be dangerous if he was as broke as I am.

But now, with all his money—

He could destroy me any way he wants.

"Now you know how I feel," I say. "When you go home with strange men."

He sits back, studies the photo on his phone. Adam and his late brother, Sebastian, at a gala. Sebastian is giving him bunny ears. Adam is shaking his head *my silly younger brother*. "You trust him?"

I trust him not to hurt me. Maybe I shouldn't, but I do. "Yes."

"He's super hot."

I nod.

"There's nothing post-accident. Is he all mangled now?"

"He has scars," I say. "But the imperfection is beautiful."

His eyes fill with doubt, but he shakes it off. "Are his eyes that blue?"

"They are."

"And his bod?"

60

I haven't seen it up close, but I can tell he's in good shape. "It's good."

"Are you serious, Danny? Good. Good is your detail?"

"Sure is."

"You're horrible."

"Thank you."

He laughs. "He looks like he has a big dick."

"Oh my god."

"What? He does?" Remy sets his phone on his thigh and he looks to me. "Promise you'll tell me if you need help."

I'm not sure if that's a promise I can keep, but I nod anyway. "I promise."

Chapter Eight

DANIELLE

After we finish our coffee, Remy and I say goodbye, and I meet Bree in the private dressing room on the first floor.

It's the size of my apartment, complete with a small stall, a three-panel mirror, a podium, a leather armchair, and a matching fainting couch.

Bree already has half a dozen racks of clothes in the space.

Casual, work, cocktail, activewear even.

For an hour, she dresses me in proper winter clothes. Sweaters, jeans, tall boots, thick dresses, scarves in accent colors.

Then she really kicks into gear. "Let me measure you properly, sweetheart. I want to see if you're wearing the right bra size."

I do away with my current outfit—a snug magenta dress and impossibly tall boots—and turn to face her.

It's funny. I'm comfortable posting nude photos on my site, but with Bree studying my unmatching bra and panties, I feel impossibly naked.

My cheeks flush. My chest too.

She doesn't notice. Or she doesn't mention it. Just wraps the tape around my bust, ribs, waist, hips.

She takes another half a dozen measurements, scribbles them in a tiny leather notebook, steps back to admire her blank canvas.

"You have a lovely figure, Danielle," she says. "Quite the hips."

"Thanks." I think.

"I'd like to show them off, if that's all right with you."

"Adam didn't offer instructions?"

"He trusts me." She turns to the rack of lingerie. Plucks three black bras from the rack. "Try this one. It should fit better than what you're wearing."

Holy shit, is that the price? I swallow my shock.

Bree turns, giving me a tiny hint of privacy. "You're the first. If you were wondering."

"Huh?"

"The first woman Adam has sent to me."

"Do most men send women to you?"

"It's common. Especially when wealthy men are dating younger women, women who are still early in their careers."

Women without money.

Sugar babies.

Mistresses.

Girlfriends.

At the end of the day, it doesn't matter what you call it. Rich men use their money to score time with pretty young women.

"Are you finished, sweetheart?" she asks.

I do away with my cheap bra. Try on this obscenely expensive piece of nylon. "About."

She turns. Adjusts the straps. Studies the fit. "You don't like the idea of it?"

"Huh?"

"Being shown off."

"That's what Adam is doing, isn't it?" I ask.

"He sent you here to build your wardrobe. So you'll be comfortable in his circle."

"And I won't look cheap?"

"You work in a gallery. You know what it's like."

I nod. "If you look like the help, people treat you like the help."

"If you wear Louboutins, they assume you're one of them."

"Are those Louboutins?"

"Don't pretend you didn't notice." She studies my reaction. "Don't worry. I won't put you in anything showy. People who come from money don't shout their designers from the rooftop. They do it subtly. So people notice their style, not their label."

That's true. The really rich collectors never show up with a purse bearing the Louis Vuitton label. "It's all confidence."

"It's always confidence." She motions for me to turn.

I do.

"How is the fit?"

"Different. But good."

"Very good. Try the dress again." She motions to the snug black dress on the wall. "It will look different."

"Right."

"With these." She hands me a seamless black thong.

Not what I usually wear—this is one thing I don't need riding my crotch—but hey, when in Rome.

This time, she steps outside the dressing stall.

I change into the black underwear, rise to my tiptoes, check my reflection.

The overhead light isn't the most flattering, but the lingerie fits well.

I push the strap of the thong down my hip. Curl my fingers into my skin. Snap a photo with my cell.

It's not the kind of picture I normally take. Certainly not what I post on my website.

Nudity is one thing. It's not necessarily sexual.

But lingerie?

There's no other way to interpret the scrap of black fabric.

And this picture, with my fingers curling into my skin, the nylon thong sliding down my hips, the close crop—

It might as well say *I'm about to fuck myself and I want you to watch.*

What would Adam say if he saw it?

If I posted it on my site?

I adjust the exposure. Try a filter. Tweak the crop.

It lacks depth and precision but it looks good.

It looks really fucking hot.

I can post it now.

I can force him to react to me.

"Ms. Bellamy."

Shit. I slip my cell into my purse. Pull the dress over my head. Pretend I'm not imagining Adam fucking himself to my image. "Come in."

Bree steps inside. She nods *that's it.* "Perfect. I'll pull more in that size." She adjusts the shoulders. "How do you like the dress?"

The stretch fabric is thick and soft, warm yet breathable. With the short hem and the low scoop, the dress is sexy. "It's beautiful."

"Try this." She holds up a pair of wine-red ankle boots. "Sexy, in charge, and still practical for winter."

Practicalish. Those are three-inch heels. But they're gorgeous.

I sit and slide into the boots. They're a soft suede and they're beautifully saturated. Rich and lush. Like everything in Adam's world.

"With this." She holds up a necklace. Motions to a tailored black coat. "Perfect." Bree looks to me. "If you love it."

"I do." It's perfect, actually. Sexy, artistic, expensive. And still me. "You're good at this."

"Wait until I put you in evening wear."

———

AFTER I TRY ON ANOTHER TEN BRAS, THREE DRESSES, AND six pairs of shoes, Bree sends me to lunch.

I order a twenty-dollar salmon Caesar at the department store restaurant. A week ago, I would have balked at the price tag. Today, I shrug it off. I've got a hundred grand in my bank account and a credit card from my fake boyfriend.

The salad is delicious. Fresh salmon, crisp romaine, creamy dressing, the hint of lemon. Then another cappuccino and a chocolate truffle that costs as much as the coffee drink.

Anything and everything I want.

Sure, it's anything on the menu at this mid-range restaurant, but it's still intoxicating.

No wonder rich people are so annoying and bossy.

I sip my cappuccino. Pull out my cell. Check the image again.

A tight crop of my thigh, hip, waist. My hand on the curve of my hip, pushing the black fabric down my leg.

Removing my panties for someone.

Myself.

Him.

Both of us.

Adam didn't say anything about the image I posted last night. Because he's buried in work, because he hasn't seen it, because he has incredible restraint?

One of the three.

Or two maybe.

I read our text thread again. All those terms and deals. Dry and proper. Until the last line.

Then you're mine.

I've never felt I belonged to someone. I've certainly never felt anyone belonged to me.

I don't know if I want to belong to Adam.

But I want someone to need me that badly.

I return to the dressing room. Let Bree have her way with me.

We try gown after gown.

An A-line with a cape.

A backless black.

A silver mermaid.

A snug champagne number with sheer sleeves.

A strapless gold sheath.

Bree embraces her earlier edict on the ultra-rich. She tosses aside anything too fussy, too bold, too bright. Sticks with the elegantly understated.

Then we move on to matching shoes and bags.

Hair.

Makeup.

Bree is merciful enough to put me in a "normal outfit" for an hour-long session at the makeup counter.

I try to pay attention—makeup is a great skill for a photographer to learn—but I'm too worn out to absorb much of the lesson.

The artist takes me through a day look. Then he adds until it's a night look.

When we finish, it's dark, and I'm exhausted. I want to change into my workout gear, sweat off my foundation, shower, and climb into bed.

But I'm not going to the home I've known for the last twenty-two years.

I'm going to Adam's place.

Louis humors me with a short walk, then we get into the car and start the long drive.

For a while, I watch the city whiz by the windows.

My thoughts wander back to the reclusive billionaire.

What the fuck does Adam actually want with me? Does it matter?

I have a year to work on my art and save for my future. I'm using every single day wisely. Including today.

Tonight. After he dismisses me. In whatever space is mine.

My camera is in the trunk. Sure, it's buried under thousands of dollars of designer gowns, but it's still there.

That's still mine.

I'm still Danielle Bellamy. No matter how expensive my dress, heels, lipstick.

When we arrive, Louis insists he'll unpack and leads me inside.

Straight to the dining room.

To the candlelight and the scent of basil and Adam Pierce standing at the table, staring at me like he's going to consume me.

Chapter Nine

DANIELLE

"**M**r. Pierce." Words refuse to form on my tongue. He became more handsome in the last twenty-four hours. I'm sure of it.

Adam's eyes stay fixed on me. "Are you going to call me that after we marry?"

Right. We're going to convince the world we're happily married. I should call him by his first name. "Adam."

"Danielle." He almost smiles. "You look beautiful."

"You too."

"Beautiful? Really?"

I nod.

"You mean that."

"Why wouldn't I?"

He raises a brow *really*. The way he did in the photos with his late brother. With ease, joy, love.

I almost see the possibility in his eyes.

Adam Pierce is capable of happiness.

I'm not sure he believes it. I'm not sure anyone does, not if the gossip online is any indication.

I don't have a camera. I can't capture his expression.

But I still commit it to memory. Every curve of his lips, every shade of blue in his eyes, every jagged line on his skin.

"Imperfection is what makes a piece of art interesting," I say.

"Is interesting a compliment now?"

"From me it is."

He stands there, tall and broad and imposing, absorbing my words, remaining a stone wall. "Bree asked me to be gentle."

"Really?"

He takes a step toward me.

My body buzzes. I want him closer. I want every inch of him pressed against every inch of me.

"She was excited to call. We haven't spoken since..." His eyes flit to the window behind him. The dark sky, the manicured garden, the miles of ocean. "She styled my first suit."

"When you were what, five?"

He half-smiles. "Did you like her?"

"She worked me hard, but the results were good."

His eyes pass over me slowly. "If you're tired, I won't keep you."

"A little." I'm exhausted, but I want to sit with him. "But I'm starving."

He pulls out my chair for me. After I sit, he signals the kitchen and pours two glasses of wine.

Mine first.

He really is a gentleman.

Usually, I don't see the appeal in chivalry, but it suits Adam.

He really does seem like the prince in a fairy tale.

Trapped in his castle, surrounded by wealth and possibility but still miserable.

If I lost my brother—

I don't know how I'd get out of bed.

I drink my wine quickly. Too quickly. It's not smart. I need to keep my wits. But he makes me nervous.

His gaze lingers on the empty glass, but he refills without comment. "You must find me strange."

"No stranger than the other men who offer me a million dollars to marry them."

He half-smiles. "How many are there?"

"You know what it's like, being a broke young woman in a city full of wealthy men. A new suitor every other day."

His lips curl upward. A full smile.

It lights up his expression. Brightens the room. The house.

For one perfect moment, the world is a place full of love and joy. Then Adam blinks and his smile disappears.

I miss it instantly.

"It's true," I say. "Rich people are always strange."

"Used to getting our way?"

"Yes. And unaware of the hoi polloi."

"Is that how I seem?"

"A little." I take a long sip.

"A little…"

"A little out of touch. But I don't blame you. If I lost my brother… I'd lock myself from the world too."

Adam barely frowns, but I still feel the change in energy.

I miss his smile. His laugh. His potential for joy.

"I'm sorry," I say. "I shouldn't… I shouldn't bring that up."

"No. It's why you're here. You don't need to pretend it didn't happen."

"I am sorry. That you lost your brother."

"Thank you."

I take another sip. Try to find something to say. I don't want to be one of those obnoxious people who makes someone's grief about me.

Who fills the silence with bullshit platitudes.

"You've mostly stayed here," I say. "Since then."

He nods.

"Is there a reason?"

"It's easier."

Right. Of course. There are so many rumors about the accident. If he went out, he'd have to hear the whispers. Endure the stares. "Your brothers?"

"Liam and Simon."

"You said they worry. Do they visit?"

"At first, all the time. Now, on occasion. Liam likes to pop in. He will, if he gets word you're living here."

"You didn't tell him?"

"Not yet."

My eyes meet his. "Will he be surprised?"

"Yes."

Adam really is the king of short answers.

"I don't date often," he says.

"Any reason?"

"I work too much. It wouldn't be fair."

"Now?"

"I'm taking the time." He doesn't add *and I'm paying you a million dollars, that sounds fair.*

But it still fills the room.

Fuck, this is awkward.

Thankfully, Trish arrives with dinner. A seared white fish and sauteed root vegetables. Tiny bowls of salad. Not like the salad from this afternoon. Arugula, sunflower seeds, long slices of carrots and parsnips, fresh herbs.

Is that dill?

I'm not sure I've ever seen dill in person.

"I hope you'll forgive me for serving the first two courses together." She sets both plates in front of me then does the same for Adam.

"No. I'm starving. Thank you, Trish," I say.

She beams. "You're very welcome, Danielle. It's nice to have someone so polite here." She shoots Adam a knowing look.

He almost smiles. "I'm at the table."

"Today." She shakes her head *he really is difficult* and exits through the kitchen door.

The scents of citrus, olive oil, and fresh herbs fill the room. I didn't know food could smell this good.

What's the rule about dinner ware? Inside to outside or outside to inside?

I watch Adam pick up the outside fork. Do the same. Taste the salad.

Mmm. Long strips of carrots and zucchini, dollops of hummus, olive oil, and lemon. Everything crisp and fresh.

Adam watches me taste the food. "How do you like it?"

I chew and swallow. "Perfect. Thank you." And this is exactly what I like. Am I obvious? Or did he find that while digging? "How did you know I'd like it?"

"I didn't."

"You didn't research my preferences?"

"Where would I find those?" he asks.

"I'm not the one who owns a tech company."

"Hypothetically?" He takes a slow bite, chews, swallows.

Maybe I'm not as unique as I want to believe. Maybe this is what he serves all his guests. "Sure. Hypothetically."

"I'd go through your social media accounts. See if you post pictures of food."

Right. That's obvious.

"Check which restaurants you like and follow."

That too.

"Or I could access your takeout apps. See what you order."

That would do it. "You didn't serve curry."

"Should I?"

"No."

"You don't like it?"

"You don't know?" I ask.

"No." He takes another bite. "But I can find out."

"By checking my order history?"

"Asking you."

"Oh." My cheeks flush. "Right. That would be the easiest way."

He half-smiles.

My heart thuds against my chest. It's such a nice smile. It lights up the room. "I do. Like curry. More Thai than Indian, but my family isn't from India. You probably know that. But my mom was from the Caribbean. People assume, but I don't know anything about India." I swallow another sip of wine. "I like anything spicy."

His eyes stay fixed on me. Not tearing apart, just watching carefully.

I take another bite. Mmm. Dill and lemon and arugula. "Does that say something about me?"

"People who like spicy food have higher pain tolerances."

Ah. That explains that.

"They're usually risk takers."

"What about you?"

"What about me?"

"Do you like spicy foods?"

"I do." His eyes meet mine. "And I drink my coffee black. You prefer almond milk and honey."

"How did you—"

"Louis."

Oh. Right.

"People who like bitter foods are more likely to be psychopaths. Or sadists."

My cheeks flush at the thought of his palm on my ass. "We're a good match then. A masochist and a sadist."

He actually smiles. "Is that where you go first?"

"Of course."

"Is it true?" His gaze travels down my body. "Do you like being hurt?"

"I've never tried it." Not the way he means.

"Do you want to?"

Despite my thick dress, I feel impossibly naked. "Are you asking because you're going to fuck me?"

"No."

"But you want to fuck me."

"Was I unclear last time?"

No, but—"You left before we started eating."

"I didn't want to lose control."

Lose control and touch me.

Fuck.

For a few minutes, we eat in silence, the suggestion heavy in the air.

I want to fuck him.

He wants to fuck me.

But we're sitting here, eating dinner, not making any attempts to fuck each other.

The main course is even better than the salad. Tender fish with a light lemon and olive oil sauce, crisp potatoes, sauteed spinach.

Everything fresh and flavorful. The best meal of my life. And the strangest.

Adam waits until he's finished with his plate to speak. "You looked me up. I did the same with you."

"Did you find anything interesting?"

"You love pictures of naked women."

My cheeks flush.

"You're constantly giving quotes for the gallery. Always photographers who specialize in artistic nudes."

Oh.

"But then, I knew that a minute after meeting you."

"*The Voyeur* is my favorite."

"It's beautiful."

"Did you know me before that?"

"Yes." He takes a long sip of his wine. "I read all your quotes when I stumbled on *The Voyeur*."

"Is that why you paid for home delivery?"

"I rarely leave the house."

"Wouldn't that be an easier way to convince your brothers? Go out, hit the clubs."

He shakes his head.

"No?"

"No. They'd think I was replaced with a robot."

"You don't like dancing?"

"Dancing, yes." He finishes his wine. "Loud, crowded spaces, filled with drunk assholes? No."

"Are galas that different?"

"They're not as loud or crowded." He almost smiles. "But, yes, I could meet Simon or Liam at a quiet bar. Have a few drinks. Show up with a pretty girl on my arm." He stands. "Kiss her."

So that's his plan.

His eyes meet mine. "Have you ever been in love?"

"Never."

"You've dated."

It's not a question, really, but I answer anyway. "Yes. Not casually. It's not for me."

He nods with understanding.

"I've had three boyfriends. A cute nerd in high school. He was sweet. The first time he kissed me, he asked permission."

"Did you like that?"

"I did. But after a while, I wanted him to know without asking. I wanted to feel like he needed to kiss me."

"You wanted him to read your body language."

"Yes."

He takes a step toward me. "The others?"

"After school. Both artists. One when I was working as a waitress. He, uh, he helped me get the job at the gallery."

"There's no shame in that."

Maybe. It is how the world works. "We were together for a year, then he found a new muse. And I met another artist who was showing at the gallery."

"Of course."

I raise a brow.

"You're beautiful, smart, articulate. You wear your love of art on your sleeve. What artist would be able to resist you?"

"Men are easily threatened."

He actually chuckles. "Yes."

"Male artists… they like me when I'm gushing. When I talk about selling photographs. But when I show them my own?"

"They want to be the artist in the relationship."

I nod. "They want me to be their groupie. Or their muse."

"Men who take photos of naked women?"

"Yes."

"I'd want you to be my muse too." Intent drops into his voice.

My body buzzes. I want him. Badly. "You're not a photographer."

"My cell phone has a camera."

"Have you ever used it?"

"Have I taken a cell phone picture?"

"For illicit purposes?"

"No."

"Would you?" I ask.

"If I trusted someone enough."

If he trusts me enough, maybe.

I've never wanted a man to send naked photos before. But I'm desperate to strip Adam out of his suit, watch him wrap his hand around his cock—

"Did you pose for them?" he asks.

"No."

"Why not?" He takes another step toward me.

This time, I raise my brow *really*. "Why didn't I let a man take naked photos of me?"

"Was that it?" He offers his hand.

I take it. Let him pull me to my feet.

"Were you doing the practical thing?"

"Partially."

His fingers curl into my palm.

"I wanted to be the one behind the camera. And they couldn't handle that. The first was threatened by me owning a camera. The other... I offered him a deal. I'd pose for him if he'd pose for me."

His hand curls around mine.

I look up into his eyes. "He said no."

"And that was it?"

"It was the beginning of the end."

"Because he turned you down?"

"It wasn't that he said no. It was how. The idea of posing disgusted him. He'd never lower himself to that level. He'd never be an object for the camera. That was a job for women. They were supposed to be objects for his viewing pleasure. Pretty and pliable."

"How do you see it?"

"There's a power in standing in front of a camera without your clothes. Saying *this is me, world, in all my glory.*"

"You've done it?"

Does he really not know? Maybe. Or maybe he's pretending. "Only for myself. I can't afford models. That's the easiest way."

"How long have you been practicing your photography?"

"Three years."

"That's a lot of naked photos."

"Only naked for the last two. And not always. Sometimes draped in a sheet." Or lingerie. Like the one I took today. I swallow hard. Meet his gaze. "Would you do it?"

"Pose naked?"

I nod.

"I wouldn't pose clothed."

"It's easier being naked. No one judging your cheap dress or your mismatched lingerie."

"No pretenses."

"Exactly. Nowhere to hide. No way to pretend. It's terrifying. And freeing too."

His eyes fix on me. "Do you talk to everyone like this?"

"Are you going to tell me I'm irresistible again?"

He nods. "You are."

My cheeks flush. "Thank you."

"Will you show me your photos?"

Has he really not seen them? "Tomorrow. It's late."

"I won't keep you long." He offers his hand. "But we need to practice."

Right. We're convincing the world we're in love. We need to look the part.

"Are you ready?"

Chapter Ten

ADAM

"**A**re you going to ask next time?" Danielle's eyes fix on me.

"No." The words barely leave my lips. I'm not like her high school boyfriend. I'm not a fumbling teenager.

I know how to read women. I know how to watch their cheeks flush and their lips purse.

Or I did.

I've never slept around. Not the way my little brother does. Certainly not the way Bash did.

I was more like Simon, with his long-term arrangements.

A part of me wanted love, intimacy, connection.

Most of me preferred work.

A relationship wouldn't be fair. I didn't have enough of myself to give. Friends with benefits worked fine before the accident.

When I was first recovering, my brothers checked in every other day. When I was ready for visitors, they brought friends.

Attractive women.

I never knew how they'd react.

Disgust, fear, fascination.

The scars were harsher then. Red and angry, like my soul was trying to express something on my body.

Some of the women tried to touch me.

Some offered to fuck me.

A few times, Liam sent in professionals. His idea of help.

None of the women appealed. Even the beautiful, sweet women who said all the right things.

I didn't want to feel pleasure.

Certainly not the pleasure of sex and all the intimacy and vulnerability that came with it.

I didn't even fuck myself.

Until Danielle.

For days, I stared at her photos.

The jut of her hip or the arch of her back.

Her lips parting with a groan.

Her fingers tugging at her long, wavy hair.

For days, this foreign sensation built inside me.

Desire.

It built and built, until it was agony as much as it was ecstasy.

Finally, I gave in.

I fucked myself the way I did as a teenager, like I'd just discovered the secret to the greatest pleasure in the universe.

For ten minutes a day, I felt only bliss.

Then guilt consumed me.

Stop overthinking it, Adam. There's a babe six inches away, and she wants to fuck you.

It's rude to keep a lady waiting, you know.

If you want to punish yourself, fine, but don't punish her.

If you must punish her, do it the fun way.

At least make the woman come.

And save all the details for me.

Her fingers brush my chin.

My thoughts scatter.

The rest of the universe disappears.

"I'm ready to practice." She runs her fingers over my jawline. "Are you?"

No. But I can't wait until I'm ready. I'll never be there. "If I lead."

"You kiss me, not the other way around?"

"Yes."

"In front of your brothers?"

"When we're alone."

She traces the line of my jaw. "Is this too much?"

Yes. "No."

She brings her free hand to my waist. Slips it under my suit-jacket.

Her fingers dig into the soft cotton of my shirt.

All of a sudden, I'm a fumbling teenager. The dorky kid with glasses, who's never kissed a girl.

"You're nervous." Her voice is tender. Gentle. "I am too." Her hand curls around my neck. "I haven't kissed anyone in a long time."

"Your photographer?"

"We broke up last summer." Her eyes fix on mine. "And he wasn't a very good kisser. You have a low bar to clear. Besides, this is practice."

I bring my hand to the small of her back.

She shudders from the touch. "If it's not perfect the first time, that only means we need more practice."

The possibility terrifies and thrills me in equal measure.

I want to kiss her.

I want to run far away from the hint of intimacy.

She rises to her tiptoes.

For a moment, she stares into my eyes, then she leans closer.

My eyelids flutter together.

Her lips brush mine.

It's soft. A hint of a kiss.

The taste of wine and lemon and Danielle.

Need overwhelms me.

I have to pull back, open my eyes, break our touch.

She looks up at me, still nervous, but no longer scared.

She steps backward. Picks up the bottle of wine. "I could go for another glass." She fills hers. Then mine.

My fingers brush hers as I take it.

She raises her glass to toast. "To good kisses."

"To good kisses."

The clink echoes around the room. She brings the glass to her lips. Drinks with greedy sips.

I finish in two gulps. It's wrong to drink good wine this fast, but I need something to lessen the voice in my head. The one whispering *what the fuck are you doing?*

It's not Bash's voice. He wouldn't approve of this plan, but if it got me to fuck Danielle—

If that's what it takes, Adam. Must be miserable to spend so much energy hating yourself. Why not spend it loving pussy?

I almost hear his voice.

I almost laugh.

Fuck, I miss him so badly. The world isn't the same without him.

How is it turning?

How are Simon and Liam surviving?

How am I standing?

None of it makes sense.

Her fingers brush mine as she takes my glass, places it on the table next to hers. "Again?"

I nod. Again. Until I can handle the intimacy of a kiss.

This time, I try to channel my brother. What would he do, after he finished teasing me for my stupidity?

I bring my hands to her waist. Press my palm into the small of her back, over the smooth fabric of her dress.

I pull her closer.

Closer.

Her eyelids flutter together.

Mine follow.

My lips find hers.

Softly, at first.

The light pressure of her mouth against mine. The hint of wine and Danielle.

Then harder.

Her lips part.

Her groan vibrates against my mouth.

For a few beautiful moments, she yields to me, then she pulls back with a heavy sigh.

Her eyes open slowly. Her expression fills with desire. And something else I recognize.

She wants to melt into me. To melt into a puddle of desire. Into that perfect space where she trusts me to fill every one of her fucking needs.

I don't ask permission this time. I don't channel Bash. I let that other part of me take over.

The man who knows exactly how to read his partner.

She wants me to kiss her.

I can kiss her.

I can handle it.

I bring my hands to her hips and pull her body into mine.

Crotch, stomach, chest.

Lips.

I kiss her softly.

Then harder.

Her lips part.

Her tongue dances with mine.

Strange for a second.

Then familiar.

Intoxicating.

I hold her close as I swirl my tongue around hers.

Blood rushes south.

She groans against my mouth. Pushes closer, pressing her pelvis against my hardening cock, beckoning me to take her.

Here.

Now.

On the big, empty table. Her panties at her ankles, her legs spread, her cunt pulsing against my lips.

Then around my cock.

Her fingers skim my neck. My jaw. My cheek.

The scar running across my cheekbone—

I pull back.

"Adam." Her expression stays heady. Her eyes stay fuzzy.

I can't do this.

"Are you..." She blinks. "Am I moving too fast?"

I need to get the fuck out of here. "You're perfect."

She stares at me like she doesn't believe me. "One more time then." Her voice softens. "Please."

Fuck, the need in her voice.

"I need the practice." She takes a half-step toward me. "And I like kissing you." She looks into my eyes. "I know this is only pretend. I know you have no plans of falling in love with me."

I just barely nod.

"I don't want to fall in love with you either." She takes

another half-step. "I know this isn't a normal job, but it is a job of sorts. And I don't like doing things half-assed."

"You don't want to pretend you love me half-assed."

"Not if I can help it." She takes another half-step. Into my space.

Desires surges through my veins.

I need her.

It's different.

Everything is different now.

This time, she moves slowly. She rests her hand on my cheek, the unmarked one, the side of me that's still man.

She runs her thumb over my temple, rises to her tiptoes, brings her lips to mine.

It's a soft kiss.

Slow, tender, intimate.

My head swims.

My body buzzes.

When she pulls back, I'm dizzy with desire.

Another three hundred and sixty-four days of this.

How the fuck am I going to survive that?

Chapter Eleven

DANIELLE

Adam makes an excuse about a work call. He leaves so fast he bumps into Trish as she rolls in dessert.

Trish shakes her head, but she doesn't stop him. "Don't mind Adam. He's not used to having company."

It's more than rusty manners. It's more than an addiction to work.

It's me.

Kissing me, specifically.

It's not hard to do that math. He's cool and in control all through dinner. Then, bam, the second he kisses me—

Time to run.

Which is fine.

Yes, I want to keep kissing him. Yes, I want to unzip his slacks and wrap my hand around his cock. Yes, I want to hear him groan.

But I—

Fuck, I can't think.

My head is flush with images of Adam.

His soft lips.

His hard chest.

That thin layer of fabric between my hand and his skin.

The pressure of his palm on my back.

He wants to fuck me.

I just have to ask. That's what he said. He'll fuck me if I ask.

If I go to his office right now and knock gently—

Will he say yes?

Or will he lock every part of himself away?

Dessert is raspberries and dark chocolate. Everything fresh and rich and delicious. None of it eases the tension in my sex.

I want him.

I want him badly enough I consider going to his office. Speaking in a gentle voice. Dropping to my knees and begging for whatever he'll give me.

My dress on the floor.

His hand in my hair.

His cock in my mouth.

Fuck.

I try to push the images into something appropriate for a photo shoot, but they stay illicit.

After I finish my tea, Trish shows me to my room. The spare room with the four-poster bed and the framed photos.

I studied these images for weeks. I dreamed they'd hang on my walls.

Now, they're mine.

"Mr. Pierce thought you'd enjoy this space," she says. "If it's not to your liking, I can find something else."

"It's perfect."

"It suits you." She smiles. "And it's yours. Mr. Pierce

asked me not to enter without permission. Promised the same."

A room that's all mine. Is it a gift or a curse?

"Adam's office and room are off-limits. And the old bedroom..." Her voice trails off as she fights a memory. "It's locked. You're welcome anywhere else in the house. The movie theater. The study. The gym."

"The gym?"

"Yes. On the first floor. Past the ballroom."

Past the ballroom. Of course. That's a normal sentence.

"Mr. Pierce uses it every morning. Mostly weight training equipment. You know men and their muscles." She chuckles. "It's a marvel. Adam was the skinniest boy I'd ever seen. His brothers called him string bean. He never wanted to play sports with them. He preferred to sit inside, with his fantasy books and his video games."

"Really?"

She nods. "Until Bash was old enough to get into trouble." She smiles wistfully. "He was an adventurous boy. Adam followed him everywhere, to make sure he wouldn't get lost or hurt himself. He even coached Bash when he started playing soccer."

"Really?"

"Oh yes. He was like the Adam you see now. Tough. Unyielding. But full of love and joy too."

Like in the old pictures.

"He always kept that part of himself hidden. It only came out with Bash. And Bash... he was trouble, but he was bright. Passionate. The way you are. I could hear you gushing over these photos downstairs."

"I can't help it."

"I know." She turns to the door. "Adam saw it too. He didn't say it, but I could tell he couldn't stop thinking about you. He's a good man. And he means well… He may not deserve your patience, but I'll ask for it anyway. As a favor. To me."

"I don't know you."

"Then an exchange. You give Adam time. I fix your favorite breakfast every morning."

"Oatmeal."

"You don't want something grander? Chocolate chip pancakes. Or stuffed French toast?"

"Grander than oatmeal? I thought you wanted to be friends."

She smiles. "Oatmeal it is."

"What does Adam eat?"

"Whatever I fix. He isn't picky."

"Really?"

"Not since Bash passed. He wouldn't eat if I didn't force him to do it." Her lips curl into a frown. "I'm not sure he tastes his food."

"He must. Dinner was great."

"It will be nice to have someone around who appreciates the effort." She shakes off her frown. "And I will fix oatmeal if that's your preference. But I hope you'll let me fix something more complex on the weekends."

"I can't turn down chocolate chip pancakes."

She nods. "What time do you rise?"

I guess the rest of the night is mine. And the morning too. "I think I'll sleep in tomorrow if that's okay."

"I'll guard your room."

"Thank you, Trish."

"I run the house, sweetheart. Anything you need, you let me know. Even if it's unusual. Even if you have to wake me at three a.m."

I'm not waking her at three a.m., but I might be able to

get used to someone cooking and cleaning for me. "I appreciate it."

"Anything you tell me stays between us, Danielle. Anything. I promise."

"Thanks."

She looks at me the way my mother did. Like she can't believe I've grown into this beautiful young woman. Then she says, "Good night," and she leaves.

I spend a few minutes exploring the room. The closet is already packed with today's finds. The dresser is packed with undergarments and lounge wear.

I find my camera in the corner, set up my laptop, unpack my books.

There isn't much. I'm used to a smaller space. But between the stack of photography books and the images on the wall, the place already feels like it's mine.

I move into the attached bathroom—it's as luxurious as the rest of the house—and shower off the day. Then I slip into a new set of pajamas. Wine-red silk. Smooth. Sensual. Begging for touch.

Begging me to slip into Adam's bed and strip.

Maybe one day, but not tonight.

First, I need to get my bearings.

I explore the rest of the house. The first floor is just as grand in the dark. Dining room, kitchen, foyer, ballroom, gym, study, some kind of coffee room. There are speakers hidden in the walls, but there's no sign of a TV anywhere.

The second floor is a mix of offices and bedrooms. Adam's is the furthest on the left. His door is closed. The room is silent except for the soft hum of instrumental music.

I don't recognize the piece, but the melody catches me all the same. It's beautiful, and somehow, bombastic and reserved at once.

The third floor is more open. A home theater. A library. A big window with an ocean view. And a clean white room, with hardwood floors and bare walls. The perfect space for a studio.

I don't ask. I claim the room immediately. I set up my lights, reflectors, camera.

The soft light of the night sky flows through the window. It's not like the city. It's all starlight and silver moon.

Have I ever seen stars this brilliant?

They're beautiful flecks of light in the dark sky.

I open the window, set my aperture, move the tripod, snap a photo of the sky.

It's too dull.

I lower the aperture. Try again.

There.

Perfect.

It's not as brilliant as the sky itself, but the photo is still a beautiful canvas of light on dark.

I want it as my backdrop.

I move the camera further from the window. Frame the photo.

My shirt unbuttoned, my back to the camera, my gaze turned to the viewer. *Click, click.*

Then I face the camera, leave the shirt open, do away with my pants, bring one hand to my thigh.

As if I'm fucking myself.

Head turned, hair in front of my eyes. *Click, click.*

My head thrown back as if I'm lost in pleasure. *Click, click.*

The wind whistles through the room, breaking me from my photographic trance. It's freezing outside.

I shut the window. Slip back into my new sleepwear. Return to my room with my camera.

The photos are more erotic than what I usually post.

Yes, my face is mostly hidden, but Adam will know it's me.

What will he say when he sees it?

Take off your dress and sit on my cock.

Or *what the fuck do you think you're doing posting photos like that for strangers?*

Or *I fucked myself to you a hundred times.*

I have no idea how the moody mogul will react, but I know I need him to react.

I post the photo.

Then I close my computer, climb into bed, let images of him fill my mind.

His eyes on my skin.

His teeth on my neck.

His cock driving into me again and again.

I come fast, but I'm not satisfied.

I only want him more.

Chapter Twelve

ADAM

New post on *Broken Beauty*.

Danielle's site appears in my RSS feed.

Another new photo.

Taken here.

I recognize the pattern of the window. The slope of the ceiling. The cut of the shirt falling open.

Bree bought the same pajamas for the last woman Simon dressed. In slate grey, not Merlot, but her handiwork is obvious.

That's Danielle, with her silk shirt falling open, her breasts on display, her head thrown back in bliss.

Her take on *The Exhibitionist*.

Cropped at the hips, like that photo.

Is she fucking herself or simulating it?

Does it matter?

Her tits are on display for any asshole who stumbles on her site.

There must be a thousand men gawking right now.

A few hundred fucking themselves.

Picturing Danielle, naked, under them.

Picturing her body splayed over their beds.

Picturing her pretty red lips around their cocks.

Fitzgerald sees these.

This is how he found her.

Is he picturing her right now?

The thought makes me sick.

Because I want to destroy him.

Because I'm already desperate to protect her.

It's ridiculous. This is the point of my mission.

Make the asshole jealous. So jealous he can barely live with himself.

And I'm worried about him wanting her?

I take a deep breath. Push an exhale through my teeth.

Calm eludes me.

Sense eludes me.

Instead, my thoughts go to Danielle. Her, in this office, sitting on my desk, peeling her dress to her waist, spreading her legs.

I need her. Here. Now. All fucking day.

It's the only thing that matters.

Not convincing my brothers.

Not revenge.

Not even playing fair.

Only this, watching pleasure overtake her expression, claiming every inch of her.

This is a dare.

But is she daring me to fuck her?

Or daring me to admit this is how I found her?

I stare for too fucking long.

Until a familiar sound interrupts me.

The door downstairs.

And my brother Liam, yelling, "Lucy, I'm home."

Chapter Thirteen

DANIELLE

"Hello." A tall man in jeans and a t-shirt shoots me a devilish smile. "I didn't realize Adam had company." He notes my outfit—the silk pajamas and fancy slippers—with a knowing look. "An overnight guest."

Shit. What do I say here? Adam and I haven't exactly worked out our story. "Danielle Bellamy."

"Liam Pierce."

So he's Adam's younger brother. That explains the easy access to the house and the deep blue eyes. Adam hired me to convince his brothers he's okay. That might not be the whole story, but I've got a million reasons to play along.

I'm Danielle Bellamy, Adam Pierce's loving girlfriend.

I offer my hand.

Liam takes it. Drops to his knees. Places kisses on the back of my palm. "Nice to meet you, Danielle Bellamy." He stands and offers his arm. "Have you eaten breakfast?"

"Not yet."

"Escort me to the dining room?"

"Sure." I take his arm.

He turns toward Adam's office and raises his voice. "And promise you'll tell me every one of Adam's secrets?"

"Every one?"

"All right, only the sex ones. He's a freak, isn't he?"

"Completely."

"Should I check you for rope burns?" He raises a brow. "Or maybe check him for rope burns?"

"A lady doesn't kiss and tell."

"Don't tell me you're a lady." He exaggerates a frown. "That won't be any fun."

A laugh spills from my lips.

His eyes perk. "A woman with fine taste in humor."

"You remind me of my brother."

"Danielle." He takes his free hand and mimes stabbing himself in the gut. "A man never wants to hear that."

"No?"

"No. The only thing worse than 'you remind me of my brother' is 'you're like a brother to me.'"

"We've only just met."

"So there's time for the mighty to fall." He shakes his head *the tragedy* and leads me into the dining room.

Trish appears out of nowhere. She smiles warmly at Liam. "You didn't tell me you were coming."

"It's a surprise," he says.

"You know how I feel about those," she says.

"You love them as much as you love me?" he asks.

She chuckles *ah, silly boy*. "I'll serve your coffee black next time."

"You'd have told Adam. And then I might not have met his overnight guest. Though…" His eyes go to my pajamas. "This is a familiar look."

"Liam, it's rude making references Danielle doesn't understand," she says.

He pouts.

"Save it for someone who buys it." She shakes her head. "Did you eat?"

"Not yet," he says.

"Coffee?" After he nods, she turns to me. "And you, Danielle?"

"Please," I say.

"Do you mind if I make pancakes?" she asks. "Liam has never been one for porridge."

He sticks his tongue out. "Tastes like paste."

She chuckles *ah, what a silly boy*, and moves into the kitchen.

Liam pulls out a chair for me.

I sit.

A sound upstairs calls my attention.

Adam.

Did he see the photos already?

Did he wake up, see them first thing, fuck himself to them?

Is he desperate to throw me on his desk?

Or maybe desperate to order me to cover up, keep my body hidden, keep my images for his eyes only?

If he orders me not to post, I have to comply.

My stomach churns. Not taking photos, not posting them—

I can't do it. I need the outlet or I'll find another. And exercise won't be enough.

I can't go back to bad habits.

I just can't.

"Damn. There goes our time for gossip." Liam sits across from me. "Quick. Something juicy."

I'm getting ahead of myself. Adam might not even know about my site. Or he might love it. Maybe he hired me because it gets him off, knowing his fake girlfriend is naked on the Internet.

"Danielle?" Liam nudges me. "You already thinking of Adam naked? Didn't get enough last night?"

"How did you know?" I force a smile.

He doesn't buy it, but he doesn't call me on it. "My gossip for yours."

Right. I'm the happy girlfriend. I'm playing my part, teasing Adam's brother. "You first."

"The outfit. It's what Bree buys whenever we ask her to dress a *friend*."

"That isn't juicy."

"All right. I lost my virginity on this table."

"Really?"

He nods *really*. "That side." He motions to the other side.

"Ambitious for your first."

"Older woman. She knew what she liked."

"How much older?"

"It's your turn."

Okay, this is why I'm here. But what can I actually tell Liam? Adam and I barely touched. "Your brother likes to make me wait."

"Cruel." He looks to the open side of the room.

Adam steps into frame.

He's already dressed. Grey suit. Patent shoes. Deep blue tie.

His scars are more obvious in the morning light. Jagged pink lines on pale skin. Well, not pale, exactly, but lighter than his brother.

Liam is unusually tan for a white guy in the middle of a New York winter. It's one of those signs of wealth. He can afford to fly to St. Barts for three weeks of sand and sun.

But then I can't curse people with money anymore.

I'm a billionaire's fake girlfriend.

And Liam seems like a good guy. Difficult, yes, but caring. If he came from the city, he came a long way.

His eyes are a little lighter than Adam's. A little greyer. His hair is a sandy brown whereas Adam's is dark.

They're both conventionally attractive. At least, before the accident.

Now—

God, I want to trace every line on Adam's skin. I understand his fear. I understand why he pulled away last night. God, how I understand.

But that does nothing to lessen the ache in my chest.

"Is that true, Adam?" Liam shakes his head. "It's rude to keep a lady waiting, you know."

Adam's eyes meet mine. He raises a brow *really*. The way he did last night. As if we both know I've said something ridiculous.

But this is true. I return the gesture.

He chuckles and turns to his brother. "She's just as bad."

Liam looks between us. "Interesting." He settles on his brother. "And you weren't going to tell me about your new… friend."

"Do you tell me every time you have an overnight guest?" he asks.

"You really want me calling three times a week to brag about getting laid?" Liam looks to me. "Maybe only twice some weeks."

"No judgment," I say. "As long as you're safe."

He motions *mostly* and looks to his brother. "How long has this been happening?"

"Long enough," Adam says.

Is he defensive on purpose, because that's his usual MO?

Or because he's nervous his brother will find the truth?

"Uh-huh." He turns to me. "What about you, Danielle? Are you going to confess?"

"It's new. But… when you know, you know, right?" I look to Adam. Shoot him a loving smile.

His eyes meet mine. For a second, they fill with surprise, then they fix on me in a way that screams *I need to see you naked*.

He can't sell love.

But he can sell that.

Fuck. My cheeks flush.

Liam chuckles. "Should I leave you two alone?"

"Would you, if we asked?" Adam says.

"You know the answer to that, Adam." He turns to me. "Is it really that serious?"

"Why are you asking me?" I ask.

"Adam is a vault. Don't tell me you haven't noticed." He turns back to Adam. Raises a brow. "Or is it different when you're in *lurrve*."

"You'll find out one day," Adam says.

Liam shudders. "I hope not. I don't need the commitment, the compromise, the pain."

"Not a one woman kind of man?" I ask.

"No. But it's not about adding notches to my bedpost," he says.

"Uh-huh," I say.

"I enjoy the freedom. I do what I want, when I want, how I want. How many people in a relationship can say that?" he asks.

"How many people without money can say that?" I ask.

Liam chuckles. "True, very true. Astute observation."

"When did you learn the word astute?" Adam asks.

"New friend. Smart girl," he says.

"The kind of girl you'd like to do whenever you want?" I ask.

Again, he chuckles, delighted. "That's a new one. I'm going to add it to my repertoire." He looks to me. "I'm surprised to see Adam with someone so clever. How did you two meet?"

"Work," I say.

"You work at Pierce? And you came here?" he asks.

"My work." Ex work but same difference. "I sold him some art."

"Snoozeville," Liam says.

I look to Adam. Raise a brow. "Should we tell him?"

"Not yet." He smiles.

A full-blown smile.

It lights up his eyes.

My heart.

The entire fucking room.

Adam Pierce is smiling.

I need to see him smile again. Now. Later. Forever.

"Secrets!" Liam shakes his head in mock protest. "Rude! But I understand. You can't admit you secretly want me."

"How did you know?" I tease.

"I see the look in your eyes, Danielle. The lies that I remind you of your brother. To hide the truth that you want to throw me on the table and have your way with me."

"I guess I'm obvious, huh?"

"I'm used to it. But I can't. I'm sorry. I know you want me and I hate to turn down a beautiful woman, but I could never betray my brother." He holds his hand to his heart like he's reciting an oath.

"I guess I'll have to live with that," I say.

Adam laughs.

Actually laughs.

It lights up the entire house.

His joy is the most beautiful thing I've ever seen.

"You're delusional." Adam sits next to me. "You've sold your story for so long you believe it."

"There's nothing to believe, big bro." Liam taps his t-shirt. "The ladies go wild." He pulls the v-neck low enough to show off his chest-piece. "It's the tattoos."

"Did you mention the nude pictures yet?" Adam asks.

"Nudes?" My tongue slides over my lips.

"See." Liam winks at me. "The ladies want to see as much skin as they can."

Adam chuckles.

"And when you have a body this beautiful, it's an oblig-ation." He looks to me. "You must understand, Danielle. You're as beautiful as I am."

"I'm surprised you admit that," Adam says.

"You've always had good taste in women," Liam says. "But only women. Has he asked you to sit through Bach yet?" Liam rolls his eyes. "Or, god forbid, watch one of those horribly depressing foreign films?"

"I love depressing foreign films," I say.

"Don't tell me you love Bach too." Liam makes a *gag me* motion.

A laugh spills from my lips. "You're so much like Remy."

"A hot man you're desperate to fuck?" he asks.

"Her brother," Adam says.

"Danielle. No. We're so close to perfect here." Liam shakes his head *the horror, the horror*. "I send you my nudes. You send me your nudes. We think of each other when we fuck other people."

"Sorry." I shrug as casually as I can. Liam is mentioning naked pictures like they're a fact of life. Not like he's seen me naked.

Has he?

Does he recognize me?

My social media is popular. And, yes, I don't show my face. But there aren't a lot of brown girls posting artistic nudes.

And Adam did invite me here.

Maybe his brother knows something I don't.

Maybe Adam fucked himself to my picture first thing this morning and that's why he's so relaxed and easy.

God, I like seeing him relaxed and easy.

"Coffee." Trish saves me from over-thinking overload. She places mugs in front of me and Liam, then she drops a pot and fixings in the middle of the table. "You too, Adam?"

"Share with your girlfriend," Liam says.

Adam's eyes meet mine. Something passes between us. Some knowledge we're playing a part and pulling it off.

It's easier than I expected.

I like him.

I don't have to pretend.

"Sure." I take a long sip of my coffee. Mmm, sweet, creamy, deliciously full of caffeine. "Drink as much as you want."

His fingers brush mine as he takes it. He brings the mug to his mouth, wraps his soft lips around the rim, takes a long sip. "Too sweet."

"Isn't that you in a nutshell?" Liam shakes his head. "Everything is too sweet for the most miserable man in the world."

"What about the most miserable man in the mansion," I offer. "Alliteration."

"A beauty and a poet." Liam blows me a kiss. "I like you more than... shit, when's the last time Adam had a girlfriend?" He makes a show of scratching his head. "College, maybe. What was her name? The nerdy redhead with the thick glasses?"

"Lauren," Adam says.

"Lauren. She was cute. Whatever happened to her?" Liam asks.

"Last I heard from her, she was moving to California with her husband," he says.

"Getting away from the cold." Liam nods. "Genius. I was freezing my balls off outside. How do you deal with it?"

"You don't live in the city?" I ask.

"It's ten degrees colder here. And then the breeze." He shakes his head *no thanks*. "But now we're getting off track."

"We are?" I ask.

He nods. "You want to see me naked."

"She's a photographer," Adam says.

"Oh, so you want to photograph me naked. Kinky. I like it." He stage whispers, "But we can't tell my brother."

"Do you think this will make me jealous?" Adam asks.

"I think it is." Liam draws a line around his brother's face in the air. "You rock the poker face, Adam, but I see the envy in your eyes. It's a classic fear of having a smaller dick. But I talked to Lauren. You've got nothing to worry about. Right, Danielle?"

I nearly spit out my coffee.

"What?" Liam plays dumb. "Is it not true? Did Lauren lie? Is it tiny?"

"Oh my god." I barely stifle a laugh.

Liam looks to Adam for support.

Adam chuckles.

Then it's a full-blown belly laugh.

Beautiful and vibrant and bright.

"You're just like my brother," I say.

Liam draws a tear running down his cheek, but he persists. "But you do want to photograph me naked?"

"If you'll sign a release," I say.

"Only if you show me your work." Liam looks me in the eye. "I need someone who knows how to capture true beauty." He pulls out his cell. "Do you have a site?"

So he doesn't know.

"Social media maybe," he says. "Give me all the details. Where can I find Danielle Bellamy's work?"

Chapter Fourteen

DANIELLE

A dam watches his brother carefully. Looking for signs to Liam's intentions.

Because he's used to his brother ribbing his girlfriends?

Or because he knows I'm naked on the Internet?

"You should see the way Danielle's decorated the spare room," Adam says.

"You put your girlfriend in the spare room?" Liam shakes his head *how awful*. "Really?"

"It's my studio," I say. "Well. Half of my studio. I'm using the empty room on the third floor too."

"You're living here?" Liam asks.

"I am," I say.

Liam makes that *hmmm* noise, adding everything up in his head. Then he shrugs, back to effortless playboy. "So you can take my picture here anytime."

"I don't remember agreeing to this." I try to keep the tone light. As if I don't have an anonymous site full of half-naked photos. As if Adam and I aren't pretending we're in love and the three of us aren't awkwardly avoiding the subject of their brother's death.

Totally and completely light.

No problem.

"Right." Liam perks. "Naked people. You were going to show me some."

Adam's eyes flit to me. He looks me up and down carefully.

Like he's seen me halfway out of these pajamas.

Or maybe like he spent the night picturing me—

Well, he hadn't seen me in the pajamas. But he does want to fuck me. It's entirely possible he spent the night picturing me naked.

"Danielle?" Liam asks.

Right. "I did pick out photos for the spare room. They're on the gallery site." I tell him the address to buy myself time to think.

Liam's eyes go wide as he pulls up the gallery's site. The collection is still on the home page. It's still named after my favorite photo, *The Voyeur.* "These pictures are there." Liam points in the direction of the spare room.

"Do you want to see them?" I ask.

"Fuck yes." He jumps out of his seat. "You two will give me twenty minutes in the room alone, right?"

"That's eighteen more than you've ever lasted," Adam says.

Liam isn't remotely insulted. He smiles with pride. "Did you just make a sex joke?" He beams. "Am I finally corrupting you, after all these years? Or is it your beautiful new house guest?"

"I can only hope," I say.

"Did you take these?" he asks.

My cheeks flush. "I haven't taken anything nearly as well composed or interesting. Not that my photos are bad.

But I'm still learning. This artist... she's a master. She has another set we sold last year—"

Liam holds up his cell phone, displaying one of Dana DeLaney's older sets. Naked women, posing together, inviting the viewer to enjoy the girl on girl action, then turning it on its head as the girls embrace awkward poses and uncomfortable emotions.

"She's not afraid to make people gasp. Or make them uncomfortable. I'm not quite as provocative."

"You don't have any of babes fucking themselves?" he asks.

I can't honestly answer that with a no. "Not explicitly."

"So... un-explicitly?"

"I've tried to riff off her set. But I, uh, I mostly take self-portraits." My eyes meet Adam's.

He holds his poker face.

"And I'm not showing you those," I say.

"Wait. You're telling me there are photos, of you, without clothes."

"They exist," I say.

"And, yet I'm sitting here, looking at... you're beautiful in your pajamas, Danielle, but I'd rather see you naked." He looks to Adam, waiting for a response.

"Why are you looking at him?" I ask.

"You know men," Liam says. "They're territorial."

"Still. You could ask my permission first," I say.

Liam looks to Adam again.

He nods. "She has a point."

"You don't mind me staring at your girlfriend's tits?" Liam asks.

"I respect her as an artist," he says.

Is that part of our ruse? Or does he mean it?

My entire body buzzes with equal parts warmth and need.

Adam wanting me is one thing.

Adam respecting me as an artist?

It's hot in here. Way too hot.

"Well…" Liam raises a brow. "I want to see the best you have. If that image happens to include your tits…" He shrugs *so be it*.

Thankfully, Trish saves me from picking a photograph.

A mug of coffee for Adam. Full plates for me and Liam.

A fluffy stack of chocolate-chip pancakes, topped with sliced strawberries, fresh whipped cream, and rich maple syrup.

Mmm, just the right mix of cake and chocolate and sugar. A groan spills from my lips.

Adam's entire body tunes to mine. The subtle movement sends an electric charge through the air.

Liam notices too. He looks to me and raises a brow. "I can leave you two alone."

With my next bite, I stifle my groan. "This is amazing."

Liam nods *it is*.

"Do you eat like this every day? Every meal?" I ask.

"Trish is a fantastic cook. Had to get out so it didn't all go to my hips." Liam taps his narrow waist. "The ladies like a man with abs."

I tease him. "And since you're a giver, you had to oblige them."

He nods *of course*. "And little did I know it would earn me a gig modeling for the world's sexiest photographer," he says.

"I didn't offer you a job," I say.

"And you didn't show me your work yet." He swallows a sip of coffee. Motions for me to hand over my cell phone.

I can't do that.

There are too many explicit photos in my gallery.

But I can find something appropriate. "I'll text you something."

He looks at me curiously—no website, no social media—but he doesn't call me on it. He relays his number.

I tap it into my phone. Pull up my Dropbox app. Find a recent photo that isn't overly revealing. Okay. There. *Woosh.* "What do you do when you aren't harassing your brother?"

"World domination," he says.

"He works with me," Adam says. "Finance for Pierce."

"Oh, he said with me, not for me. That's progress." He stage whispers, "Adam likes to believe he created the entire company himself."

"He didn't?" I ask.

"He and Simon did most of the paperwork, but they needed my beautiful face to charm early investors."

"But you're rich." My cheeks flush. "I mean, this house belonged to your parents. Your family has money."

"Oh yeah. We're loaded," Liam says. "Spoiled rich boys all around." He motions to Adam. "Look at him, wearing a suit to breakfast."

"It's eleven," Adam says.

"It's a long drive." Liam shakes his head *obviously*. "We've always had money, but he and Simon tripled our net worth."

Ding

The picture message delivers.

Liam's eyes go wide. "Fuck, Danielle. You took this?"

"I did." It's one of my better photos. The curves of my neck, chest, stomach, hips. My fingers curling into my thighs. My nails painted black. My hair falling to one side.

Cropped at the edge of my breasts.

Sensual without actually revealing anything.

Liam turns the cell to Adam. "Have you seen this?"

"No." His pupils dilate.

"It's hot. But classy too." Liam nods with approval. "You have to do me like this."

Uh...

"If Adam approves." He looks to Adam, giving him a chance to object.

But Adam holds that poker face.

"If you can afford me," I say.

Liam smiles and offers his hand. After we shake, he shifts his troublemaking tactics, starts telling stories about Adam as a dorky kid.

Apparently, even when he was a skinny dweeb, Adam attracted all kinds of female attention. But he barely noticed. He was always focused on something else.

School or work or family.

Liam is surprised he finally found time for a girlfriend. He didn't think it would ever happen.

He doesn't add anything about the accident, the scars, the loss of their brother, but it's in every sentence.

Adam was never a social butterfly. He was never a happy-go-lucky guy. But since the accident—

He's different.

I piece that much together.

I eat too many pancakes and drink too much coffee. By the time Liam announces his departure, I'm jittery from the caffeine.

"You should really move back to the city," Liam says. "You have any idea how long it takes to get here? Even in a fucking helicopter." He shakes his head *ridiculous*. "You're going to have two hours in your limo Friday. Four if you hit traffic."

"Friday?" I ask.

He nods. "Next week is the Pierce quarterly meeting." He turns to his brother. "Or did you forget?"

Adam fails to hide his discomfort. "I remember."

"You two are going to dinner with me after. No excuses. If you won't meet me in the city, I'll come here, stay the entire weekend."

"Simon too?" Adam asks.

"Up to him," Liam says.

Adam stares at his brother for a minute, then he nods. "We'll be there."

Liam pulls him into a hug. Whispers something in his ear.

Adam releases him with a nod. "Until then."

Liam hugs me goodbye, then he motions *call me* and he leaves the two of us alone in the big empty house.

"He's a lot," Adam says.

"Like Remy." I move toward the dining room. "Funny."

"The court jester, as Simon says." He says it with affection. "Simon is as serious as I am."

"That's hard to believe," I say.

Adam actually smiles. "Older and wiser."

I guess Adam isn't the oldest, even though he acts like it. He wears the same burden I do.

If Remy died on my watch—

No wonder he locks himself in his office. I'm not sure I'd ever face the world.

It almost makes sense. He's sure he'll never be happy again, and he doesn't want his brothers to worry. So, being rich and powerful and used to getting his way, he tried to buy a solution.

A million dollars for an elaborate ruse.

But did he really pick me because he liked my passion for art?

It's more likely he bought the photos and specifically requested I deliver them, because he enjoys my photos.

But then Mr. Davey said Adam didn't specify who should bring the photos.

Was that true?

Something is missing.

I know he's seen my pictures. I can feel it.

Last night's photo wasn't enough.

I have to push him harder.

"Would you mind?" I ask. "If I shot your brother?"

"He offered because he knew it would vex me. But he meant it. If you'd like to take his photo... I trust your judgment."

"But you'd prefer I didn't?"

"Yes."

Okay. I guess that's clear enough.

"You were great today." He stands. Looks at me awkwardly, like he's not sure if he should hug me, kiss me, shake my hand. "Perfect."

"Thank you."

"I have to get back to work." He doesn't hug me, kiss me, shake my hand. Instead, he nods goodbye. "Thank you, Danielle. Really."

"Sure thing." I nod back. Watch him walk up the stairs.

He slips out of his role as lovebird as easily as he slips into it. That's all it is.

Pretending.

He doesn't love me.

I don't love him.

Yes, I want him. I want him so badly I can't breathe but—

Well, I have my own set of tools there.

I'm going to post pictures until he breaks.

I don't care what it costs me.

We might be lying to the world, but I'm not letting Adam Pierce deceive me this time.

Chapter Fifteen

ADAM

Danielle is daring me.

There's no other explanation.

Two hours after I return to my office, she posts a photo taken in her room. Her, draped in the sheer curtains, bathed in soft light.

At dinner, she doesn't mention it.

She doesn't ask me to stay.

She doesn't make conversation.

She says goodbye when I excuse myself. Then she watches a foreign film in the home theater.

I wake to another photo.

This time, Danielle in the boots she wore to dinner, her body bent over the bed, her panties binding her thighs.

Again, she makes small talk at dinner.

Again, she says goodbye without complaint.

Again, she posts an erotic image.

Her body splayed over the soft sheets, her fingers curling into the white cotton.

There's nothing explicit, but I can feel the bliss emanating from the image.

She *is* fucking herself.

She's not pretending.

For days, she toys with me.

She dares me to divulge my intentions, demand she stop, claim her completely.

For days, I resist.

I run an extra mile, spend an extra hour at the gym, work late.

I hold it together through dinner Thursday.

Until she's sipping her limoncello, looking at me like she's going to consume me.

"We're meeting Liam tomorrow." I'm facing the world tomorrow. I'm not sure which scares me more.

"When will we leave?" she asks.

"Late morning." I stand. Call on all my composure. I'm wary of the looks I'll get from investors. But this, standing here and kissing her?

That's terrifying.

"We should practice." I have to control myself. After a week of seeing her naked, in increasingly erotic images, I have to control myself.

"We should." She finishes her last sip. Stands. Offers me her hand.

I take it. Pull her closer.

She hooks her arms around my neck.

I place my hands on the small of her back.

She rises to her tiptoes and presses her lips to mine.

Sugar and lemon and Danielle.

She tastes so fucking good.

Her lips part.

My tongue slides between them.

Her fingers curl into my skin.

She arches her back, rocking her hips against mine, groaning against my lips.

"Adam." She whispers my name as she pulls back.

Every molecule of my body begs me to claim her. To pin her to the wall, push her panties to her ankles, dive between her legs.

This is too complicated.

That makes sense.

It's the only thing that makes sense.

This is it.

I leave or I fuck her.

Those are the only two options.

Her fingers brush my neck. My chin. My cheek.

Fuck. I can't.

I'm a monster now.

I can't let her see that.

"Perfect." I step backward. "Good night."

Her expression deflates. "Good night, Adam."

———

ALL NIGHT I TOSS AND TURN. I TASTE DANIELLE'S LIPS. I see the need in her dark eyes turn to disappointment.

I imagine her here, in my bed, in those sleek silk pajamas.

Undoing the buttons.

Slipping her bottoms off her hips.

Climbing into my lap.

Touching me tenderly, the way she did when we kissed.

Her hand on my chest, neck, chin.

It's too much. Even in my head.

I can't handle her touching my scars.

And the jagged lines on my cheek are nothing compared to the markings on my body.

I've never been driven by sex. I had needs. I filled

them. Sometimes, those needs involved a rough touch, a stern order, a rope around a woman's wrists.

I enjoyed being in control.

It sated something in me.

Now, the only thing I need is Danielle.

Her long, soft body bent over the bed. Her face wracked with bliss. Her wine lips parting with a groan.

Adam.

I wake sweaty, tense, frustrated.

My morning workout fails to help. A cold shower does nothing. After breakfast, I make an excuse about an early meeting. Leave instructions with Trish and Louis and head into the city alone.

It's a long drive.

I've only made it a few times since the accident. Only when it was strictly necessary.

It's strange, being behind the driver's wheel. Familiar and foreign at once.

I keep my attention on the road. Drive straight to my apartment building, head upstairs, to the penthouse apartment I've been avoiding since Bash died.

The place I called home for most of the last decade.

It's still clean and modern, with big windows and sleek furniture. The perfect place for Danielle.

To curl up on the couch.

Or study the morning light.

Or bend over the dining table and beg for my cock.

Fuck.

Take a chill pill, Adam. She wants to fuck you. You want to fuck her. Stop making it complicated.

She's obviously into your scars.

Yeah, you're a freak show now. But let's face it, you've always been a weirdo.

Why not use it to bang a hottie?

I celebrated Bash's last birthday here. Toasted to him finally dating the same woman for more than three months.

And he joked about fucking her on the table when I was away.

Or have you beat me to it, Adam? Someone has to christen this thing. Wood on wood. It's poetic.

Of course, I didn't know the details.

I didn't know he was fucking a married woman with a vengeful husband. Only that he was over the moon.

This place is beautiful, but I don't see the perfect view of the modern appliances.

Only the lack of Bash.

It's in every room, corner, piece of furniture.

He's gone.

And I don't know how to survive without him.

Chapter Sixteen

ADAM

"Hey kid, nice of you to finally make it." Liam meets me at the elevator with a smile. He pats me on the shoulder. "Where's your girlfriend?"

"Why would I bring her to a meeting?"

He shakes his head *don't be ridiculous*. "She's a hottie. You can see that."

"I can."

"You need coffee or something? You're not getting this. I get to look at her. She gets to look at me." He motions to his face. "And find entertainment for hours."

"She is an artist," I say.

He nods *exactly*.

"Someone as hideous as you must be fascinating to her."

He chuckles. "Good one." He pats me on the shoulder again. "You don't shoot often, but when you do." He makes a finger gun and points it in the direction of the windows on the other side of the building. Slowly, he narrows in on the tip of the Empire State Building, shoots, blows invisible smoke. "You ready?"

"Are you going to be an idiot?"

"There's no helping that."

A laugh escapes my lips. It's impossibly light. So light it floats.

"You know what they say. Fish gotta swim, birds gotta fly—"

"Idiots have to idiot."

"Liam Pierce has to light up the room with his vibrant personality."

"Is that what you call it?"

"Oh yeah." He places his hand on his heart. "Everybody loves me." He motions *follow me*.

Liam is teasing, but he's right. Everyone loves him. Yes, his class clown antics occasionally rub someone the wrong way. But he always wins them over eventually.

He's always bright. Even at the fucking funeral.

I understand his impulse to hide his pain behind humor. And I love him. I'd die to protect Liam, even if he's the most annoying person on the planet, but I'll never understand him.

This—

This is the best I can do.

"You bring your a-game?" He nods hello to a pretty young woman with short hair and an edgy style. "Black coffee for Adam."

"Another cup for you, Liam?" she asks.

"As sweet as your smile," he says.

She laughs. "So black then?"

"As sweet as my smile."

"Still black." Her smile lights up her face. It may not be as sweet as Liam takes his coffee, but it's awfully sweet.

Is she another person who responds to his charms?

Or does she actually like him?

For a minute, the thought of Liam settling down steals

my attention. I almost laugh at the image of him buying a ring, proposing, walking down the aisle.

Then we step into the boardroom, and my ease evaporates.

A dozen executives, sitting in expensive ergonomic thrones, trying to pass off bragging as small talk.

A new yacht, a new mansion, a new wife.

They see Liam and smile.

Then they see me.

The room falls dead silent.

The same silence that overtook the house when Bash died.

Liam says hello, introduces me as our CTO, pulls out my chair.

He makes a point of asking about some rich man's wife.

Whispers fill the room.

Is that really Adam Pierce?

I thought he never left the house.

My daughter always found him handsome. Not so much now. What a waste of a nice face.

Good thing he's rich.

I don't know. The scars add character. Like that R&B singer. Didn't he marry a supermodel?

Liam's assistant interrupts with our coffees. He takes a long sip and lets out an over-the-top sigh. "Ah, as sweet as my smile."

She shakes her head *ridiculous,* but again, she laughs at his antics.

I sit.

Liam takes the spot next to me. He keeps that wide, easy smile as he talks numbers. He drops a joke every few minutes, keeping the room engaged even during painfully dry spreadsheets.

He finishes with a bow and hands the room to me. "Now, for someone who actually knows what they're talking about. Adam Pierce, our CTO."

Before the accident, quarterly meetings were a necessary evil. I didn't enjoy presenting, but I was passionate. That kept my nerves at bay.

Now, with everyone staring, deeming me a monster, wondering if the rumors are true—

My stomach churns.

My shoulders stiffen.

My thoughts refuse to straighten.

"That's just it," Liam says. "You use our new privacy suite, you go silent. No one else will hear a peep."

I nod as if I'm staying quiet on purpose.

"They'll have no idea who you are, where you are, what you do."

I can do this. I can explain. "You control how much you share." I take a deep breath. "We've responded to our major competitors' technology. Including investigator databases." I find my footing enough to finish the rundown.

The room quiets. That familiar quiet I used to claim all the time. Respect. Interest. Admiration.

When I finish, and Liam takes the floor, the quiet shifts. Half attention on my brother. Half whispers.

I guess the accident didn't screw up his head too bad.

He's slower now.

You know why he's upgrading the privacy, don't you?

Because he did it and he doesn't want anyone to know.

How's the software going to help with hiding evidence of murder?

I focus on my coffee. Dark, strong, warm. Comforting in its familiar bitterness.

The meeting ends. My brother shakes hands with our investors. Charms every single one.

I find privacy in the bathroom. Piss. Wash. Check my cell.

Messages from Trish, disapproving of my unplanned exit this morning.

Updates from Louis. He dropped off Danielle an hour ago. Along with everything she needs for dinner. And enough to spend the weekend here. Just in case.

A new image on her Instagram.

Danielle in a long silk robe, standing in front of the wide windows of my penthouse.

Setting up for my next shoot. What do you think of the wardrobe?

Her back is to the camera, but her intent is clear.

She's stripping.

She's taking naked pictures.

In my fucking apartment.

Another dare.

And the only fucking thing that makes sense.

The Bash in my head is right.

She wants me.

I want her.

Why make it complicated?

Chapter Seventeen

DANIELLE

The afternoon light fades into the orange glow of sunset. The cozy warmth is the perfect contrast to Adam's cold, modern apartment.

I check the light, adjust my aperture, frame the photo just so.

It's difficult, getting into position for a self-portrait without the help of the display screen, but I do my best.

There. Halfway between the dining table and the kitchenette, in front of the window.

I close my eyes. Try to channel the expression I need.

My thoughts go to Adam immediately.

His hands on my lips, his lips on my neck, his cock driving into me.

Snap, snap.

It's a gorgeous photo. Riding the line between sensual and erotic.

Easier because it's my body, because I don't have to blush over a naked model.

Harder because it's my body, because I'm revealing myself to thousands of anonymous strangers.

My photos are sexy. Sometimes, they turn me on. Not the images as much as the feeling of exposing myself.

Usually, the thought stays in the back of my mind.

Today, it's at the front.

I don't focus on composition, or presentation, or figuring out exactly what I want to say with these images.

I think of Adam.

His deep blue eyes on me.

His steady voice in my ears.

His hand wrapped around his cock.

God, I want to watch him fuck himself. I want to know he craves me. I want to see him see me.

As an artist.

As a woman.

As a person he wants to fuck.

He wants me.

And this—

There's no way he can resist this photo.

I slip into my robe to check my social media. My last post is already popular. It's enough to test him.

I add more anyway.

A cell phone snap, from the front this time. My hand on the bottom of the robe, pulling the fabric up my thighs.

Me, ready to fuck myself.

It's cropped innocently enough, but the intent is clear.

I'm here, in his gorgeous apartment, touching myself.

Woosh.

I post the image.

Return to the camera. Take a bigger, broader, better version.

Then another.

Another.

I lose myself in the rhythm of pose and picture.

My phone buzzes, but I ignore it.

Footsteps in the hallway call my attention.

The jingle of keys in the door.

I can stop now. Close my robe. Hide my camera.

This is it. My last chance to back off.

I don't.

I let my robe fall open, turn my head to one side, dig my fingers into my thighs.

The door opens.

Steady footsteps move closer.

Adam's footsteps. I recognize them.

"I'm not the only person with a key." His voice is steady. No anger, no hurt, no passion.

I don't respond.

"What would you do, if I'd sent Liam to fetch you?" he asks.

"You wouldn't."

"I wouldn't?" He takes a step toward me.

"You disagree?"

"No." Another step.

Is that seriously his response? No.

"Do you care I'm naked?"

"Yes."

"Do you care I'm taking photos in your apartment?"

"Yes."

"Is that the only word you can say?"

His eyes meet mine. "You wanted me to find you like this."

"Yes."

"You want me to see you, posing for your camera." He moves closer. Close enough to touch me.

My chest heaves with my inhale. My body moves toward his. It's an involuntary reaction. An instinct as strong as turning to the sun or pulling away from a fire.

"You want me to see you flushed and panting."

"Yes," I breathe.

His fingers skim my chest. He pushes the robe off my shoulders.

It falls open, revealing my breasts, stomach, thighs.

"You're beautiful," he says.

"Thank you."

His eyes fix on me. "Show me. Here. Now."

My cheeks flush.

"Take off the robe."

I step away from the window. Drop the silk at my feet.

"Turn around."

I do.

He lets out a soft gasp. "What do you want?"

"You."

"How?"

"Whatever you'll give me."

"You think of me when you fuck yourself?"

"Constantly."

His voice hardens. "Turn around."

I do.

"Touch yourself."

My breath catches in my throat.

"Now."

"Will you…" I'm not sure what I'm asking, only that I want it. "Can I touch you?"

"After."

"You promise?"

"No." His eyes move over me slowly. "Fuck yourself. Now. If I'm feeling generous, I'll give you more."

"Adam—"

"Now."

Fuck. The cold disappears. The nerves in my stomach disappear. I'm terrified. But I want him too badly to care.

"Don't make me ask twice." His voice drops to something deep and rough.

He wants me as badly as I want him.

He has to stay in control.

Fuck, I want him in control.

I want him touching me. I want every inch of his skin against every inch of mine.

But if this is the only way I can have him—

As long as I can have him—

I meet his gaze and I slip my hand between my legs.

He watches intently as I bring my index finger to my clit. I work myself with slow strokes.

I'm already keyed up.

I'm already so fucking close.

He stares at me with fascination. Like he's been waiting to watch me for a thousand years. Like I'm finally releasing him.

I watch him for as long as I can.

Then my eyes flutter closed.

It's too much. Too intense.

Pleasure threatens to overwhelm me.

"Come for me, Danielle." His voice is soft and rough, yielding and hard, in control and completely unraveled.

For a second, the dichotomies threaten to derail me.

Then he lets out a low, deep groan, and I go over the edge.

The tension inside me winds to a fever pitch. With my next stroke, I unravel.

My sex pulses as I come.

His name falls off my lips.

I work myself through my orgasm, then I blink my eyes open.

He moves closer. Close enough to touch me.

But he doesn't. Not the way I expect.

He brings his hand to my chin, and he pulls me into a soft kiss.

I pull back with a sigh. "Adam."

"We don't have time."

"But later—" I reach for him.

He wraps his hand around my wrist. "I stay in control, angel."

Angel. It suits the soft lighting here. The look of my images. My desire to take his pain away.

"Please." I look up into his eyes. "Please, Adam."

"Later."

"You promise?"

"Ask again and the answer is no. Understand?"

I barely manage to nod.

"We're late. You should get dressed." He pulls me into another slow, deep kiss.

I have to drag myself away.

I change into my evening attire in the bedroom. Adam's bedroom.

He's slept here.

Fucked himself here.

Fucked other women here, probably.

Will he fuck me here tonight?

God, I want that so badly.

But he's so... controlled.

I don't get it. I don't get him.

But right now, I don't care.

I only care about touching him again.

I wash up, retouch my makeup, grab my bag.

He helps me into my coat, then into the elevator, onto the street. We walk four blocks in silence.

Take another elevator in silence.

Step into the lobby in silence.

Just when I'm ready to declare Adam as cruel as he is

cold, he wraps his arms around me, and he pulls me into a slow deep kiss.

It's not loving or romantic.

It's pure sex.

He kisses me like he's claiming me. Like he's going to spend his entire life watching me come.

Touching me.

Savoring my touch.

I pull back with a sigh. Whisper his name.

But he isn't looking at me anymore.

He's looking at a man in the lobby.

He's familiar. A client.

Cole Fitzgerald.

But what the fuck does he have to do with Adam?

Chapter Eighteen

DANIELLE

"**M**s. Bellamy. Is that you?" Mr. Fitzgerald nods hello.

Adam's grip around my waist tightens.

"You must introduce me to your date," he says.

Adam's eyes meet his.

They stare each other down. The way men do. That territorial pissing contest.

But why?

Mr. Fitzgerald is a client. Yes, he flirts sometimes, but he's never expressed an interest. He's married.

And he's not like other married men who whine their wives don't understand them. He speaks highly of his wife's wit and taste.

"Adam Pierce." Adam offers his hand. "We've met."

"Pierce Industries. Of course. I'm sorry." He takes a wide step toward us. Studies Adam carefully. "I didn't recognize you."

"Yes, the shorter hair confuses people," he says.

I fail to stifle a laugh. "Oh my god." I press my forehead to Adam's chest.

He wraps his arms around me. Pulls me closer.

"You have a dark sense of humor," I whisper.

"I know."

"Always?"

He runs his fingers over my chin. "Always."

"You don't make a lot of jokes."

"Should I?"

"I like it when you do." I soak up the warm, hard feeling of his skin. The soft wool of his suit jacket. The Earthy smell of his soap. Can I stay here, in his arms, forever?

Maybe without the clothes.

But absolutely pressed against his warm, hard body.

"Of course. The accident," Mr. Fitzgerald says. "I was sad to hear that news. Your brother was a force of nature."

Adam's grip tightens. "He was."

"He'd do whatever it took to get his way."

"You must understand that." He catches himself. Releases me. "Angel, let me take your coat."

Right. I'm wearing my coat inside. I could have his hands on my bare skin. I could remove one of the horrible layers of fabric between us. "Thank you."

He slips it off my shoulders, one at a time, brings it to the host.

"I didn't see you at the gallery last week," Mr. Fitzgerald says.

"I'm not working there anymore."

"Oh?"

"I had another opportunity."

He motions for me to continue.

That's the polite response, yes, but there's something strange about it.

Something between him and Adam.

Mr. Fitzgerald was interested in *The Voyeur*. He was

going to come in and buy it, have his assistant pack it up and hang it in his study. He was going to do it the day Adam paid double the asking price.

Is he that territorial about his art?

I want that to be true. I want to believe someone is as passionate about photography as I am.

But there's a more likely answer.

Adam bought the painting to fuck with him.

Or he tried to buy it to fuck with Adam.

Rich men think nothing of dropping five figures as a fuck you.

But they're acting as if they barely know each other.

"And, well—" I can figure out what Mr. Fitzgerald wants later. Right now, I have to earn my million dollar pay day. Time to play pretty, supportive girlfriend. "Things with Adam are moving fast."

"Oh." He tries to hide his disappointment.

"He asked me to move in with him. I know, we sound so young. I'm sure it was a million years ago you asked your wife to live with you," I say.

He frowns. "No. Back then, you didn't live with someone before you married them."

"Oh. Of course. My mother's family was..." Not traditional, exactly. And I can't really say they were wrong for disapproving of my father.

Mom never gave me the full story. But the facts are clear. He married her, stuck around for long enough to knock her up again, left for a younger woman.

Asshole.

But, hey, I'm not here to work out my daddy issues either. I'm here to make everyone jealous.

And while I can't push everyone's buttons, I can push Mr. Fitzgerald's.

"My mom was wild," I say. "She didn't care who

approved of her choices. Short hair, tattoos, leather pants. The whole nine yards."

"Did you rebel by wearing pencil skirts?"

"No. She was always supportive of my passion for art." I'm not telling him about my personal rebellion. "I just don't like pants. Dresses are much more comfortable." I spin on my heels. Show off the low back of my gown.

When I put it on, I thought it was too much.

With Adam staring like he's going to consume me, it's too much in a different way.

I need the fabric gone.

I need his hands on my skin.

Now.

Here.

I don't care who sees, as long as he touches me.

"And easier too," I say. "A dress is an entire outfit."

"Is that dress really easier than jeans and a t-shirt?" Mr. Fitzgerald asks.

"I can never find jeans that fit." I smooth my dress. "The curse of wide hips."

His eyes follow my hands. "You wear it well."

"Thank you."

Adam slips his arm around my waist. "Liam is running late."

"Oh?" I ask.

"His date." Adam shakes his head *don't ask*. "Let's have a drink."

"On me," Mr. Fitzgerald says. "To celebrate your new love."

I look to Adam, but he's back to perfect poker face.

"That's kind of you, Cole," he says, suddenly familiar.

"It's nothing, Adam. Only what your brother would have wanted." Mr. Fitzgerald motions *after me.*

Adam shoots him a sickly sweet smile. One equal parts *you're full of shit* and *I'm going to kill you with kindness.*

Or maybe just *I'm going to kill you.*

I have no idea what the fuck these two are doing.

And I lose interest the second Adam presses his palm into my lower back.

His hand feels right on my skin.

Warm and steady and sure.

He leads me to the bar on the right side of the restaurant. It's like Adam's house, something out of an old movie. High ceilings, chandeliers, curved windows letting in the skyline.

A dozen tables, well-spaced, quiet, classy.

The bar is the same. Long with plenty of room between stools and a cute blonde bartender in a snug black dress.

Adam's fingers glide over my lower back as he leans in to whisper, "I can order a bottle."

"Is that what you're drinking?"

"Only when Trish insists."

"What do you normally drink?"

"Whatever the lady is drinking."

"You're a charmer now?"

"When I have to be." He traces a line up my spine. Then back down it.

"A grapefruit martini. With gin please," I say to the bartender.

When she asks if I have a preference, Adam names a top-shelf brand. "Two."

"Make it three." Fitzgerald brandishes his credit card. "On me. Please."

Adam pulls me closer. "Only if I can buy you and your wife a round. To celebrate your love."

"How is Celine?" I ask. "She has such great taste."

"Celine. I'm not sure we've met," Adam says. "How do you know her, angel?"

"I don't. Only through Mr. Fitzgerald." I lean into his touch. "You buy for her, don't you?"

"Some for her. Some for me." He looks to Adam. "You know women. They always have final approval."

"Danielle is the artist. I trust her taste," he says.

"Have you bought pieces for the Pierce manor?" Mr. Fitzgerald asks.

"Yes," I say. "I bought the DeLaney set. I know you were interested, but I had to have them."

"And I offered double asking the second I saw her eyes light up." Adam turns to me. He keeps one hand on the small of my back. Brings the other to my chin.

He cups my cheek as he pulls me into a soft, slow kiss.

The rest of the world disappears.

It's only Adam's hands on my skin and his lips on my lips and his hard, warm body against mine.

When he pulls back, I'm dizzy.

My surroundings return to me slowly. Adam's deep blue eyes. His slate grey suit. The shimmering crystal of the chandelier.

The bartender, placing our drinks on the counter.

Adam's fingers brush mine as he passes me the drink. He holds his up to toast. "To *The Voyeur*."

"To young love," Mr. Fitzgerald butts in.

"To love. Yes." Adam shoots him a smile. "To love and the lengths we'll go for it."

Mr. Fitzgerald returns an equally sharp smile as he raises his glass.

He toasts Adam. Then me.

Then Adam turns to me, and the world disappears again.

His blue eyes are so gorgeous.

And he's so close.

Because of our ruse.

Because he wants to prove something.

But then I want to prove something too.

Fuck Mr. Fitzgerald for staring at Adam like he's a deformed creature who can barely survive.

I'm not letting him get away with that.

Adam taps his glass against mine. Brings it to his lips. Takes a long sip.

"How is it?" I ask.

"Liam said something to his assistant today," he says.

"Oh?"

"He asked her to bring him coffee as sweet as his smile," he says. "Of course, she said, 'black then.'"

I can't help but smile. Liam is even more ridiculous than Remy.

"This is… almost as sweet as you. And as sour as me," he says.

"Sour isn't the word I'd use," I say.

"Tart?"

I shake my head.

"Bitter?"

"Strong."

His pupils dilate.

"Intoxicating." I take a long sip. Mmm. Fresh grapefruit, high-end gin, some delicious orange liqueur. Tart and sweet and strong. "Completely intoxicating."

He kisses me softly this time. It's quick, a second maybe, but my knees still threaten to crumble.

"Do you get used to drinking and eating like this?" I take another sip. "It's overwhelming."

"You're asking the wrong person, Danielle," Mr. Fitzgerald says. "Mr. Pierce has always had money."

"You too," Adam says. "But I spent my college years rebelling. I drank my share of cheap vodka."

"Really?" I ask.

Adam nods.

"Did you wear jeans too?"

"I did."

"I can't imagine that."

"It was a long time ago."

"Were you really a dweeb in school?"

His eyes flit to Mr. Fitzgerald. "A dweeb in a boarding school uniform."

"I've seen pictures, I know, but I still can't believe it." I slide my arm around his waist.

He stiffens for a moment, then he leans into the pose.

"You've always been sure of yourself," I say.

"In photos," he says.

"And handsome." I run my finger over his chin. I shouldn't do this. I know better. But I can't stop myself. "More every day."

His eyes flit to Fitzgerald again.

The asshole is watching like Adam is an animal at the circus.

Fuck him.

Maybe this is too much for Adam. But I'm not letting that asshole think Adam's scars make him a freakshow.

I cup his cheek the way he cupped mine.

He stiffens again. But, this time, when I kiss him, he kisses back.

Softly at first.

Then harder.

My lips part for his tongue.

That perfect, deep kiss. Claiming my mouth, my body, my heart.

This time, my knees go weak when he pulls back.

He catches me. Holds me close.

Mr. Fitzgerald tries to interrupt. "Another round?"

"If you'd like one, angel. Liam will be here in fifteen."

"Okay." I stare back into his eyes. This is fake. For the benefit of the asshole behind us.

I need to believe that.

But my heart still screams *love him, love him, love him.*

Chapter Nineteen

ADAM

Danielle's fingers curl into my neck. Her dark eyes fill with affection.

Desire.

Love.

Or something close. I've never been in love. I've been intimate with women, cared for them, wanted the best for them.

I had other concerns. School, work, family. At least, that's what I told myself.

Who has time for love?

Who has space?

Then dad died and—

There wasn't room in my heart for anyone or anything. I had other concerns. I still have other concerns.

Then Danielle's lips brush my neck and I forget every one.

I barely remember why I'm here.

Or the asshole standing behind me.

What the fuck is he doing here?

Why am I thinking when I could take her home?

I need to see her come again. I need to taste her, touch her, fuck her.

"Adam." She whispers my name like it's our secret. Her fingers skim my chin. My jawline. The scar running across my cheek.

My head turns. A reflex. I can handle it when she's kissing me, but not now.

I try to lean into the gesture. I press my lips to her neck.

She lets out a soft groan.

It's not appropriate for the restaurant, but at the moment I don't give a fuck.

"Your drinks, sir," the bartender interrupts.

The asshole Fitzgerald tries to pay, but I cut him off. "You got the first round."

He nods *of course*. Looks to Danielle as she brings her drink to her lips. "I never pegged you for a gin drinker."

"No." She takes another sip. Lets out a soft sigh. "What did you think I drank?"

"Wine." His eyes flit to her lips. "Red. Something rich."

"I did drink red at our showings." She leans closer. "It's always wine and cheese. Sometimes grapes if you're lucky."

"Grapes and wine?" I ask.

"Redundant, I know," she says. "Some galleries serve cheap stuff. But we went all out. I spent the entire day gathering supplies. The best red wine under twenty dollars a bottle."

"Is there good wine under twenty dollars a bottle?" I ask.

She laughs. "For some of us, that's an expensive bottle. And the cheese. From a specialty shop. Extra aged. Fancy crackers. Fig jam. Raspberries. Really, whatever I could justify serving. I got to take home the extra."

"You were allowed?"

She motions *sorta*. "My boss would have been mad if he caught me. But they'd go to waste otherwise."

"You're always enterprising," I say.

She beams. "Thank you."

"What was your favorite?" I ask.

"The figs and goat cheese," Fitzgerald answers. "You were always eating that."

She looks at him funny. Surprised he remembers.

As far as she knows, he was a regular customer, period. Yes, he probably attended quite a few showings. Maybe even with his wife.

But that's all.

Could she tell he had an interest?

Men aren't as discreet as they think they are.

"My wife was always glad you had them," he says. "She talked about it all the time. 'Finally, a proper appetizer. Not the bargain bin cheese tray.'"

"Oh, you're right. I did meet Celine." Danielle wraps her hand around my waist again. "I completely forgot. She was staring at DeLaney's first set and I confessed I never thought I'd meet someone who loved it as much as I did."

"She adores them," he says.

"She's beautiful. And funny too. You're a lucky man." She raises her glass to toast.

"Yes, to your wife," I say.

His eyes narrow for a split second, then he smiles. "Yes, to Celine."

Danielle beams as she toasts. She takes a long sip. Sets her drink on the counter.

Fitzgerald leers at her bare back. It's hard to fault him for looking—her black gown barely covers her ass—but his stare is transparent.

He's seen her in less.

Does she know?

Or is she used to men gawking?

Danielle is beautiful. Of course men stare.

And this is what I'm doing, isn't it?

Fucking with him the only way he understands.

I had no idea the asshole would be here. But I may as well make something out of the occasion.

There's no way it's a coincidence.

Him following her. Or following me, because he knows I have her.

He'll go to great lengths to hurt people who try to take his women.

My stomach churns.

Then Danielle's lips brush my ear and I forget everything.

I bring my hands to her back. Pull her into a soft, slow kiss.

She tastes so fucking good, like grapefruit and gin and sugar.

The rest of the world disappears.

Until a familiar voice interrupts. "Holy fuck, is that Adam?" Liam cuts through the room.

"Hmm, we're meeting your brother and his girlfriend here, and we're late. What a shock to see him at the bar." Then his assistant, Briar.

"You don't understand," Liam says.

"I don't?" she asks.

"Adam is making out in public."

"Yes, I see that."

"It's Adam."

"Okay."

"Making out."

"Yes, in public. You said that." She turns to us. "Which part of that is exciting?"

"Both."

"Why?"

"Because it's Adam."

She shakes her head *if you say so*. "Sorry. He's not that bright."

"Undoubtedly. But this is Adam. Making out. In public," he says.

"It's nice to see you, Liam." Danielle turns to him.

"My uh… if I'm your muse, what does that make you?" he asks.

"You aren't my muse," she says.

"But you promised to photograph me naked," he says.

"Uh. No." She laughs. "I'm Danielle."

"Briar."

"How do you know Liam?"

"Bad luck," she says. "He's my boss."

"That is bad luck." Danielle winks at my brother. "Should we sit? And stop shouting across the restaurant?"

"I'm liking the shouting," Liam says.

Briar whispers something in his ear.

"Does that mean you'll give me a spanking," he teases.

She laughs. "Like you'd let me."

"Baby, I'm game for anything. You know that." He winks at her.

She shakes her head. "In your dreams."

"The dream I had about you last night… It started a lot like this." He leans in to whisper.

She flames red. "Order me a drink, please."

"Are you bossing *me* around?"

"Am I doing *you* a favor?"

He blows her a kiss.

She pretends to dodge it as she moves to the hostess stand.

"You look gorgeous today, Danielle." He greets her with a hug. "And who's your friend?"

"Cole Fitzgerald." He holds out his hand.

"Ah, yes, the guy with the spyware." Liam shakes. "Our sworn enemy."

"Something like that," Fitzgerald says.

Liam laughs as if it's typical CEO ribbing. For him, it is. He has no idea Fitzgerald was behind Bash's death.

Why would he?

Until I hired someone to investigate, I believed the story the mechanics told. The car malfunctioned.

And besides, who would try to kill Bash? Everyone adored him.

More likely, someone was after me. A competitor. Or a person who didn't believe in our mission.

Not Cole Fitzgerald. A CEO who's barely in the same industry. He ran an e-commerce company.

He didn't move into spyware until after Bash's death.

He was no one. Another rich asshole.

But I was looking at it all wrong. It wasn't about money.

It was a woman.

Bash was fucking his wife.

Reckless. As usual. *Adam, if you saw her, you'd understand. Especially if you saw her coming on my cock. It's a thing of beauty. Elegant and depraved at the same time. And the mouth on her? I've never heard dirty talk that poetic.*

"Is it National Pink Drink Day?" Liam taps Danielle's martini glass. "Am I missing out?"

"Mine," she says.

"Adam?" he asks.

"If he touched it, let him take it," I say.

"Do you have cooties?" she asks.

"All of them." He winks.

"Do you flirt with any woman in front of you?" she asks.

"Any cute woman, yeah." He takes her drink and takes a long sip. "Shit, that's sour." He offers her the rest of the drink.

She shakes her head. "You lick it, it's yours."

"A good policy, yeah, Adam?" he asks.

"That's what Bash would have said." My eyes flit to Fitzgerald.

He fights a frown.

"I did teach him well," Liam says. "The kid knew what mattered in life," he continues, completely oblivious to Fitzgerald.

"Eating pussy?" Danielle asks.

"Did your girlfriend just say pussy?" Liam asks.

"Why are you asking him? I'm right here." she asks.

"Do kids still say pussy?"

She shrugs. "My brother is gay."

"A different brother?"

"No. The one you remind me of," she says.

"Danielle... I don't know how to feel about it."

"Should we call your therapist?"

"No. I think..." He turns to Briar, as she returns from the host stand. "I need a different intervention."

"I should let you go," Fitzgerald says. "You have a busy night."

"I do," I say.

"Briar, baby. I need a special kind of help," Liam calls.

"Where's my drink?" she asks.

"You want to try this?" he holds up the martini glass.

They're in a different world. An easier one.

Danielle looks to me for direction. "Should we sit?"

"You sit. I'll walk you out, Cole," I say.

"Of course." He sets his half-drank martini on the bar and smiles smugly. He motions *after you*.

I lead him into the lobby. Call the elevator.

He looks to the inside of the restaurant. Liam, Danielle, and Briar are still at the bar. Danielle is sipping what's left of my martini.

Briar and Liam are arguing over hers.

They look easy. Comfortable.

I told Danielle this was for my brothers. Because they're worried. If I was a better man, it would be the truth.

Instead, I'm here, challenging the asshole who had my brother killed.

Without her proximity, my plan is clearer. Make him hurt. Period. The end.

No distractions of her soft lips or her lush curves.

Fitzgerald follows my gaze. "Do you love her?"

"Yes." It doesn't feel like a lie.

"It's not right, bringing her into this," he says.

"I don't have the faintest—"

"You're not a good liar."

"My love life isn't your concern," I say.

"Of course. It's a coincidence you started dating Ms. Bellamy after everything."

"We have the same taste in art."

"Art, is it?"

"I'm sure it broke your heart, losing *The Voyeur*. I understand. You don't like when people take things from you. I don't either. Even if it takes everything I have, I make it right."

"It's a beautiful painting."

"Yes. And Danielle adores it. You should see the way she gushes."

"I can imagine."

"Yes, your wife is the same, isn't she? She loves beautiful things."

The elevator dings.

"You'd do anything for her. I understand that, because I'm the same with my family." I hold the door open for him.

"You're in over your head, kid."

"Good night, Cole. Send Celine my regards."

His eyes narrow. "Yes. And let your brother know how sorry I am for your loss."

Fucking asshole.

I step backward.

He smiles, triumphant.

I watch the doors close and the elevator descend.

I try to find some peace.

I join my family at the table.

But I no longer taste victory.

Bash is gone.

Whatever happens, Bash is gone.

How can anything else matter?

Chapter Twenty

ADAM

"**A** busy club is the perfect place to be anonymous," Liam says. "It's so crowded and loud, no one has a clue who you are."

"It's true. Once, I was out with a friend, and I danced with Liam by accident." Briar makes a *gag me* motion.

"Was he a good dancer?" Danielle asks.

Briar motions *okay*.

Liam chuckles. "That isn't what she said at the time."

"It didn't even happen! I was telling a tall tale."

"Damn, was that another dream?" He makes a point of giving her a long once-over. "You were wearing something like that."

"Was I?" she asks.

"Oh yeah. You know I love your refusal to wear a suit," he says.

Danielle smiles. "Your outfit is fierce."

"This old thing?" Briar blushes and motions to her sheer blouse and leather skirt. "No. It cost a fortune."

"Whatever I can do to help the see-through blouse cause," Liam says.

"I should sue you for sexual harassment."

"You know you can't."

"You know you're an asshole," she says.

"I do know that." He looks to me. "Adam? Anything to add?"

"She covered it," I say.

He raises a brow *all right, but you're not fooling anyone with the aloof shit.* "Do you like to dance, Danielle?"

"Who doesn't?" she asks.

"A lot of men feel awkward," he says.

"You're aware of that possibility?" she asks.

"Crazy, I know. Me. Awkward. There's only one time it happens," he says.

"When you can't rise to the occasion?" She blows him a kiss.

He catches it and presses it to his crotch. "No, baby. Happened in college a few times. Did what I do best." He puts his fingers in the shape of a v.

Briar actually grabs his hand. "Do not do what I think you're going to do."

"Well, if you want to volunteer for an explicit demonstration."

She giggles. "Liam." Her voice is pure schoolgirl crush.

"Okay. No demonstration. Because I aim to please my audience. But you understand, Danielle. Whiskey dick. It happens to all of us." He motions for me to join. "Back me up, Adam."

"I know my limits," I say.

"Boring." He shakes his head. "Is there a version of ladies? Whiskey—"

"Schnapps Snatch," Briar says.

"Did you make that up?" he asks.

"My best friend used to say it," she says. "You're horny but you can't cross the finish line."

"Really?" Liam's eyes go wide. "Tell me more."

"I've told you enough," she says.

"So when do I have to cut you off?" he asks.

"Depends. Do I need to be drunk enough to find you attractive?" she teases.

"Absolutely. That's two or three, minimum," he says.

She smiles, charmed.

He does it every time.

"This is two," he says.

"And, yet, I can't get past your horrible personality," she says.

"Not when I'm dressed. But when I'm naked." He calls to Danielle. "And soon, I'll have photos that are pure body. No personality."

"What do I need you for then?" she asks.

He chuckles. "Baby, if you're fucking yourself to my photos, that will be enough for me."

She makes a *gag me* motion.

"The human body is a work of art," he says.

"That is true," Danielle agrees.

"See," he says. "My photographer finally has her muse."

"You have to pay women to look at your naked body, huh?" Briar shakes her head. "Sad."

He laughs. "That was good. I walked into that."

"It's true," she says.

"I'm paying Danielle for her time and talent," he says.

"It would take a lot of talent to make you look tolerable," she says.

"Absolutely. But you're good for it, right?" he asks Danielle.

She laughs. "I've never shot a man before."

"No? You and Adam aren't getting freaky?" he asks.

"Sexts are private," Briar says.

"I didn't ask to see them," he says.

"You know your brother as well as I do. He's not the type to flaunt," she says.

"Wait. Are you saying there are men out there who don't flaunt their bods?" he asks.

"Or brag about their dicks maybe. Imagine that." Briar laughs.

"He won't pose for you?" He looks to me. "Really, Adam? That's cold."

"How could I compete with you?" I try to tease him, but it doesn't land. The three of them are light and easy.

The gin is making them effervescent.

It's an anchor around my ankle.

I need to get out of here.

We're done with dinner—some grilled fish and lemon vegetables. A fruit tart dessert. Plus espresso that will keep them going all night.

Liam didn't fight me over paying the check.

We can leave now.

I need to leave now. Before I ruin something else.

"Okay, I'll cut you off at five, Briar." He takes her hand and holds it up. "So you can come as you think of me tonight."

"Uh-huh." She plays coy, but she doesn't hide her blush.

"What about you, Danielle? When should I cut you off?" he asks.

"I've got it under control. But thanks," she says.

"And Adam? You said you know your limits?" he asks.

"We should go," I say.

"Ready to party already?" Liam jumps to his feet. "I know the perfect place. And they play eighties music all night. The only pop you like."

"You like eighties music?" Danielle asks.

"You mean you haven't seen the man singing about the plains in Africa?" He looks to me and raises a brow *really*. "He lights up like a pinball machine." He holds up a fake mic and mouths the chorus.

"Adam is more New Wave, actually, Liam," Briar says. "The only time I ever saw him smile was when you sang *Tainted Love* to him. Well, until tonight."

"I do a good Soft Cell," Liam says.

"Soft, huh?" Briar asks.

"Baby, you know what will happen if you bait me," he says.

She laughs *I do*. "One of my regular hangouts has a new wave night. It's a dive, but the music is great."

"I'm not really dressed for a club," Danielle says.

"You look fabulous though. You can't go home until you show that gown off again," Briar says.

Danielle smiles. "Thanks."

"One drink. A bar. Someplace quiet," Briar says.

"Quiet enough, you have to talk to me?" Liam asks. "That means she likes you, Danielle."

Briar laughs. "I do like her. I'd say more than I like you, but we all know that's setting the bar low."

"I love when you tease me, baby," he says.

She lets out another schoolgirl giggle. "One drink. Please." She looks to me. "You'll like the place, Adam. I promise."

"Yes, Adam. Don't be a party pooper." Liam presses his hands together as if he's about to drop to his knees and beg. "Or is this too close to what gets you off."

Danielle's chest heaves with her inhale.

I want to touch her.

That makes sense.

It's the only thing that makes sense.

But not now, not with my head this messy. I don't trust myself.

I stand, offer my hand, help her up.

She hooks her arms around my neck. "We can go home." Her fingers curl into my skin. "Or go somewhere else. Be alone."

Every molecule of my body begs me to say yes. To pin her to the wall, peel her panties to her ankles, fuck her until she's screaming my name.

But I can't risk hurting her.

Is it better to leave now?

Or go with her?

Liam is all talk. I trust him to protect her.

"Go." I suck a breath through my teeth. "Have another drink."

Her lips curl into a frown.

"I'll be there when you get home." I lead her to the lobby, fetch her coat, slide it over her shoulders.

We take the elevator together. Walk to the car Liam called. He helps Briar into the back seat. Then he shoots me a *don't fuck this up* look and climbs in after her. "You have one minute to make out. Two if you send pictures." He blows Danielle a kiss.

She waits until he shuts the door. "Are you okay?"

"Tired."

Her fingers skim my neck. My jawline. My cheek.

I step back.

"We can go home," she says. "Finish what we started."

It's too fucking tempting. "Later."

She stares back at me for a minute, but she doesn't ask again. She kisses me goodbye and gets into the car.

Chapter Twenty-One

ADAM

After a year in the mansion, I'm not used to New York City at night. With every turn, I expect darkness to fall, but the city stays light.

A softer shade of blue. Brightened by the flickering bulbs of apartment dwellers and office workers. It's Friday night. Late by normal standards. Certainly by the standards of the financial district.

Early for the rest of Manhattan.

For the people like Danielle, Liam, Briar, the ones searching for fun, love, connection. Or enough alcohol to fake it.

The building is strangely familiar. A memory of a dream. Cream and silver lobby. Shining elevator. Clean hardwood floors.

And my apartment, quiet and still, lit only by the skyline.

Come on, Adam. Even you appreciate the view. The Empire State Building in one direction. The Hudson River in another. On a clear day, you can see the Statue of Liberty. Don't tell me you're unmoved by those massive phallic symbols.

The babe in a sheet is holding a torch. A torch!

I can still see him standing at the table, raising his glass to toast.

To the miserable among us.

I can hear his laugh.

Feel his smile lighting up the room.

He thought he was the funniest asshole who ever lived.

And he was.

Now, he's gone.

It doesn't make sense.

It will never make sense.

I understand why Liam wanted to drag me to a bar. After doctors weaned me off prescription painkillers, I tried to find solace in alcohol.

A few drinks dulled the pain.

A few more and the dam broke.

Loss consumed me.

There was no joy, no purpose, no want.

Only emptiness, in every direction, as far as I could see.

I didn't find pleasure in music, film, food.

I've never been like Bash, with his love of sensory delights. I never learned to cook anything fancier than grilled cheese or chicken and rice.

Why go to all that trouble? The nourishment is the same.

I enjoyed food, sure, but I didn't live for it. I didn't seek out novel experiences. It was like sex.

A need I filled when it nagged at me and ignored the rest of the time.

Then, after the accident—

I barely taste anything.

There's gin in the fridge. Bottles of freshly squeezed citrus. Orange, grapefruit, even lemon and lime.

Louis already knows Danielle's preferences.

Or Trish relayed them.

They know my fiancée better than I do.

She's probably spent more time with them in the last week.

Who the fuck do I think I'm fooling? I'm avoiding her. She's a smart girl. She must see it.

But what else can I do?

I don't trust myself with her.

I consider the gin. Another drink will dull my inhibitions. Quiet the voice telling me not to touch her.

The selfish part of me begs me to swallow a mouthful.

But I can't hurt her.

I won't forgive myself if I hurt her.

I pour a glass of water. Drink it in three gulps. Wash in the shower. Wrap myself in a towel.

The door opens.

Familiar footsteps move closer.

"Adam." Danielle's voice is soft. "Are you there?"

I'm not dressed.

The ugly scars crisscrossing my torso are on display.

I'm half monster now.

I can't let her see me that way.

I press the door closed. "Here."

"Hey." She moves across the living room. Into the hallway. The master bedroom. "Are you going to bed?"

Maybe. I'm still wound tight. I won't fall asleep in this state. "Soon."

"Can you unzip me?"

It's a normal request.

It shouldn't feel like she's asking me to jump into the freezing Hudson.

I'm capable of honoring a simple request.

I am. "Close your eyes."

"Okay." Her breath stills. "I, uh, I'm right outside the door."

I suck a breath through my nose. Push it through my teeth. I built a multi-billionaire dollar company with my brother. I survived the last year.

I found her, convinced her, paid her.

I can unzip her fucking dress.

As long as she doesn't look at me.

I swallow hard and open the door.

She's standing there, her back to me, her hands at her sides.

An angel in the soft blue light.

What does that make me?

My hands disobey my command. One goes to her hip. The other to her neck.

I trace a line down her spine.

She shudders. "Adam."

"Say it again." I trace the line up, then down again.

"Adam." It falls off her lips like poetry. "Please."

"Please?"

"Fuck me. Please."

She doesn't want to talk about the pictures? Dinner? Me abandoning her after?

"Adam?"

"I don't want to hurt you."

"You won't."

"You don't know that."

"I do."

"How?" I bring my hands to her hips. Pull her body hard against mine.

She gasps. Blinks her eyes open.

I cover them with my hand, but I'm too slow. I hear it in her gasp. She saw a glimpse of me.

We're in front of the fucking mirror.

When I bought the place, I appreciated the mirrored walls. Extra angles to watch women I wanted.

Useful when I filled certain needs.

Decorative the rest of the time.

But now—

"Adam." She rocks her hips against my hardening cock. "Please. Fuck me. Now. Here. Tie me up. Blindfold me. Bend me over the bed. Whatever you need. As long as you fuck me."

My body threatens to take over.

"Do you need me to beg? I will. I'll get on my knees and plead."

"Don't. I'll get carried away."

Her breath catches in her throat. "Please."

Fuck, how can I say no to that? "You do exactly what I say. Nothing more. Nothing less. Understand?"

Her chest heaves with her inhale. "Yes. Please."

She wants that too. She wants to follow my orders. To slip into the state where I command and she obeys.

Fuck.

I struggle to hold on to conscious thought.

I want to let go. I want to give in to my body's demands. But there are practicalities to consider.

The usual.

And new ones.

"Are you safe?" I ask.

"Safe?"

"Have you been tested for STDs?"

"Yes. It's been awhile. And I'm on the pill. If you… if you're safe too. I… fuck." Her fingers curl into her sides. "Will you fuck me bareback?"

There goes my self-control.

"Please."

"You trust me?"

"Yes."

"You barely know me."

"I don't care. I want to feel you against me. If you're safe."

"I am." I find her zipper. Pull it over her ass. "I haven't been with anyone since the accident."

"No one?"

"No one." I didn't even fuck myself until I found her.

I push her dress off her hips.

It falls to her feet. I bend to gather it, rise, drape it over the dresser.

I want to be inside her.

I want to feel her pulsing around me.

Why the fuck am I arguing with her?

That's one practical concern down.

For the other—

I find a blindfold in the dresser. Pull it over her eyes.

She gasps as the silk brushes her skin. "Adam."

"You are beautiful." I run my hand over her side.

"Thank you."

"Sometimes, I can't believe it." I push her panties off her right hip. "That someone as beautiful as you wants anything to do with me."

"I do."

"Tell me." I push them off her left hip. "When you fuck yourself, thinking of me, what do you imagine?"

"I'm in that bedroom, in those silk pajamas. It's dark. Late. The house is quiet. You slip into my room. Climb into my bed. Your lips are on my neck as you undo the buttons, one at a time. Then you pull my pants to my ankles. Gasp when you see I'm not wearing anything under them."

"You want it soft?"

"Sometimes. Sometimes, you start soft, then you get

rough. You flip me over, bind my wrists with your tie, fuck me so hard I can't breathe."

"Which makes you come faster?"

"Rough."

"You want that now?"

"Yes." Her chest heaves. "Do you?"

"More than anything."

"Please."

Fuck.

"Adam, please."

My resolve crumbles. The voice whispering *be careful with her* disappears.

Does she know she's found my weak point?

I can't resist the need in her voice.

It's impossible.

"Put your hands behind your back," I say.

She does.

I find a tie in my dresser. Use it to bind her wrists.

Then I guide her to the bed. Sit her on the edge.

Even though she's blindfolded, she looks up at me expectantly. She trusts me to guide her.

"Spread your legs," I say.

She does.

I drop to my knees between them. "Beautiful." I lean in. Press my lips to her thigh.

She shudders.

I do it again. Then again.

Closer.

Closer.

There.

My lips brush her cunt.

She falls onto her back. "Please."

I pin her thighs to the bed, then I brush my lips against her again.

It's been a long time since I've done this.

Not since the accident.

Not since I turned into a monster.

The part of me that's man takes over. This is still the only thing that makes sense.

Me making her come.

What could be better?

I tease her with another soft brush of my lips.

Again and again.

Then I pin her harder and I lick her up and down slowly, tasting every sweet inch of her.

Mine.

The thought threatens to overtake my brain. I've been with other women. Done this with other women.

But I've never wanted to claim them. Not the way I want to claim Danielle.

Mine.

I want her mine forever.

I want her here, tied to my bed, groaning my name as she comes forever.

I take one more taste of her sweet lips, then I test her with softer strokes. Harder.

Longer.

Shorter.

Up and down.

Left and right.

Slow circles.

Her hips buck against me.

There. That's it.

I try another slow circle.

"Adam." Her thighs fight my hands. "Please."

I scrape my nails against her thighs.

She lets out a soft groan.

I try a little slower, a little faster. Faster. There.

She lets out a low, deep groan.

I want to tease her forever. To keep her in sweet anticipation, in this place where I'm the only thing she wants.

But it's been too long.

I need to be inside her.

I dig my nails into her thighs as I work her with those soft circles. Again and again.

Until she's bucking against my lips.

"Adam."

Another circle.

Another.

Another.

"Fuck." She pulses against me as she comes. She groans my name like it's a curse.

I lick her through her orgasm, then I stand, turn her over, pull her to the edge of the bed.

Her fingers dig into her palms.

Her wrists fight her restraints.

She groans as the fabric digs into her skin.

Being bound turns her on. And she's so fucking beautiful, wracked with pleasure.

I bring my hands to her hips. Hold her in place as I tease her.

She groans as my cock brushes her cunt.

Again.

Again.

With one steady stroke, I drive into her.

Her warmth overwhelms me. It's been a long time. Too long.

My body threatens to take over. Use her for its satisfaction.

That might be what she wants.

But I need to make her come again.

I need to feel her pulsing around me.

She groans as I drive into her again.

A little harder.

Then softer.

Slower.

Then faster.

I test different rhythms until I find the one she needs, then I hold her in place and drive into her with steady strokes.

Her nails dig into her palms. Her toes curl. Her hips buck against me.

She groans as I pin her to the bed.

"Come for me, angel." I slip my hand between her thighs. Hold my thumb against her clit.

Her head falls to one side. Her hair goes with it. She nods into the sheets as she rocks her hips.

Slow circles that drive me out of my fucking mind.

"Adam." My name falls off her lips. "Fuck, Adam." Another slow circle. Then she's pulsing around me, groaning my name as she comes.

Her body pulls me closer.

Deeper.

Pleasure overtakes me.

I rake my nails over her thighs as I come. I work through my orgasm, filling her with every fucking drop.

She's mine.

Maybe not anywhere else. Maybe not any other time.

But here and now.

And the entire fucking world makes sense.

Even as I untangle our bodies and help her clean up.

For a moment, I savor the feeling of her body in front of mine. The long line of her back. The soft curves of her ass.

She sighs as I unbind her.

She reaches back, trying to find a grasp of my skin. I grab her wrist too hard, but that only makes her gasp.

"Not yet." It's the only thing I can say that won't steal the magic.

"One day?"

The thought threatens to overwhelm me. I want her hands on my skin. I want her looking at me the way she does now, like she sees the best in every broken part of me.

But she won't.

She'll see the monster I've become.

And I can't lose this. Not yet.

"One day." When I have to release her.

"Can I sleep with you?" she asks. "Here. In this bed?"

"Yes." The word falls off my lips without passing through my brain. It's not smart. She'll get the wrong idea. Believe I'm capable of loving her.

Her lips curl into a smile. "I'm wiped. I should shower. Can I use this one?"

"Go for it."

She motions to her blindfold.

Of course. "I'll use the bathroom in the hall."

She pulls the blindfold over her head, but she keeps her back to me. "Good night, Adam."

"Good night." I brush her hair behind her ear and press my lips to her neck.

She lets out a soft moan as she leans into the gesture.

Then she releases me. Moves into the bathroom without looking back.

Because she respects my wishes?

Or because she can't bear to look at a monster?

Chapter Twenty-Two

DANIELLE

Adam's bathroom is as modern and sleek as the rest of the apartment.

It's easy to imagine him here. Stripping out of his suit after a long day of work, savoring the warm water and its perfect pressure, running his hands over his skin as he soaps and shampoos.

It's easy to imagine the two of us here together, his hard, warm body against mine. The streaming water between us. Every inch of his skin on display for me.

Is the blindfold a kink?

Something to enhance my experience?

Or because he's afraid to reveal himself to me?

He's shy about his scars. But I can't tell if it's the circumstance—he got them in the accident that killed his brother—or the scars themselves.

Has he seen mine?

Does he find them equally disgusting?

I run my fingers over the scars on my left forearm. They're faded now. Barely raised. Barely visible.

Did Adam notice?

I hide the newer ones under my watch. Those are impossible to miss. Big, red lines. Raised and angry.

I don't want strangers to see.

Not even when I'm in control, behind the camera.

Sometimes, they show up in my photos. I know how to light them to look harsh and ugly or faded and beautiful.

Sometimes, I consider claiming triumph. *Look at how I used to hurt myself to cope. How I stopped. Found peace and mental health and well-being.*

It was true for a while.

But when everything started feeling hard again—

I gave into old habits.

I'm not showing these to Adam. I'm not peeling back the walls around my heart, revealing my ugly parts, hoping he'll accept me.

How can I expect him to do the same?

Maybe that's it. Maybe I need to lead by example.

But the thought of sitting down and pointing out my scars—

It's terrifying.

I finish washing, wrap myself in a towel, find clothes in the dresser.

Adam is in the main room, in his own set of silk pajamas (slate grey, like most of his suits), sitting on the leather sofa, leafing through an old paperback.

Wearing glasses.

Holy shit.

Hotness overload.

I...

He...

Fuck.

"What are you reading?" Shit. "Sorry. I hate when people ask me that."

"You can sit. If you'd like."

Yes, I'd very much like. I cross the room. Take a seat next to him on the couch. "It's dark."

"It is."

"Doesn't that hurt your eyes?"

"It would if I was trying to absorb the words."

"Isn't that reading?"

He nods as he turns over the worn paperback. "Bash's favorite."

"Oh?"

"He was a man of action. He could barely sit still for school. He wasn't ever going to read voluntarily."

"Not an intellectual type?"

"No. A doer, not a thinker. But one day, he came out of his room—it was summer. We were all home. Even Simon. And Bash wanders down the stairs, holding up this book and he says, 'I just read the greatest thing in the world.'"

"Yeah?" I ask.

He smiles at the memory. "I'm sitting there thinking he finally did his summer reading. Was it *Romeo and Juliet*? *To Kill a Mockingbird*? *The Outsiders*? What great work of art finally moved him? So, I asked him. I named the books, and he looked at me like I was an idiot." Adam copies his brother's expression. "Please, Adam, you really think I'd like something so stuffy?"

"Would he?"

"No, but those books aren't stuffy. Of course, Bash would write them off just because they're on the list."

"I was the same way, with some more popular artists. Do we really need to see another impressionist bridge? Or a photo realistic vase." I smile. "I'd never admit it to Remy, though. He's always rolling his eyes at pictures of fruit or flowers."

"You like them?"

"Sometimes. I'd rather look at people. They're much more interesting than fruit."

"Bash would have liked you." His smile is sad. "But then he always liked pretty girls."

"Hey."

"He knew what he wanted."

"Pretty girls?"

He nods. "It got him into trouble sometimes." His eyes flit to the window. The dark sky. The deep blue Hudson. "A lot of times."

The view is unbelievable, but I don't want to look at the city. I want to watch him.

No, I want to pull him back to the room.

To me.

"What did he say about the book?" I ask.

Adam turns to me. Slips back into his memory. "He didn't read a classic, so I named a few books I read when I was his age. Harry Potter. Percy Jackson. Still, he shakes his head. And holds it up proudly." He holds the book in the air. "The greatest book of all time, *Detectives in Togas*."

"Did you read it?"

"Eventually."

"Is it the greatest book of all time?"

"No. But it's Bash. Troublemakers determined to get their way. He kept this copy for years. Took it with him to boarding school, college, his first apartment. He gave it to me when I moved here. So I'd finally have something good in my library."

"That's sweet."

"He didn't want to let on how much he cared, but he did."

"You're the same way."

"Maybe."

"Maybe? You spent three hours in a car to have dinner

with your brother," I say. "And you'll spend another three on the way back."

"I had to come into the city today. Quarterly meeting."

"You can't skip them?"

He nods. "I missed the first one, after the accident. People talked. A few investors pulled out. Liam was sure he could win them back, but..."

"You didn't want to put that burden on him?"

He nods.

"How was it?"

"Difficult."

"I can come with you next time. If that helps." I turn toward him. "At least keep Liam busy."

"He's not as easy to distract as he seems."

"He forgot I existed every time Briar giggled."

"He likes her."

"Is there something between them?" I ask.

"He wouldn't tell me if there was."

"They have that ease with each other," I say. "The ease people have after they've slept together." I can feel it now, with us. One of the walls around his heart is gone. There are plenty left, but I'm a little closer. And a little less scared to reveal myself to him.

He makes that *hmm* noise that means he's considering it.

"I'm sorry you lost your brother. When I lost my mom, people said so many stupid things. There's nothing worse than some idiot saying 'she's in a better place now.'"

"They're uncomfortable."

I nod. "Grief is scary. For everyone near it. I... I lost a few friends who couldn't handle my anger." Then I redirected it to someone who could take it: me. "It was funny. I was overwhelmed by how little time we have with people we love. I didn't want to waste any more. But I lost my tolerance for bullshit too. I didn't have patience to deal with people."

"It doesn't show."

"I found other ways of coping. I had to... Remy needed me."

"You're a good sister."

"Thanks." I want to touch him. Reach for him. Put my arm on his shoulder. Something. Anything, as long as I can comfort him. "I was thinking... about that man, tonight. Mr. Fitzgerald."

His eyes darken.

"The way he stared... it was so awful. Would it be ridiculous to make sure he's around when we announce our engagement?"

He stares into my eyes for a moment, then he nods. "I can arrange it."

"Oh. Good. Maybe in a few weeks. So it doesn't seem too rushed."

He nods. "Yes, that's smart."

"And I want you to meet Remy first. We're already in the city. It would be easy to do it tomorrow. For brunch maybe. There's a place in this neighborhood we went once. It had great French toast. And good coffee."

"Of course."

"Really?"

"He's your brother. He needs to believe it too."

Right. Adam wants Remy to buy into our ruse. He doesn't want to meet him because he's my brother.

Because he wants into my life.

We may be fucking, but we're not lovers. We're not even friends really.

Still.

He understands a part of me. And I understand a part of him.

Not most of him. But a part. Is that enough for a relationship? Or am I thinking with my libido again?

Maybe I need to meet with Remy on my own. Let him talk me into seeing Adam as a nice dick with a man attached.

"It's late. I'll text him in the morning," I say.

Adam nods *of course*.

"I should get to bed." I stand. "You wore me out."

For a second, his face fills with pride.

It warms me everywhere.

Then he stands, wraps his arms around me, pulls me into a soft slow kiss, and whispers, "Good night, Danielle."

And I float away completely.

Chapter Twenty-Three

DANIELLE

I fall asleep quickly. Wake warm and safe, with memories of Adam's body against mine.

He's already out of bed. The sky is already blue. The sun is already shining.

A cold, sunny day. Classic New York winter.

If it was a normal Saturday, I'd slip into my workout gear and dance in the living room. Then I'd drag Remy out of bed, go to brunch, drink too much coffee.

Spend the day wandering around the city, trying to soak in as much sun as possible, despite the cold temperature.

Now that I'm here in Adam's apartment, in his life?

I want to spend the day in bed with him. On the couch. In the shower. I don't care, as long as his body is pressed against mine.

I rise, wash, find coffee in a French press and a note on the counter.

There's almond milk in the fridge and honey in the pantry. Drink as much as you desire.

- Adam

It's a note, not a love letter, but it's a start. He's communicating with me. And casually. Well, casually by Adam standards.

I stretch my arms over my head. Let out a yawn. I want to move too, but I need to touch base with Remy first.

I find my cell, fix a cup of coffee, and curl up on the couch.

Danielle: What are you doing today?

Remy: Listening to your gossip about Adam's dick.

Danielle: We're in the city for the weekend.

Remy: Please tell me it's so you can fuck someplace new. Some rich person place, like a private room in a restaurant, or the balcony at the opera.

Danielle: Wouldn't someone notice?

Remy: Maybe not full on fucking. But you could drop to your knees and unzip his slacks. And time your finishing move to the uh, what's the climax of an opera called?

Danielle: I would know?

Remy: Yeah. You're a fancy rich girlfriend now. You've got the clothes. You've got the knowledge of visual art. Next step, opera oral.

Danielle: Why are you so obsessed with oral sex?

Remy: I don't understand the question.

Danielle: Never mind.

Remy: Danny, don't tell me you're not generous.

Danielle: Why aren't you concerned he's not generous?

Remy: He had generous energy.

Danielle: Based on what?

Remy: His photo.

Danielle: And I don't?

Remy: You could go either way.

Danielle: Asshole.

Remy: You love it.

I do.

Danielle: Can you do brunch today? Adam wants to meet you.

Remy: Really?

Danielle: What's surprising about that?

Remy: What isn't?

Danielle: Yes or no?

Remy: I can't promise I won't ask about your generosity.

Danielle: You think I just met you?

Remy: If you'll allow it.

Danielle: I'll allow inappropriate sex questions on the condition you don't mention his scars.

Remy: Are they as nasty as everyone says?

Protective energy fills my veins. Who's talking about Adam that way, and where can I destroy them?

Danielle: No, they're beautiful.

Remy: Danny.

Danielle: Not because I have some fixation on scars. Because they are. He's still handsome.

Remy: To a normal person?

Danielle: Are you the normal person in this situation?

Remy: Yes.

Danielle: I didn't know you looked at guy's faces. I thought you only looked at dicks.

Remy: Well…

Danielle: You know I won't tell you.

Remy: Above average though? Tell me he's above average.

Danielle: I'm satisfied.

Remy: Danny!

Danielle: Above average. But not too much.

Remy: Too much?

Danielle: Too much is as bad as too little.

Remy: No.

Danielle: Really?

Remy: No such thing as too much.

Danielle: What if he had a horse dick? Didn't some guy die from that?

Remy: Yes, but he actually fucked a horse. Do you think I'm into bestiality?

Danielle: You're pretty freaky.

Remy: Danny!

Danielle: Not full-on animals, but maybe furries.

Remy: I would never!

Danielle: No? What if the guy was really hot?

Remy: That's not a toll I'm going to pay. And you won't distract me from this important topic? What's too much to you?

Danielle: No comment.

Remy: No fun.

Danielle: Does one work for brunch? Maybe two?

Remy: Nine inches? Eight?

Danielle: We're in the financial district right now. Near the brunch place with the French toast. And the single-origin coffee.

Remy: Seven?

Danielle: I'll meet you there at one.

Remy: Not six, Danny! Tell me it's not six!

Danielle: I'll see you at one.

He sends me a sad face emoji.

Then an eggplant and a sad face.

Remy: You're the worst.

Danielle: Love you too.

It's almost eleven. One is two hours away. That's just enough time to work out, shower, dress, fuck Adam.

Will he?

Or will he make me wait?

It feels strange texting him, but I do it anyway.

Danielle: Told Remy we'd meet at one. Does that work for you?

I leave my cell and coffee cup on the counter. Look for workout clothes in the dresser. Of course, it's stocked. There's even a sports bra in my size. A nice one, made out of nylon, in an actual bra size and not the boob smooshing small, medium, large nonsense.

Then leggings, socks, shoes, a tank top, one of those sleek zip up jackets.

I look like a space commander. An overly curvy space commander with too much hair, but a space commander still.

Adam already has the TV set up for my workout streaming service. And the couch and table are a little farther back.

He rearranged the room for me.

It's sort of absurd, working out in the living room of his multi-million-dollar penthouse. If we really lived here, I could go to actual classes, in an actual studio.

Before, they were out of my price range.

Now, I could rent my own studio room and hire a private instructor.

Whatever I want.

The world is my oyster.

I stream my dance workout. Lose myself in the rhythmic movements. After forty minutes I'm sweaty and spent and buzzing with endorphins.

I do a quick cool down stretch then I strip and step into the shower.

The door opens.

Adam's footsteps move closer.

Into the bedroom.

Then he knocks.

"Come in," I say.

He's in his own set of high-tech workout gear. A sleek jacket and running leggings.

Why don't men wear leggings more often?

I can see all the muscles in his legs. They're as broad and built as the rest of him.

And I need my hands around them.

If he wants the leggings between us, fine, I can do that, as long as I can touch him.

"Adam." My eyes fix on his. "Are you going to stand there and watch?"

"Do you want me to?" His eyes move over my body. Lips, neck, chest, stomach, pelvis.

"Yes." My cheeks flush. "But I'd rather you fuck me."

He actually smiles. "You're persistent."

"Isn't that what you like about me?"

"Besides your tits?"

My cheeks flush. My stomach warms. "You made another joke."

"Did I?"

I want to laugh, hug him, and tear his clothes off in equal measure. "I like it."

"I know."

"It changes the mood."

"I know."

"Because you're not going to fuck me?"

He nods.

"But maybe later?"

"Maybe."

I turn to him. His image is fuzzy through the fogged glass. He's impossibly far away. I need him in here with me. "I need help."

"You were fine last night."

"It's a different help." I arch my back. "Your hands on my skin."

"You want me to fuck you?"

"Yes."

"Then do what I ask."

How can I say no to that? "Will you promise?"

"No."

A whine falls from my lips.

"Do you fuck yourself in the shower?"

"Not usually."

"Why not?"

"The water makes it difficult. Not enough friction."

He nods with understanding. "Wait here."

Uh, okay...

He slips out of the bathroom.

I try to ignore the desire building in my stomach. I want to fuck him. No, I need to fuck him. I don't care what I have to do to make that happen. I'm doing it.

Finally, my hair is wet enough to wash. Adam returns halfway through the process. Watches as I comb conditioner through my hair, soap my skin, shave, rinse.

Then he holds out something for me.

A bright pink vibrator.

"You bought it for me?" I ask.

He nods.

"It doesn't bother you?"

"Why would it bother me?"

"My ex-boyfriend."

"The photographer?"

"Yeah, the one who wouldn't pose for me. He got upset when I mentioned toys."

"What about them?" he asks.

"He saw them as a threat, I think. If a vibrator could make me come, what was he there for?" I can't help but laugh. "I sound like Remy."

"What would he say?"

"If a man isn't better than a toy, kick him to the curb."

"Where do I rate?"

My cheeks flush. "I haven't tried the toy."

"But you have your own?"

I nod. "And hands too."

"I've seen."

My blush deepens.

"Which do you like better?"

"You."

He half-smiles. "Your hands or the toy?"

"My hands."

"Why?"

"More precise. More intimate."

"Intimate with yourself?"

"Of course," I say. "It wasn't always easy for me. I haven't always felt at home with my body." Even now, it's a struggle.

His eyes rake over me slowly. "Show me."

"I am."

"No." He takes a step toward me. "With your hands."

"Last night—"

"If you want me to fuck you again, show me."

"Please—"

"Now."

I barely manage to nod. I turn to him, rest my back against the wall, spread my legs, slip my hand past my bellybutton.

It's different in the shower. More and less friction at once. And with Adam watching me, I'm already wound so fucking tight.

I try to look him in the eye as I draw circles on my clit.

A little softer.

Then harder.

There. I find the right pressure.

He watches intently as I bring myself to the edge.

Almost.

Almost.

My eyes flutter closed.

The tension in my sex winds to a fever pitch, then

everything unravels. My world goes white. The beautiful, soft, blinding light of bliss.

His low, deep groan.

The warm water.

The heat of his gaze.

His eyes meet mine. "Beautiful."

My entire body flushes. "Will you fuck me after lunch? Please."

"Yes. But not a second sooner."

How the hell am I supposed to entertain my brother with that promise in my head?

Chapter Twenty-Four

ADAM

"**R**emy is a lot, but he always means well." Danielle presses her lips together. "He'll probably ask about your dick. No. He will. It's his favorite topic." She looks at the restaurant, a French-inspired bistro on the first floor of an office building.

It's exactly the kind of place I imagine Danielle enjoying. White furniture, teal walls, potted plants as centerpieces.

And it's empty.

"I reserved the restaurant," I say.

She looks up at me with a curious expression. She wants to ask why, but she's too polite to say it. Or she's scared of my reaction.

"I appreciate privacy," I say.

She nods, accepting the answer. "Privacy is good." She looks around the space again. "Remy doesn't know about my photography. Not the details. So don't mention the whole naked self-portrait thing."

"Oh my god, that coat!" A cheerful voice cuts through the air.

Danielle lights up as she turns to her brother. She waves and rushes to meet him.

He pulls her into a tight hug. Whispers something in her ear.

She laughs. "You're disturbed."

"I take that as a compliment." He releases her. "Seriously, Danny, you look great. Did you really put this together yourself?"

"Hey!" She smooths the eggplant wool of her coat. "Rudeness will not earn you details."

"There's something that will earn me details?"

She flips him off.

"Are you going to introduce me to your boyfriend?" he asks.

"Inside," she says. "It's freezing."

He nods *it is* then leans in to whisper something in her ear.

She blushes and follows him inside.

The restaurant is warm, quiet, small.

Before the accident, this place would have been too much for me on a busy afternoon.

Now, even with the place empty, I can barely handle the attention.

"So, uh, we have any seat?" Remy asks.

"Yes. Adam reserved the place for the afternoon," she says. "Because he knew you'd make enough inappropriate comments you'd get us kicked out otherwise."

"When has that ever happened?" he asks.

"IHOP."

"Well, yeah, it was an IHOP. I can't be responsible for repressed attitudes of people who live outside the city." He looks at me. "No offense."

"You can't say something rude, then say no offense like they cancel out," Danielle says. "I will leave."

"You will not," he says.

She tries to fight a smile, but she can't. She adores him. It's all over her face.

She knows he's a handful and she loves him for it.

It does something to me, seeing this side of her. Warms me in places that are usually cold.

Even with the memory of Bash threatening to derail me.

Honestly, Adam, why are you wasting time meeting family? You fucked her for the first time last night. Get back in there.

Enough with the excuses.

She wanted to fuck you in the shower.

And you stand outside the glass door like an asshole?

Really.

I'm disappointed.

You know better than to leave a woman wanting.

He never knew me in this state.

He didn't see the way people react.

Of course, Bash would laugh it off. Find a silver lining.

Haven't you seen Beauty and the Beast, Adam? Every girl who grew up with that movie has a thing for brooding dudes with castles. Play up the temper and you're gold. We both know you want to throw her against the wall. Punish her for letting other guys see her naked.

Fuck, those pictures of her…

If you broke and fucked yourself to them, imagine what guys with less restraint are doing?

Fuck, why am I imagining dudes jacking it?

Let's get back to picturing Danielle naked.

Much better.

My head spins.

My clarity disappears.

I suck a breath through my teeth. Push an exhale through my nose. This is for Bash, but I need his voice to quiet.

I need to hear myself think.

My manners kick in.

I take Danielle's coat, hang it on the rack next to mine, pull out her chair.

"Thank you." She sits. Crosses her legs, pulling the soft black fabric of her dress up her thighs.

I need my hands on her bare skin.

I need to push the dress to her waist, bend her over the table, fuck her until she's groaning my name.

"What are you drinking?" A waitress steps out from behind the counter in the back of the restaurant. "We have four kinds of mimosas. Classic, pomegranate, grapefruit, and passion fruit."

"Really? Passion fruit?" Remy asks.

"Really." She looks at the white pad in her hands, not at all interested in selling him on the drink.

He makes a *how disturbing* face and turns to Danielle. "What do you think?"

"Almond milk latte for me," she says. "And honey, if you have it."

The waitress jots it down.

"Make it two," Remy says. "Two extra shots in mine."

The waitress barely stops herself from rolling her eyes.

"Black coffee," I say.

The waitress's eyes flit to me for a second. She notices my suit, tie, scars. Shrugs *weird rich guy*. Disappears.

It's the most normal interaction I've had in the city since the accident.

A typical brusque server.

The familiarity is strange. Like the lobby in the apartment. A memory of a dream.

"You still haven't introduced me," Remy says.

"Right." Danielle stands. Motions to me. "Adam, this is my brother, Remy. Remy, this is Adam. My boyfriend."

"Glad to see she's finally getting some." He offers his hand.

I shake.

"I told her you have a generous vibe," he says.

"Remy!" Her cheeks flush.

"Based on your old pictures," he says. "Since she wouldn't show me a new one."

"How can you tell?" I ask.

"It's a skill," he says. "I can get a lot from a picture. Not just generosity."

"Do you have to start with dick size?" She sits and hides behind her hands. "Couldn't you at least work up to that?"

"No can do, sis. I'm not a tease. I start with the good stuff," he says.

She makes an *ew* noise.

"If you told me the first time I asked, I wouldn't have to ask again." He looks to me and raises a brow. "Or should I ask you directly?"

"What is it you want to know?" I sit.

"Oh god, make it stop." She groans in exaggerated agony.

"Hmm, interesting." Remy taps his chin. "Do you say that because it's a familiar phrase? Someone torturing you with too much—"

"Too much information, yes." She drops her hands and sits up straight.

He smiles. "Aw, you don't mean me. All information I offer is beautiful and intoxicating. And the only response you could ever have is *please, more.*"

"Gross." She shakes her head. "Please stop."

"Sharing is important," he says. "Don't you think, Adam? Relationships require honesty."

"And boundaries," I say.

"Ow. That hurt," he says. "Good thing you don't throw down like that, Danny."

"Would it work?" she asks.

"Would I ever stop making sure you have the best?" he asks.

"There's more to life than dick size," she says.

The waitress emerges with our drinks. She drops them off, shrugs *weird rich people*, pulls out her pad of paper. "You still want three orders of French toast?"

Danielle shoots me a look. *You organized this?*

I nod.

"All three for me, right?" Remy teases. "That's perfect."

The waitress nods uh-huh and disappears again.

"She didn't think you're funny," Danielle says.

"She did agree about the dick size though," Remy says.

"How do you figure?" she asks.

"I can tell," he says.

"How could you possibly tell what a woman thinks about… oh my god, why are we still talking about this?" she asks.

"He is like Liam," I say.

Remy perks up. "Who?"

"Adam's brother," Danielle says. "He's also a trouble-maker. Though significantly less concerned with penis."

"Is he hot?" Remy asks.

"Very. But straight. I think," she says.

"He is," I say.

"Then why are we talking about him? Boring. Unless you have pics. Hot pics." he asks.

"Well, actually…" She brings her mug to her lips. "He offered to pose for me." Her berry lipstick marks the clean white ceramic. Her eyes close as she sips. Her face fills with pleasure. Her lips part with a groan.

It steals all my attention.

I need to fuck her.

Now.

"And you said yes, and you have the pictures on your phone of him fucking himself?" he asks.

"No." She sets her mug on the table. "I said I'd think about it."

"Isn't your family famous?" Remy turns to me. "Sorry. It is true, though."

"It's not a secret," I say.

"That would be good for your career, right?" Remy asks. "You should do it. Unless, uh... straight people are possessive."

"It's not a straight thing. It's you seeing men as fuck-toys," she says.

"Maybe," he says. "But the point stands."

"It could be awkward, yes," she says. "Thank you for stating it so eloquently."

He chuckles. "But if he'd let you show those photos, that would be a big draw."

"It would," she admits. "But what if it was Adam, offering to take naked pictures of you? It would be weird."

He looks at me and raises a brow *interesting comparison*. "It would be hot. I'd definitely say yes."

"Really?" She looks at him incredulously. "You'd let my boyfriend see your dick?"

"It deserves to be seen," he says.

She hides behind her hands. "I can't tell if you're kidding."

"It would be unconventional." He looks to me again. "But still hot."

"Stop looking at him like that. You're making it weird-er," she says.

"Like what?" he asks.

"Like you're wondering what his reaction would be to your dick," she says.

"I'm considering your hypothetical question," he says.

She lets out a low groan. "You're impossible."

"You asked," he says.

A laugh spills from my lips.

They stop at the same time. Look at me with the same *what's so funny* expression.

"You're just like me and Liam," I say.

"I still haven't seen photos of this Liam," he says.

"He's your type," she says. "Conventionally attractive."

"God forbid," he says. "Who would want to see a conventionally attractive man naked?"

"Are you going to look at his face?" she asks.

"Oh no. Is he ugly below the neck? I need the total package, Danny. You know that," he says.

She laughs. "He seems in shape."

"Seems?" He raises a brow. "Only seems."

"I didn't get him naked yet," she says.

"But you will?" Remy studies my expression.

It's not the same as other people's stares. He isn't studying my scars or creating a before and after in his head.

He's a brother, trying to figure out the intentions of a man who wants his sister.

"I gave Danielle my blessing." I look to her. "I meant it."

"Really? That wouldn't bother you?" he asks.

"Of course. That's why he volunteered," I say. "But I knew Danielle's passion the second I met her."

"Oh no, was she talking about that photographer with the dumb name?" he asks.

"Her name isn't dumb. She's a genius!" Danielle huffs. "And, yes, Adam bought one of her pieces. And I, uh… I talked him into the rest. Well, the rest of the set. She's prolific."

"She really gets into a state over those." He sips his coffee. "I don't get it. Naked women. Boring."

"She does men too."

"She does? And you haven't shown me?" He pulls out his cell. "How do you spell her dumb name again?"

"It isn't dumb!" She huffs again. "You make video games. How can you call photography dumb?"

"So video games are dumb?" he asks.

"You know what I mean," she says.

"Do I? Or did you just insult my passion?"

"Because you never insult mine?"

"It starts with a *D*, right? A *D* for the *D*." He laughs at his own joke.

"Put it away. I'll show you," she says. "If you stop asking about my sex life."

"No deal," he says. "There are plenty of naked men on the internet."

She lets out a low groan.

"Now, for the interesting questions." He turns to me. "Adam, how much of a freak would you say my sister is, on a scale of one to Rick James." When no one laughs, he continues. "*SuperFreak*. The song. Do you live in a cave?"

"From the 70s? Or the 80s?" Her brow scrunches. "The 60s maybe?"

"It's not that old," he says. "I have the wrong audience." He lets out an over-the-top sigh.

"I've only ever heard Adam listening to classical music," she says.

Remy nods *of course*. "He's a snob, like you."

"I'm not a snob," she says.

"Yeah. Carly Simon is great, but Michelle Branch? That's middle-brow squared," he says.

She fires back with her own playful insult.

They banter through coffee, French toast, a second round of caffeine.

When Remy finishes teasing her, he talks about her work, her passion for the gallery, her skill as an artist.

Then she talks about his work as a programmer, the internship at an independent mobile app developer, the game he's making himself.

He waits until she excuses herself, then he turns to me, and drops the playful smile.

"Danielle tells me you love your family," Remy says.

"I do."

"I know it's rude to bring up the rumors about your brother's accident," he says. "And, meeting you, I don't think you're the type of person who'd have your own brother killed. And, really, if you did, you'd be smart enough not to be in the car when it happened."

"Is that a compliment?"

"An observation." His eyes stay fixed on me. "I am sorry, about your brother. If I lost Danny... I'd be a fucking mess. Way worse than you."

"Your family isn't great with compliments."

"No. We're not." He chuckles. "And I do like you, Adam. You're quiet, but in a strong, supportive way. That's what Danny needs. Someone who supports her."

"I want that too."

"Our dad isn't in the picture. Our mom is gone. So it's just me, protecting her. And I will protect her. I know you're rich enough to crush me. Pay to have me killed. Whatever. I don't care. Danny is all I have. And she... she's given up a lot for me," he says. "If you hurt her, I'll destroy you."

"I appreciate that," I say.

He looks at me, waiting for me to get angry, challenge him.

But why would I?

How could I possibly object to her brother doing anything to protect her?

I'm exactly the same.

———

AFTER ANOTHER ROUND OF BANTER, DANIELLE AND REMY say goodbye. They trade whispers and laughs, then she releases him and returns to me.

She lingers there for a moment, watching her brother leave, in a state of limbo.

We're not alone yet.

We're still pretending.

But where is the fucking line?

I don't see it anymore.

Does she?

Her fingers intertwine with mine. She squeezes my hand, still nervous, but for some other reason altogether.

"Thanks for setting that up," she says. "He liked you."

"I liked him."

"Really?" Her eyes light up. "He's a good guy despite the obsession with dick, I swear."

A laugh spills from my lips. "He's teasing you because you react."

"I know. But I can't help it. He knows exactly how to push my buttons."

"You're sweet with him. Protective."

She blushes.

"I'm glad you have someone who loves you."

She looks at me funny for a moment, then she nods. "He's a good brother."

He is.

I believe his warning. I believe he'll protect her, even if it takes everything he has.

How would he react, if he knew the truth?

Would he appreciate the financial assistance? Or deck me for asking her to lie?

I deserve both.

I deserve worse.

But I…

I have too far to go. I can't quit now.

I put the thought out of mind as I lead Danielle to the penthouse. We walk in silence, absorbing the cold, bright day. The financial district is empty on the weekends, but it still hums with noise. A million times louder than the mansion.

I used to appreciate the buzz of the city. The life, the sounds, the lights.

Now—

It's too much.

There's too much in my head.

I need to be in control of something.

No, not something.

Danielle.

She moves closer as we enter the building. The shiny silver elevator. The hallway.

The apartment.

The door swings shut behind her.

I take her coat. Hang it on the rack. Do the same with mine.

She looks around the room the way she does when she's setting up a photo shoot, as if she's finding the perfect spot to place her camera.

She runs her fingers over the leather couch. The oak dining table. The tile counter in the kitchen.

The big, glass window where she fucked herself last night.

Was that only a day ago?

A single day and everything is different.

I don't understand it.

I don't understand anything but my desire to make her come.

Danielle closes the distance between us. She slips her arm around my waist. Under my suit jacket. "Please." Her fingers curl into the fabric of my shirt. "Fuck me. Wherever you want. However you want. I don't care as long as you fuck me."

Words form on my tongue. Disappear before I can articulate them. There's too much going on, too much we need to discuss. Her brother. Her living arrangements. When and where we're announcing our engagement.

It's as overwhelming as this sleek, modern apartment and the memories in it.

This makes sense.

It's the only thing that makes sense.

"Please, Adam." It falls off her lips like poetry.

It disarms me.

Yes.

Whatever she wants, as long as she says my name like that again.

"Go to the couch," I say.

She does.

"Hands on the arm."

She places her hands on the leather. Looks to me for instructions.

"Wait."

"For what?"

"Until I decide you've waited long enough."

Chapter Twenty-Five

DANIELLE

*W*ait. *Until I decide you've waited long enough.*

Adam's voice echoes through my ears as I press my palms into the soft leather.

He stands there, against the clean white wall, tall and broad and patient.

Has it been thirty seconds or a thousand years?

I'm not sure.

I only know I need him to touch me.

Fuck me.

Groan my name.

I want everything. My hands on his skin. His secrets in my ears. His hard, strong body on display for *me.*

Will he show me one day?

Or will he hide behind suits and blindfolds forever?

I understand the impulse—almost all the dresses I selected have long sleeves—but that understanding does nothing to lessen my desire to touch him.

Adam takes a step toward me.

Another.

Another.

His hands find my hips. He rolls my dress up my waist. Runs his fingers over the waistband of my silk underwear.

"Do you know what you do to me, angel?" He presses his palm against me, pressing the sleek fabric into my sex. "Do you have any idea, how badly I want you?"

I shake my head.

His fingers find my clit. He rubs me over the fabric. "You drive me out of my fucking mind."

He runs his fingers over me again.

My thoughts evaporate.

He bends me over the arm of the couch. Then he rolls my panties to my thighs.

I'm splayed out for him, helpless to do anything but take him.

And I want every bit of it.

I want it so badly I can barely breathe.

He rocks his hips against mine, so I feel him hard against me. His slacks are still in the way, but I can feel the pressure of him. The firmness.

"You're playing with fire." He takes my hand. Places it on the couch cushion.

"Maybe."

"You might get hurt." Then my other arm. On the other side.

"Adam, please."

"Please?"

"Fuck me. Please. I can't think like this." I rock my hips to reach for him. "I need you."

Without warning, he slips two fingers inside me.

Hard.

Hard enough it hurts.

But it hurts so fucking good.

"Do you have any fucking idea, how badly I want to claim you?" He drives his fingers into me again.

I nod into the couch.

"You should be more careful." He drives his fingers deeper. "I'm not the man you think I am."

A groan falls off my lips.

It's intense. Too intense.

But, somehow, still not enough.

My eyes flutter closed.

His nails dig into the flesh of my ass.

The burst of pain pushes me closer. I need it.

I need him like this.

Unleashed.

He drives his fingers into me. Again and again. Until I'm so fucking close, I'm sure I'm going to break.

Then he rubs me with those perfect circles, and I go over the edge.

My sex pulses as I come. Pleasure spills through my torso, down to my fingers and toes.

But he doesn't give me time to catch my breath. He unzips his slacks, brings his hands to my hips, pulls my body onto his.

No tease.

No softness.

No warm up.

He drives into me hard and fast. It's more than his fingers. Fuller. Deeper.

Better.

So much fucking better.

His nails dig into my hips as he drives into me again.

Again.

Again.

He presses his palm between my shoulder blades, pinning me to the couch, and he fucks me.

There's no other way to explain it.

Some animal part of him takes over. His movements are sharper, his groan is lower, his breath is strained.

He's rough. Possessive. Perfect.

He keeps me pinned as he drives into me.

The pressure is intense. Almost too much. But in the best possible way.

He winds me tighter and tighter.

Then his hand knots in my hair. He holds me in place as he tugs at my locks.

Fuck.

With his next thrust, I come.

Pain and pleasure mix together. Overwhelm my senses.

My eyes close.

My world turns white. Soft bliss. Sharp nails. His hard cock driving into me again and again.

I groan his name as I come.

He works through my orgasm, then he moves harder, faster.

His nails scrape my skin.

Harder.

Harder.

Fuck.

I blink my eyes open. See only the sleek black leather.

"Danielle." My name falls from his lips.

Then he's there, thrusting through his orgasm, pulsing inside me as he comes.

He waits until he's spilled every drop, then he helps me clean and slip back into my clothes.

And he holds me close, like I'm the only raft in the ocean, like I'm the only thing he's ever wanted.

I'm not sure how long we're pressed together. Only that I want to stay in that perfect warm, soft, safe place forever.

He pulls me into a slow, deep kiss, his tongue dancing

around mine, his hand on my cheek, his body pressed against mine.

Then he releases me. "I should clean up."

I nod. Watch him slip into the bedroom, turn on the shower, leave me alone in the big, beautiful apartment.

Is he fleeing the scene?

Hiding?

Or just... cleaning up?

It's not exactly unreasonable.

I wish he'd invite me into the shower with him. I want to see him, touch him, feel him.

It's only been a day since he touched me properly.

Of course, he's shy about showing his scars.

And it's not like I'm any better.

Maybe that's it.

I need to lead by example.

I need to reveal myself to him.

I can do that.

Eventually.

Chapter Twenty-Six

DANIELLE

I fix another cup of coffee, find my laptop, go through yesterday's pictures.

My normal Saturday afternoon routine.

Only I'm in Adam's sleek apartment.

And yesterday's pictures are incredibly erotic.

I find a potential image.

My robe falling off my shoulders. My hand between my legs. My eyes turned to the camera.

It's sexy. Sexy enough to draw a reaction from Adam.

Will he get jealous and possessive?

Storm into my room and throw me against the wall?

The mental image makes my entire body buzz.

But there's something off about it.

He fucked me.

Touched me, kissed me, made me come.

He did reveal himself to me. Not as much as I wanted, but he hasn't been with anyone since the accident.

That's big.

I can't respond with this. Even if it's what I'd normally do on a Saturday afternoon.

I need to be honest with him.

The bedroom door opens. Adam steps into the hallway, still in his suit, tie, shoes.

It's strange, but it would be stranger seeing him in jeans and a t-shirt.

He stops at the dining table a few feet from me. Runs his fingers over the thick wood. He lingers there for a moment, pulling his words together, then he says, "It's too much. Being here."

"Don't you live here?" I shut my laptop. Push it aside.

"I did," he says. "After I graduated. For years. But now... there are too many memories. Bash is everywhere."

"But not in your house?"

"It's different."

"How?"

He doesn't deliver a quick comeback. Or throw down *because I said so*. He pauses. Looks to the window, to the bright blue sky, the deep blue water, the lemon sun. "If I didn't know better, I'd think it was July."

"It's brighter in July. The sun is higher. The sky is bluer."

He nods, remembering. "I'm not used to the city anymore. It's too busy. Too loud. Too crowded."

"Here?"

"Not in the apartment, no." His eyes flit to the window, to the spot where I fucked myself yesterday. "It's quiet here."

"Isn't that what you want?"

"I don't know." He swallows hard. "The quiet is suffocating. An emptiness that used to be filled with laughter. But the noise is worse. It echoes through the emptiness. Reminds me I don't belong with other people."

"Adam—"

"You should stay. Invite your brother here. Watch that vampire show he adores."

"*Blood Borne: Legends of the Vampire Clan?*"

"Is it really called that?"

I nod. "Don't knock it till you try it."

"You think I'll like it?"

"I don't know. I don't know a lot about what you like to watch. It's possible."

"We didn't have a TV."

"There's a home theater on the second floor."

"Simon added it after Dad died, but we didn't use it often. We weren't in the habit of watching TV."

"You still don't?"

"Not usually."

"But—" I motion to the widescreen TV across from the couch. "Is it there for porn?"

His laugh is sad. "That's what Bash said."

"Oh."

"He bought it for me. He and Liam were younger. Young enough they invited girls over to 'watch a movie.'"

"Really? Liam seems more direct."

"Usually." His deep blue eyes get hazy as he slips into a memory. "He reads people well. If a girl was shy, didn't want to admit she wanted to come over to make out on the couch, he'd suggest a movie."

"Isn't that manipulative?"

"He meant it."

"Really?"

"Not your experience with boys that age?"

"I wasn't popular with guys in school. I was the weird girl with the camera. I took it everywhere. Spent lunch and break staring at the world—"

"Like it's a place of infinite wonder and beauty."

My cheeks flush. "I don't."

"You do."

"Maybe."

"It's a compliment."

"I know." That's why it steals my oxygen. Adam is sincere and straightforward when we're alone.

Why go to all this effort to lie?

Even if it is to protect his brothers?

Liam isn't a guy who needs protecting. I can't imagine Adam's older brother Simon is afraid of the truth. Especially if he's as serious as Adam is.

The Pierces are rich, yes. They've never lacked food, shelter, material comforts.

But they've been through a lot.

They're not going to fall apart because Adam is slow to let go of his grief.

"Thank you," I say.

"You had a boyfriend in high school."

"How did you know?"

"You told me."

Oh. Right. "I'm a little"—I hold up my half-drank coffee—"worn out."

"Do you want another cup?"

"Okay. Thanks."

His fingers brush mine as he takes it. He moves to the kitchen. Sets the water to boil. Grinds the beans. "I'm sure he saw it too."

"My artistic point of view?"

"Yes. But…" He actually laughs. "I was considering a more shallow angle."

"My tits."

"Your legs." His eyes flit to my short skirt. "Ass."

"I feel neglected."

"You or your tits?"

"Both."

He smiles as he scoops beans into the French press. "You're baiting me."

I motion *maybe*. "Is it working?"

"You can't tell?"

"No." I stand. Smooth my dress. Take a half-step toward him. "You're hard to read. Is that new…"

He shakes his head.

"But you… I remember when my mom died. It left me with this ache in my chest. But, more than that, it didn't make sense. She was just here. Laughing. Smiling. Fixing dinner, telling me to study, asking why I was home late, listening to bad reggae music. How could she already be gone?"

"What happened?"

"She had a heart condition. She kept it a secret. We didn't know. At first, I was mad at her. I kept thinking how I would have spent more time with her if I knew. How I would have savored every second."

"You were mad at yourself, for not appreciating what you had?"

"Yes. I missed her. I still miss her. Sometimes, I close my eyes, and I can see her smile or hear her laugh and I… It hurts, knowing I can never see her smile again. But it feels good to remember her. That night of the funeral, Remy and I had too much wine and started telling each other stories. I'd never gone from laughing to crying and back so quickly. Even now, it's such a strange feeling. I wouldn't have understood it before. And still, after three years… I still wake up some mornings and wonder what Mom will say today."

"It feels like a dream sometimes."

"Yeah." I take another half-step toward him. "Was it like that for you?"

"With my father."

"With your brother?"

"It's different. I was supposed to protect him."

"It was an accident, wasn't it?"

He turns his back to me. Keeps his eyes on the task at hand. Locks me out.

Okay. That subject is a no-go.

I take a deep breath. Let out a slow exhale. "If you don't want to talk about it, I won't ask. But... you smile when you reminisce. It's a sad smile, but it is a smile. And he... I understand if it's still too painful to remember. But if it's not, you can talk to me. I like hearing about your brother. Your life with him."

"Thank you."

"That's why you can't stay here? The memories?"

The timer beeps. He pours coffee into two mugs. Heats a half-cup of almond milk in the microwave. "Yes."

"But the house isn't painful?"

"I'm used to it."

He pours milk into my coffee. Grabs the honey and a spoon. Steps aside to leave me room to fix it.

I squeeze a drop of honey onto the spoon. Lick it off. "Tell me to fuck off if you want. I will."

"That sounds like me."

I can't help but smile. "I know. You're vulgar. Well." My eyes flit to the couch. "Sometimes."

His shoulders soften.

"But don't lock me out. Please. I know we aren't lovers. But we're together for the next year. We'll be engaged soon. In a few weeks, right?"

He nods.

"I'd like to be friends, at least. If you need space, that's okay. Just tell me. Please." I turn toward him. "It's hard for me, being away from my family, my work, my home. Especially when you storm off and lock yourself in your office."

"Okay."

"Okay?"

"Would you prefer a different response?"

"No. Okay is… okay. Just not very dramatic."

"I can yell 'fine' and storm into my office."

"That would send some mixed messages."

He smiles. "I'll try."

"Thank you." I squeeze honey into my coffee. "I don't mind staying here for a while. It's a nice place."

"It is."

"But I… I'd rather go with you." I'm out of my fucking mind. I can stay in this sweet, ten-million-dollar apartment by myself, with my camera, a massive TV, a no-limit card, access to the finest restaurants in the city.

At the very least, I can take Remy out to a bar with good drinks tonight.

Or invite him here to watch cheesy vampire trash.

Why am I arguing my way back to his secluded castle?

Am I really that desperate to fuck him again?

Or is it even worse?

Not just a physical need, but an emotional one.

His eyes meet mine. "We'll be busy soon. Meeting Simon. Maybe even Opal."

"Opal?"

"My sister. Half-sister. She lives with Simon when she's not at boarding school. But she's a senior now. Almost an adult. I won't be able to shield her from gossip."

A half-sister. That sounds like an affair. Or some other equally gossip attracting situation.

"We'll be busy announcing our engagement. You should spend time with your brother while you can."

I take a long sip.

"It's up to you. I'm leaving after dinner. You can come with me. Or you can stay here."

Chapter Twenty-Seven

ADAM

Danielle traces her mug with her finger. "Do you want me to come with you?"

I expect my head to scream *no*.

I expect my heart to beg for solitude.

The intimacy she craves is terrifying.

How can I possibly offer her the connection she's seeking?

How can I ever be enough for her?

"Yes." It falls off my lips with ease. There's no hesitation in my voice. No tension in my shoulders. No reluctance.

I want her with me.

Period.

"Oh." Her lips curl into a half-smile. "Good. I... I'd like that."

"I drove here."

"You have a car?"

"Three."

"Three?" She raises a brow. "Really?"

"I have a house and an apartment."

"You know you're ridiculous?"

I nod.

"Why three?"

"One for Louis."

"It's not his car?"

"It's a family car."

"Does he drive it when he's off?"

"Yes."

She considers it. "I guess I can count that as yours." She takes a long sip of her coffee. Lets out a soft sigh. "Why two more?"

"One for guests," I say.

"Seriously?"

"Yes."

"But you already have a driver. And your own car. You need an extra for guests?"

"The house is secluded."

"But you have everything."

"No one has everything."

"Maybe." She takes another sip. Turns. Rests her ass on the counter. "I've never driven a car. I've never even sat next to a guy I like while he was driving."

"Do you want to?"

She smiles. "I like the idea of it. Sitting next to you, listening to music, watching the scenery go by." Her cheeks flush. "It's one of those things I always see in movies. A sign of love." Her fingers curl into the counter. "I guess you're a little old for that."

"I'm too old to enjoy scenery?"

"To have sex in the back seat." She looks up at me. Rises to her tiptoes to reach for my hair.

I pull back, instinctively.

She drops her hand. "Sorry. I…"

"Don't be."

She moves closer. Curls her hand around my neck. Then my chin. Jaw. My left cheek. My unscarred side. "You're tall." She runs her thumb over my temple. "Too tall for the back seat of a car. Or do you have a mini-van?"

"A Tesla."

"Of course."

"Of course?"

"Spoiled rich tech CEO bought a Tesla."

"CTO."

She laughs. "Oh, yeah, big difference."

"It is."

"Are you going to explain it to me?"

"Does it interest you?"

"No." She runs her fingers over the scar on my right cheek. "Is this okay?"

No. But I want it to be. "Yes."

"You're shy." She traces the one below the first. Then the next. "I don't want to make light of what you went through, but I... I think they're beautiful."

My limbs go light.

"I shouldn't say that, I know, but I do."

"Beautiful?"

"You've always have been handsome. Before the accident, you were more... conventional. Like Prince Charming."

"And not the monster he destroys?"

"No." Her voice softens. "Like Prince Charming back from saving the princess." She slips her hand under my suit jacket. "Prince Charming after slaying the monster."

Not yet, no.

"I... I'm fucking this up, aren't I?"

"No."

"I just..." She brings her hand to my neck. "I've never had to work so hard to touch a guy."

A laugh spills from my lips.

She smiles. "I don't mind. It feels good to want something." Her fingers glide over my tie. "Vibrant." She rises to her tiptoes and presses her lips to mine.

It's soft, slow, intoxicating.

I want her to touch me too.

I want every inch of her skin against every inch of mine.

But I can't lose her.

Not yet.

Not now.

Not when I'm so fucking close to stitching myself together.

She pulls back with a sigh. "Adam."

My cock stirs.

"You want to leave after dinner?"

"Yes."

"It's still early." Her fingers curl into my skin. "And the light is perfect here. This place is modern and beautiful. I want to photograph it. I want to photograph us."

Fuck. "You don't mean—"

"Not pornographic. Unless you want to." Her cheeks flush. "I, uh, I wouldn't share that. Of course. But I know there are privacy concerns. Even from a guy who owns a security company."

"Especially." I know how easy it is to find information. I know the images she posts for public consumption.

Never pornographic.

But erotic. Explicit even.

If she shares something of us, strangers will see.

Fuck themselves to it.

Curse me for claiming her.

Strangers including Fitzgerald.

It will kill him.

How can I say no?

How can I agree?

"I, uh, I've never done that before." She releases me. "But I would try. With you. You wouldn't have to show your face. Or your uh… it could just be your hand."

Fuck me.

"But I was actually thinking something I could share. You'd be anonymous." She moves to the table. Opens her computer. Pulls up a photograph.

A man in a suit holding a naked woman. Her back is to the camera. His head is buried in her neck.

There's no doubt where the scene is leading, but the photo is sensual without being explicit.

"I want to pitch it," she says. "For the gallery. If Mr. Davey isn't interested, someone will be. Remy was right. Your family is famous. I'm famous by association. If Adam Pierce's girlfriend… Adam Pierce's fiancée is selling a set of nudes with an anonymous man, a man who might be Adam Pierce… people will want to see that."

"They won't be there for you."

"No. But they'll be there. And I'll make a name in the art world. And not just the Instagram world." Her eyes meet mine. "But I… only with your blessing. It would put you in the spotlight."

And destroy the asshole I'm trying to destroy.

Maybe this is kismet.

I have ulterior motives, but we want the same thing.

"Yes," I say. "Of course."

"Are you sure?"

No. Not even a little.

"Maybe we should take one to start. To see if you're okay with it."

This is terrifying, yes, but I can handle it. I will.

Her fingers curl into her thighs. "One of us has to bring it up." She swallows hard and pulls up her website.

Broken Beauty.

The homepage photo.

Danielle, draped in soft sheets.

I've seen it a hundred times. A thousand, even.

"How long have you known?" she asks.

"Always."

"How?"

"You have half a million Instagram followers."

"And you happened to be one of them?"

No. My PI brought her to my attention. I can't tell her that. Maybe one day, when I'm ready for her to see me as the monster I am, but not yet. "A friend sent me your site."

"Before we met?"

"Yes."

"Is that why you hired me?"

"Part of it." I take a step toward her. "Are you offended?"

"I don't know. What's the other part?"

"I like you."

"And that's it? You like me?"

"If I was the type to marry, I'd marry someone like you. My brothers will believe I married you for love." That's over the line. A deception. But it's as close as I can get to the truth. "Everyone will believe it."

"Because of my tits."

"Because you're beautiful and passionate, and yes, because you post photos revealing those two things online." I take another step toward her. "You didn't tell me."

"You already knew."

"You weren't aware of that."

"I suspected." She swallows hard. "Why else would you hire me?"

So I am obvious. "You've been daring me on purpose."

"It worked."

"That makes it right?"

"You kissed me and ran away."

"So you dare me to fuck myself to your image?"

Her pupils dilate. "Did you?"

"Yes."

"When?"

"Too many times to count."

Her tongue slides over her lips. "Before…"

Before we met in person. "Yes. You were the first… the first person after the accident. The only."

Her chest heaves with her inhale. "The only person you thought of? Really?"

"Really."

"Fuck, Adam. Are you seriously going to tell me that and stay all the way over there?"

"Where should I be?"

"Naked, on top of me."

A laugh spills from my lips.

"It's not a joke."

"Then ask." My eyes meet hers. "Ask me to fuck you."

"Fuck." She stands. Looks me in the eye. "I will. After this."

No. Now. No more talking. No more discussion of this terrifying possibility. I need to be in a place that makes sense. The only place that makes sense.

"I've felt guilty. Manipulative. I need to feel something else." She offers her hand. "We both knew. Neither of us said anything. We're even."

We're not even. She's on far higher ground than I am. Even if we both fucked this up, she's an artist trying to support herself, trying to develop her passion.

I'm a rich asshole using her for my benefit.

I'm paying handsomely.

I'm trying to be careful with her.

But does that really justify my actions?

"Adam." Her eyes flit to her hand. "Do we agree?"

"Not to hold our dishonesty against each other?"

"Yes."

"You should ask for more."

"Why?"

"Because you can."

"Okay. Then I'll forgive you if you let me take your picture."

"Mine?"

She nods. "Of you. And with me. You can stay in your clothes."

Fuck, there's no backing out if I agree here. I'm a man of my word. I honor my promises, whatever it takes.

If I say yes, I have to follow through.

I have to put myself on display for the entire world.

"Deal," I say.

What the hell have I gotten myself into?

Chapter Twenty-Eight

ADAM

Danielle illuminates the room with her smile.

The entire apartment.

The world.

"You can start in your suit. In fact, I want to keep you in your suit the entire time," she says. "If you're moved to strip, I won't stop you, but the vision is you in the suit. And me in less and less."

Fuck.

"You can approve the final photos," she says. "But you can't look during the shoot. Tell me if you're uncomfortable with something or if you want to stop. Otherwise, try it, take the photo, see how it turns out. If you don't like it, I promise I'll delete it."

"Are you this gentle with all your models?"

"You're my first." She wraps her hands around her mug of coffee and brings it to her lips. "I'm the only model I can afford."

"Have you posed for someone else?"

"You don't know?"

"I didn't want to imagine you naked in front of some asshole's camera."

"Even if it was for art?"

I nod.

"You were already jealous?"

"Yes."

"Are you now?" She turns toward me. "Jealous of the people who see my pictures?"

"No. You're mine." It feels too right on my tongue. I don't want to take it back. Even though it isn't accurate. "I'm the only one who sees you like this." I move closer. Bring my hand to her hips. "Who touches you. Fucks you. Makes you come."

"Adam." It falls off her lips. The perfect sound. Poetry. She rises to her tiptoes and presses her lips to mine. It's fast, rushed even. "I want to fuck you so badly." She pulls back. "But after. Save the energy for this, okay?"

"Aren't I keeping my suit on?"

"Most of it."

I raise a brow.

She smiles. "I have a few ideas. I'm sure you can imagine."

I'm not sure I can imagine anything else.

"Give me fifteen minutes to set up." She turns to the window. Surveys the light. "I like that suit. The slate grey. The blue tie. I have a lot of ideas for that. But if you'd prefer something else..." She motions to the bedroom. "I'll start here. With the window. Then the bedroom. The light will be better there as the sun moves."

There's so much enthusiasm in her voice. It does something to me. Fills me with a pride I haven't felt in a long time.

I care about her. More than I should.

And I don't give a fuck about should.

Only about seeing passion in her eyes.

And maybe seeing her clothes on the floor too, huh, Adam? Let's not lose sight of what matters here.

This idiotic plan of yours is finally making sense.

The best revenge is getting laid.

Everyone knows that.

Maybe he's right.

Fuck, my brother isn't here. He's a voice in my head. He's gone. He's gone forever and I'll never make that right.

Even with all of this—

I'll never make it right.

But I can't dwell on the loss now. I need to do this. I need to find some fucking way to do this.

I murmurer a confirmation to Danielle.

She shifts fully into photographer mode, setting up her equipment, checking the light, oblivious to everything except the photo in her head.

I move into the kitchen. Find gin in the fridge. The promise of escape is tempting.

The taste of juniper, citrus, Danielle's lips.

But I can't do it.

I need to feel this.

Every ounce of it.

Danielle moves into the bedroom. I close my eyes, try to find some way to soften my shoulders.

Then she steps into the main room in her silk robe and my other thoughts disappear.

Fuck, I need to push that off her shoulders. Pin her to the wall. Slide my hand between her legs.

I need to be in that perfect place where the world makes sense.

That's what she wants to capture—how badly I need to fuck her.

You're overthinking this, Adam. She wants to fuck you. You want to fuck her.

Why do you make everything so damn complicated?

Take the pictures. Touch her like you want her. Touch her until she's purring and coming on your hand.

Then throw her on the table and fuck her on camera.

That's the win-win here.

Not shoving it in that asshole's face.

Fucking her.

And having photos of you fucking her.

Win.

More win.

"Are you ready?" Her voice is equal parts gentle and firm. She's careful with me, but she's still in control.

I usually hear that tone with doctors, physical therapists, medical professionals tasked with my recovery.

It's different on her.

Honest.

Vulnerable.

Incredibly appealing.

"Yes." I force a breath through my nose. I can do this. I can.

"Here, to start." She motions to the wide window, the one looking out on the Hudson. "I want a few silhouettes of you."

I move across the room.

She studies me carefully. Not with concern I might break. An artist, studying her subject. "Your back to me."

I turn to the window.

"Be natural."

"Natural?"

"Look at the river."

I do.

"Put your hands in your pockets. And think."

"How can you tell I'm thinking from the back?"

"Body language." Her voice softens. "I want to capture your presence. You have a power to you when you walk into a room. You know you can control it. But you're afraid too. Because of how people see you now?"

"Yes."

"What about before?"

"I didn't think about it."

Click. She snaps a photo.

I jump.

"This is a digital camera. The sound is fake. To emulate the sound of a shudder closing in a manual camera."

"Why do manufacturers add it?"

"To make it feel more real, I guess. I can turn it off if it's distracting."

"I won't know what you've photographed."

"I'll show you everything. I promise."

"No. I don't mind it."

"Good." *Click.* "I can put on music too. Do you really like new wave?"

"I do."

"Do you want some?"

"You're the photographer."

"You're the actor. I need you in the right head space."

"I'm not showing my face."

"Even so. If you don't like the song, it will show in your body language."

Will music quiet the *what the fuck are you thinking* voice in my head? Or will it amplify it? "How do you normally shoot?"

"Usually, quiet. Sometimes, music. Sexy music." She laughs. "To set the mood."

"Then whatever you think will set the mood."

"Okay."

I turn back to her. Watch as she picks up her phone, finds the song she wants, streams it to the speakers.

A breathy voice fills the space. Then a soft jazz instrumental.

It's exactly the mood of her images.

Sexy, intimate, feminine.

Click. She snaps a photo of me watching her. "I'll keep you anonymous. I promise."

"I trust you."

"Good." She smiles. Snaps another photo. "Give me one more of your back."

I turn to face the window. Whenever people visited, they gushed over the view. Mostly Bash, Simon, Liam. The dates they wanted to show off.

Occasionally, a woman I was fucking.

A few wanted to be pressed against the glass, on display for the entire city.

I never agreed.

Would Danielle want that?

It's not the right time of year. The glass is ice cold.

But this summer—

If she's here—

If we return—

She snaps another handful of photos, then she asks me to turn. When I do, she studies me again.

It's strange and intoxicating, being her subject, seeing the focus in her dark eyes, knowing it's all mine.

"Adam Pierce in his element." She looks to my hair. Eyes. Shoulders. Hands. "What would you do, if a woman was coming over for sex?"

"A woman. Or you?"

"If I was coming over."

"You're here now."

"Imagine I'm not. I'm out with friends. I'm due home in an hour. You're home. Alone. Comfortable. Thinking of what's to come. How do you prepare?"

"Prepare?"

"Would you pour a drink? Take off your jacket? Roll your shirtsleeves to your elbows? Touch yourself?"

"Touch myself?"

"You haven't."

"Fucked myself before a date?"

She nods.

"In high school," I say. "Simon's advice. To ease the tension."

"Not recently?"

"No."

"Not to completion, then. To… stimulation."

"Do you?"

"I have."

Fuck. It's the only thing in my head.

Click, click.

I roll my jacket off my shoulders. Set it on the table.

She snaps a photo.

Then one of me taking off my watch.

The expensive time-piece next to the jacket.

I roll my sleeves to my elbows.

She snaps a photo. "It turns you on."

"What?"

"Me, touching myself."

"Of course."

"Why?"

"Move back to the window."

I do.

"Why does it turn you on?"

Click. Fuck. The thoughts in my head. The expression she's capturing. She's good at this. "The thought of your pleasure. Of you wanting me that badly."

Her chests heaves with her inhale. "I, uh… me too. I like the thought of you fucking yourself. Maybe, one day, I'll convince you to shoot that."

"Simulated?"

"Not my first choice, but I'll take it." The hazy focus fills her eyes. She slips into photographer mode. "Hands in your pockets."

I do.

"You tied me up."

"Yes."

"Why?"

"I want to be in control. To read you well enough, I know exactly what you want and how to give it to you. To push you to the edge of what you can take. To fill you with so much pleasure you burst."

"It's not just about the scars? About being in control of who sees them or touches them?"

Fuck, how can she state it so plainly?

"It's about being in control of your partner's pleasure?"

"Yes."

"And you've always been that way?"

"Yes, but before it was a sometimes thing. Now, I need it."

"Because of the scars? Or because you need control now?"

"I don't know," I admit. "I've only been with you."

Her cheeks flush. "Do you trust me?"

"Yes."

"But not with that—"

"I wouldn't do this if I didn't trust you. It's not that. I'm not ready."

She nods with understanding. "Look at me."

I do.

Click, click. "That one is for me." She lowers the camera. "Because I like the expression on your face."

"What about it?"

"No. No looking at photos until we're done. You might get insecure."

"Do you?"

"Always. But I have to look to check the framing."

"Are you insecure about your body or your photography?"

"I don't know sometimes."

"You're beautiful."

"Thank you." She sets the camera on the table. "But I... you're not oblivious enough to think that means I'm without insecurities."

"No. I am aware of the world."

"And how women are supposed to be a million contradictory things at once." She undoes the sash of her robe, showing off the silk lingerie beneath it. "I love my body. I love what it does. But I still see a closeup of my thighs and worry they're too much."

"No."

"No?"

"No." I move to her. Bring my hand to her thigh. "You're fucking perfect."

"Adam..." Her lashes fall together. "Fuck."

She is perfect. But who the fuck am I to tell her to shelve her insecurities?

I barely leave the house.

It's more than the scars.

It's more than the way people look at me.

It's everything.

But it's—

She reaches up and presses her lips to mine.

I kiss back with everything I have.

She releases me with a sigh. "I want to fuck so badly." She takes a step backward. "But not until I'm done."

"Fuck you on camera or wait?"

"Basically."

"What if I choose the former?"

"Wait here." She attaches the camera to the tripod. Adjusts the angle. Leads me back to the window. *Click, click.* She points to a remote in her right hand. "This will work with the angle. After... sometimes I put the camera on an auto mode. A photo every fifteen seconds. That's why I need the click. To know to move into the next pose." She looks up at me. Brings her free hand to my cheek.

I slip my hand around her waist, under her robe.

Click.

I pull her into a slow, deep kiss.

Click.

She turns, so my back is to the camera, so her arms are wrapped around me.

Click.

Then the other direction, so it's her back on display.

I push her hair behind her shoulder. Cup her neck with my palm.

She looks up at me like I'm the only thing she wants.

Click, click.

"Fuck." She groans as my hard-on brushes her stomach. "I might actually fuck you on camera at this rate."

I believe her.

"I'll set up in the bedroom." She kisses me softly and steps backward. "And you... it's up to you. I'll keep shooting until you say when. Even if that means I'm taking a pornographic video."

She picks up her tripod, moves to the bedroom to set up.

Reality threatens to return to my mind, but I push it aside.

How much can I handle?

I have no fucking idea.

Chapter Twenty-Nine

ADAM

I s this really the place I slept for seven years?

Between the soft light and the smooth sheets, the space is gentle, warm, inviting.

There's no sign of Bash's absence.

The cold nights I spent alone, tossing and turning.

The empty feeling in my gut.

Only the memory of Danielle groaning my name as she comes on my cock.

I need that.

Now.

Even if it's on film.

Maybe because it is.

Am I out of my fucking mind?

Or is this a sign of progress?

Finally stepping out of my fucking cage.

I don't know.

I don't care.

I don't care about anything except hearing my name on her lips again.

"This is the angle." She motions to the corner of the

bed, the one next to the window. "I'll get that half with this camera." She motions to a camera on the dresser. "And the other with this one." She smiles. "I've never done two before, but I... I want to get one in the shot. It's not set up for it yet. But with the mirror." She motions to the mirror behind me.

"Like *The Voyeur*."

Her smile widens. "More like *The Act* probably, but..." Her expression gets shy. "I, uh... let's start with that. The version I can actually show people."

"Wherever you need me."

"I like getting this side of you." She picks up her camera. Moves to me. Rests her hand on my chest. "All-powerful Adam Pierce doing exactly what I say."

"Are you baiting me, angel?"

"If I am?"

"I might punish you for that."

Her pupils dilate. "I might get it on film." She rises to her tiptoes to kiss me. "I should put on heels. Make this easier." She moves to the closet. Pulls out a pair of black heels. "You really are tall."

"Did you just notice?"

"No, but I didn't consider how it would affect the angle." She slips into the shoes. Turns to the mirror to check out her legs.

She looks fucking divine.

I need her out of that robe.

Out of her lingerie.

On the bed, her legs pressed against my cheeks as she comes on my face.

My body whines. It's without reservations. It only cares about being inside her as quickly as possible.

"Turn to the mirror," she says.

I do.

She moves in front of me. Pushes the sides of her robe apart, showing off her black lingerie.

Click, click.

She takes a few with the camera in her hands. Brings it to her eye to frame carefully.

"Touch me," she says.

I push her robe off her shoulders.

It catches on her bent arms.

She arches her back, rocking her ass against my cock. "Fuck." *Click, click.* She shifts the camera to her right hand. Slips the robe off her left arm.

Then the other.

She brings the camera back to her eye. Focuses the image.

Click, click.

It's a familiar scene. Her, in only scraps of black silk, me in my suit, the two of us turned to the mirror.

Her attention on the act.

It almost feels normal.

Even with the camera there. Maybe because it is.

Of course I feel exposed.

Who wouldn't?

I brush her hair behind her back. Bring my lips to her neck. Inhale the scent of her skin. The honey shampoo, the olive oil soap, something all Danielle.

I press my lips to her neck.

Softly.

Then harder.

She lets out a low groan. Leans into my kiss. "Adam."

My hands go to her hips instinctively. I need to hear that sound again. It's the only thing that matters.

The only thing that's ever mattered.

I pull her body against mine.

She groans as my cock brushes her ass.

Click, click. She tries to keep her attention on her mission, but she's drifting too.

She wants to be here, with me, fully immersed in this.

I want her here.

I want these fucking pictures.

For me.

For her.

Maybe for that asshole too. I'm not sure anymore.

I keep one hand on her hip. Bring the other to her chest. To the edges of her sleek silk bra.

She groans as I run my fingers over the cup. The right. Then the left.

I pull her closer. Cup her breast with my hand. Run my thumb over the sleek fabric, rubbing the silk against her nipple.

"Adam." She reaches back for me. Wraps her hands around my side. Hip. Ass. "Fuck."

I roll the fabric over her nipple again and again, teasing her with the light pressure.

She groans as she snaps another shot. "Take it off."

I tease her again.

"Please, Adam."

Fuck. I can't say no to that. It's physically impossible.

I push the strap off her right shoulder.

The left.

Her breasts spill from the fabric.

Her eyes go to the mirror. Then the camera. She snaps another photo as I do away with her bra.

Then the panties.

They fall to the floor. She takes a picture of them, then she kicks them away, presses her ass against my crotch.

"Please." She lowers the camera. Holds it at her stomach. Makes eye contact through the mirror. "Touch me." *Click, click.*

She wants this on film.

My head is supposed to step in. Say *fuck no*. Or *this is a terrible idea*. Or something else sensible.

But I'm out of sense.

I need to make her come.

Now.

"You're going to drop that thing." I press my lips to her neck. Softly. Then harder. Then the scrape of my teeth.

She groans as I bite her. "I won't."

"Are you sure?"

"No." She reaches for me. Wraps her fingers around my wrist. "Do it anyway." She takes my hand and brings it to her thigh.

I run my thumb over her soft skin.

Click, click.

Then higher, higher, higher.

There.

My thumb brushes her clit.

A groan falls from her lips.

I test different strokes. Softer. Harder. Faster. Slower.

Left.

Right.

Up.

Down.

There. I find the spot where she needs me. Harder. Faster. Until her groans run together.

"Adam." Her eyelids flutter together.

Still, she snaps another photo.

I work her with steady strokes. Bring my free hand to her chest. Roll her nipple between my thumb and forefinger.

Softly at first.

Then harder.

Hard enough, she groans.

Hard enough, her groan is equal parts agony and ecstasy.

And every part irresistible.

Click, click.

How she's holding on, I don't know.

But she is.

And the thought of looking at these later—

My cock whines.

I need to be inside her.

Soon.

Really fucking soon.

I run my finger over her clit, pushing her closer and closer.

Her groans run together.

Her fingers curl into her thigh.

Her body melts into mine.

Then she's there, groaning my name as she comes on my hand, conscious enough to take another picture.

She catches her breath slowly. Her legs straighten. Her eyes flutter open. Her attention returns to the mirror. The camera. The scene.

"Fuck." She holds the camera to her chest. "I need to touch you. Please, Adam."

Fuck. I nod.

"Can I?" She holds up the camera.

There's no doubt about her question.

Can she photograph it?

That sensible voice stays quiet.

The fear I expect doesn't come.

I'm fine with her taking pictures of my cock, but I can't let her see my chest.

What the fuck is wrong with me?

At the moment, I don't care.

I need her closer.

I need her hair in my hands and her lips on my neck.

It's the only thing I've ever needed.

"Anonymous, I promise," she says.

Anonymous. No scars. I nod a yes.

She brightens, but not the way she did before. With a mix of joy and all-consuming need.

She sets the camera on the tripod. Turns it to the bed. Sets auto mode. "It's going to take a picture every thirty seconds." She pulls something from the dresser. A tube of lipstick.

Fuck.

"I'm only going to pose for the first few. Then…"

"Whatever you capture?"

She nods, turns to the mirror, applies lipstick until the camera clicks.

She sets the tube on the dresser. Checks her perfect pout in the mirror. Turns to me like she's begging me to order her onto her knees.

Maybe she is.

It's been a long fucking time.

Too long.

"Is that for me, angel?" I motion *come here*.

She takes a step toward me. "If it is?"

"You want your pretty red lips around my cock?"

Her pupils dilate. "Adam…" Her chest heaves with her inhale.

"Is that a yes?"

"Would you?" Her voice is eager. Needy.

Would I? I've died and gone to heaven. I really have. "I don't hear an answer."

"Yes." She takes another step toward me. Another. Until her knees brush mine.

"Yes?"

"I want my lips around your cock." She runs her fingers through my hair. "I want to suck you off."

"I won't be gentle."

"Good."

Fuck. She's too good at this.

I'm the one wrapped around her finger.

But it's not like I can complain about the situation.

She wants pictures of her lips around my cock.

How the fuck can I say no to that?

I look up at her.

Her expression shifts. Still strong and demanding, but pliable. Obedient even.

She wants me to issue orders.

She wants to follow them.

I shift into my role. "On your knees."

"Help me."

I do.

She places her hands on my thighs. Runs her thumb over the fabric of my slacks. "Please, Adam."

Fuck. I take her hand. Bring it to my cock.

She rubs me over my slacks.

It's only a hint of friction, but it's enough to overwhelm me.

It's been a long time since anyone has touched me.

Since I've let anyone touch me.

I'm not going to last long.

"Unzip me," I say.

She does.

My cock springs from my slacks.

Her eyes go wide. "Fuck, I… fuck."

"Wrap your hand around me."

Her thumb brushes my tip. Then her fingers. Her palm.

Danielle.

She is a fucking angel.

And she's begging for my cock.

She runs her hand over my shaft. With a soft grip at first. Then harder. Harder.

Until a groan falls from my lips. "Fuck, angel. Don't make me come yet."

She looks up at me, asking for permission.

I nod.

She wraps her hand around my base, then she leans in, wraps her pretty red lips around me.

My eyes close.

My body threatens to take over.

The soft pressure of her mouth overwhelms me.

She explores me with her tongue.

A soft flick. A slow swirl. Then harder. Faster.

Fuck.

She's perfect.

It defies explanation.

I give her one more stroke, then I bring my hand to the back of her head.

I guide her gently.

She takes me deeper.

Deeper.

As deep as she can.

Then she pulls back and does it again.

I keep my hand on her head, pushing her forward, pulling her back.

Softly at first.

Then harder.

My hand knots in her hair.

The other slips down her chest. Finds her breast.

I toy with her nipple as I guide her over me.

Again and again.

She groans against my cock.

Takes me deeper.

Deeper.

Again and again.

Harder and harder.

I move faster, rougher, tugging at her dark hair, rocking into her pretty mouth.

She stays glued to me, taking me deeper, working me harder.

Perfect and soft and wet.

Until I'm there.

I hold her in place, groaning her name as I come.

My cock pulses as I spill into her mouth. Pleasure rocks through my pelvis. Consumes every one of my senses.

Everything is Danielle.

Her red lips. Her soft tongue. Her sweet groan.

Her gorgeous, curvy body.

Mine.

She sits on her heels. "Fuck." She wipes her mouth with her hand. "That was... fuck."

I'm not coherent enough to respond. I barely manage to offer my hand, help her to her feet, pull her into my lap.

She wraps her arms around me.

I hold her like I'm never going to let go.

For a minute, I believe it.

The world is a beautiful, perfect place.

Only bliss.

Connection.

Need.

Love even.

For a minute, I believe I'm a prince who's found a princess, and a possibility of happily ever after.

Chapter Thirty

DANIELLE

After I climb out of bed, wash, dress, pack, we eat in the kitchen. A quick meal he prepared. It's nothing fancy—box pasta, a jar of sauce, shrimp fried on the stove—but it does something to me, knowing he made it.

I'm still in a daze. I don't have much to say during dinner. As we clean, say goodbye to the space, head to the parking garage, to his shiny black Tesla.

He slips our suitcases into the trunk. Opens the passenger side door for me. Motions *after you*.

I slide inside.

He follows. Turns the car on (it barely hums). Taps the stereo. "Whatever you want to listen to."

"What if I like terrible pop music?"

"I've heard the music in your room."

My room. Because it's mine. I have my own space in his house. Not our space. Not a shared space. Mine.

It's the first time something has felt mine in a long time.

But I want an ours.

Because I fucked him a few hours ago?

Or for some other, deeper, scarier reason?

Maybe all I need is our bed.

"What would you listen to?" I pull out my cell. Connect it to the Bluetooth. Try to decide what will set the mood.

"I don't drive often."

"On the way here?"

"Soft Cell."

"What did Liam say?" I ask. "New wave. Like that song." Shit. What's it called? I hum the melody of the song Liam mentioned.

Adam nods. "*Tainted Love.*"

Yes, that's it. A fitting song? Or just a song? I type it into Spotify. Find a new wave playlist. Go straight to *Tainted Love.*

An energetic electronic opening fills the car.

Then a singer with the perfect amount of passion.

It's a famous song. I've heard it on a thousand TV shows.

And it's...

It's so not Adam.

"Really?" I scroll through the playlist, trying to find songs I recognize. "This is so... alive."

"I'm not?"

"You're more restrained."

"He's restrained."

The song isn't really, but the performance is. "It's like someone compressed the emotional range."

He nods.

"What else?"

"The rest of the album."

Right. That's what he played on the way here. I let the song finish, then I play the album from the first song.

I can picture him in his car alone, letting the music fill

256

the space, understanding the flat affection, wishing for the energy and passion.

"I like it," I say.

"I can tell."

My cheeks flush.

"You were listening to Joni Mitchell the other day."

I nod.

"Is that what you like?"

"Singer-songwriters." I slip my cell into my purse. "Mostly the music my mom played. Well, the singer-song-writers she played. She had eclectic taste. Played Joni Mitchell then the Black Eyed Peas." I used to hate *Let's Get It Started* because I'd heard it too many times. But now it feels like home. Like a home I can never see again. "How can she see the brilliance of Joni Mitchell and still like the Black Eyed Peas?"

"People are complicated."

They are. "I love every era of singer-songwriter, but the seventies are my favorite."

"Why?"

"There's a beautiful simplicity. I can't explain it."

"It suits you."

"Are you trying to make me blush?"

"If I was trying to make you blush, I'd say something dirtier."

Do it now. Let's pull over. Stay in that place where we understand each other.

His eyes flit to me, then they're back on the road. He must decide to take mercy on me, because he shifts the conversation away from sex. "What else?"

"When I'm not listening to singer-songwriters from the seventies? Mostly, singer-songwriters from the eighties. Or nineties. Aughts. There's a lot of good stuff."

"Do you have a favorite?"

"I have to choose between Carole King and Michelle Branch?"

"No."

"Okay. Then I won't. I love them all."

He nods, absorbing the information.

"When I'm home, I let Remy pick the music. Mostly, he plays video game soundtracks."

"Do you like them?"

"Sometimes. After hearing them so many times, the songs make me think of him. Of that feeling of Sunday afternoons. We'd drink too much coffee. He'd sit on the couch with his laptop. I'd stretch out on the floor with my latest set of photos."

"You edited naked photos next to your brother?"

"I didn't take anything explicit yet. It took me a while to build up to that. A few months of landscapes. Then portraits of strangers. Headshots. Careful crops."

"When was your first?"

"The first time I got naked on camera?"

He nods.

"It was after I saw Dana DeLaney's first set. Well, the first set we sold at the gallery. I stared at the photos for three days straight, trying to figure out how she got the light to fall on the model just so. I was at home, trying to recreate it, but it didn't work in my white shirt. So I took that off. And I felt this thrill from snapping a photo of myself topless. Then bottomless. It was… intoxicating."

"Did you fall in love then?"

"Once I posted on my site. I thought I'd feel embarrassed. Nervous. Ashamed. But I didn't."

"You didn't feel exposed?"

"I did. But in a way I liked. Like if you asked me to take off my clothes and fuck myself."

"Are you baiting me, angel?"

"No." Maybe. "Not on purpose."

He half-smiles. "I'll get you back for that."

"That sounds like a dare."

"Maybe."

I bite my lip. It's a long drive. Really long. I won't survive that much desire. I need to think of something else. Anything else.

My gaze goes to the scenery. Brick buildings bleed into the dark sky. The city shines in the rearview mirror.

We're already over the bridge, on the freeway, on the way to Adam's secluded castle.

I miss the city, but I want to be at his house.

Not just because I want to be alone in a place where I can actually touch him.

Because I want to be there, in the space he's called home for the last year, in the room he created for me.

The beautiful, soft, white space with its erotic art and its soft bed.

And the possibility of Adam fucking me.

Fuck.

I try to push thoughts of sex aside. "How did you get into Soft Cell?"

"My dad. He wouldn't admit it to friends. He knew he was supposed to love Bach, Mozart, opera. Something respectable. Not the popular music of the day."

"But he did?"

He nods. "At first, he only played it when he thought no one was listening. Then for Simon. I caught them singing in the kitchen."

"Yeah?"

"Yeah. Somehow, Liam picked it up. I don't know how he remembered, but he... you've met him. He always needs to be the center of attention."

I nod. "Is that why you love it?"

"Part of it." He looks to the stereo, considering the question. "The rest, I can't explain. It moves me. I don't know why. I only know it moves me."

"That's love. This feeling inside us we can't explain." I swallow hard. "At least, I imagine. I, uh, it's different. Familial love. I guess I can't explain why I'd do anything for Remy. He's my brother. My best friend. Of course, I'd move the stars for him. But I can't really say why. Not logically."

"He shares similar DNA. You're older. Socialized to feel responsible for him."

"How dreamy."

His laugh is soft. "I understand. I'd do anything for my brothers. Even now. Even though they're adults."

"Yeah." I know that feeling well. I find the bottle of water in the cup holder. Take a long sip. "You were listening to something orchestral."

"Bach." He laughs. "What my dad played when we had guests."

"You like it?"

"It envelops you."

That sounds more like Adam. "That suits you."

"You too."

"How is that?"

"It reminds me of your work. The boldness that consumes you."

"No one's ever called it bold before."

"It is."

"Thank you?" I swallow another sip, but my mouth stays dry. It's hot in here. Way too hot. I need to take off all my clothes. And climb into his lap.

Why are we driving?

Why does he live so far away?

Liam was right. This is way too far. We should stay in the apartment forever.

In his bedroom forever.

"It does consume me," he says. "Every time I look at one of your photos, I struggle to pull myself away."

"Always?"

"Always."

"Because of the composition. Or because——"

"You're naked."

"Yeah." My blush deepens.

"I don't know. I can't separate the two." His eyes flit to me. "After the accident, I had that urge, physically, but I wasn't willing to give in. I tried thinking of other women. Looking at other pictures."

"Porn?"

He nods. "And photos from exes."

My stomach churns. "You have photos of other women?"

"Fuck buddies."

"Oh."

"I can delete them."

"You would?"

"If they upset you."

My stomach settles.

"What if it upset me? That other men can see you naked?"

"Technically, you can tell me what to do for the next year. You know that."

"Yes."

"You can forbid me from posting for the next year." I press my palms into my thighs. "You wouldn't though." There's no conviction in my voice. "Would you?"

"No."

"It wouldn't be fair. Since you knew when you

hired me."

"I said no. You don't have to convince me."

My shoulders settle. "You promise?"

"Yes."

"Good. You shouldn't. I mean. Thank you." I don't know what I mean. Only that I need my photos out there. I didn't realize how badly until right now. "Is it because it turns you on, knowing other men can see me?"

"Yes. And because I know it gets you off."

It does. But I've never said it out loud. "It's generosity?"

"You're right. It's selfish too. I like knowing other men see you, want you, wish they could have you, curse me for being the one who has you." Intent drips into his voice. There's something there. Something he isn't saying.

But I'm losing interest in the more philosophical parts of this conversation.

I want to take off all my clothes.

Then all of his.

"You've taken explicit photos before," he says.

"Only alone."

"But you have?"

"Yes."

"You never post them."

"I don't want to be a pornographer."

"But you want to post erotic photos?"

I nod.

"Where's the line?"

"That's the point of the photos," I say. "To ask the viewer. Is this art? Is this pornography? Is the model an object for you to consume? Or is she using you?"

"Because it gets you off, being on display?"

"Because… I'm using the only currency I have as a broke young woman."

"Because it gets you off," he says again.

"Turning it against the patriarchy."

He looks to me, daring me to admit it.

"And because it gets me off." My blush spreads to my chest. "But I could argue… that's, uh, that's another way of taking back the power. Using men looking at me for my own sexual enjoyment."

"Angel, you don't have to justify yourself."

"You promise?"

He nods. "Explain if you want. I enjoy the insight. But you never have to justify your art to me. Even if I don't understand it."

"What if it was photos of your brother naked?"

"Are you touching him?"

"No."

"Are they sexual?"

"Well, he's naked."

"Explicit?"

"Him touching himself? No."

"Then no."

"What if it walks up to the line?" I ask.

"Where's that?"

"I don't know it until I see it."

"Can you walk up to the line with a woman instead?"

I laugh. "What a guy thing to say."

"It's not a sapphic fantasy."

"Did you just say sapphic fantasy?"

"Yes," he says.

"Why not say 'girl on girl action'?"

"All right." He chuckles. "It's not dreams of 'girl on girl action.'"

"Uh-huh."

"You're not attracted to women."

"Are you sure? I'm obsessed with photos of naked women."

"Yes." There's no doubt in his voice. "You're obsessed because you're an exhibitionist."

Fuck. There it is, without adornment. I, Danielle Bellamy, am an exhibitionist.

"I'm glad. I enjoy watching you."

Fuck.

"I went eight months without fucking myself," he says.

"Eight months without orgasm?"

"No. My body wouldn't allow that. But never intentionally."

Ah, yes, the perks slash horrors of being a man.

"Until I found you."

"Did it happen that fast?"

"It felt fast. It must have been a few days. I kept trying to tear myself away from you, but I couldn't."

"Why did you go so long?"

"Guilt." He looks to the road. "I didn't believe I deserved to feel anything else."

"Do you still feel that way?"

"Sometimes."

"But you… you want to be with me?"

"Yes."

Fuck. That's… fuck. "Are we really two hours from your house?"

His laugh eases the sexual tension in the air. "Ninety minutes."

"That's too far."

"I can take a detour. Make it further."

"Adam." My voice is a whine. "Please."

"Don't."

"Don't?"

"Don't say my name in that tone when I'm driving. I'll crash the fucking car."

"Oh."

"I can't deny you. I'm not physically capable."

"Please."

"That either," he says. "I want to live to fuck you."

"Will you? When we get to the house?"

"Maybe."

"I don't know if I can wait for a maybe. It might be better to risk death."

"It will be a no if you do it again."

"But…"

His voice drops an octave. "What are you wearing under that?"

"Underwear."

"Show me."

"Adam—"

"You want me to fuck you later?"

"Yes," I breathe.

"Then show me."

I pull the dress up my thighs. Over my hips.

His eyes flit to my exposed panties, then they return to the road. "Take them off."

"But—"

"Now."

I raise my hips. Slide my panties to my ankles. Then over my boots.

"What do you want? Right now?"

"I want you to fuck me."

His eyes flit to my thighs, but his hands stay on the steering wheel. "You have to wait."

"I know."

"No. If you want me to fuck you at home, you have to wait. If you touch yourself, I won't."

"But—"

"Your choice, angel. Do you want to come now? Or do you want to come with me later?"

Chapter Thirty-One

ADAM

Danielle's red lips part with a sigh. Her dark eyes fill with an intoxicating mix of need and fire. "You're cruel."

"Yes."

"Would you really—"

"Ask again and you'll find out."

"But you... you were talking about fucking yourself to my photo."

"I'm aware."

"Not fucking yourself for eight months. Until you found me. Do you have any idea what that does to me?"

"Yes."

"But you—"

"Are you unclear?"

"No," she admits. "I just... I can say I won't fuck you if you don't give me what I want now."

"You can." I dare her to do it.

She doesn't. "Ad—" She catches herself. Stops.

I keep one hand on the steering wheel. Set the other on her thigh.

She lets out a slow groan as I run my finger over her skin.

We stay like that for a long time. Through the first album. A second. A third.

As we pull off the freeway, turn onto the main drag, onto the road that leads only to the mansion.

Through the gate.

All the way to the garage.

I park.

She nearly jumps out of the car. She leaves her clothes, her camera, her purse. Moves into the house, through the foyer, the empty kitchen, the big open ballroom.

"Where?" Danielle looks to the stairs, her bedroom, my office. The study down the hall. The gym. Even the quiet, dark garden.

"Where?" I play dumb.

"Where will you fuck me?"

"Did I say I'd fuck you?"

She turns to me. Pulls her dress over her head. Undoes her bra.

She's standing in the ballroom in only her black boots.

She's fucking divine.

"I should punish you for that," I say.

"Then do it." She stares back at me, defiant, proud, beautiful.

I close the distance between us. Wrap my arms around her.

She groans as my fingers brush her hips. Yelps as I take her into my arms.

I hold her to my chest and carry her up the stairs.

Down the hall.

To her bedroom.

I lay her on the soft white sheets, then I spread her legs, unzip my slacks, fuck her until she's groaning my name.

She comes twice.

Pulls me over with her.

I linger in her arms until I'm too stiff to stay still.

She peels her body away from mine, cleans and dresses in the bathroom, whispers good night and slips into the study.

I don't expect to miss her, but I do.

I change into my pajamas, find something to read, retire to my room.

An hour later, she knocks, slips into my room, into my bed. Whispers, "Can I stay with you tonight? Please."

I expect my head to step in, say *no*, make some excuse. But I don't. I bring my hand to her cheek, I pull her into a slow, deep kiss, and I whisper, "Yes."

———

I WAKE TO THE ORANGE GLOW OF SUNRISE AND THE SIGHT of Danielle in my bed. She's sleeping on her side, her arms wrapped around a pillow, her expression serene.

She looks right, draped in my silk sheets. In my bed. In my life.

I linger for longer than I should, watching her chest rise and fall with her breath, soaking in the warmth of her skin.

Then I move through my morning routine—run, weight training, shower.

She rouses as I step into the room. I'm in a robe. It covers the parts I can't let her see.

But something inside me is desperate to shrug the fabric from my shoulders.

Take it off, Mr. Broodypants. She wants to fuck you. You want to fuck her. Jump on that bed and ride her like a stallion. Is stallion the metaphor I want here? No, that was a simile.

We're getting distracted, Adam.
This isn't an English lesson.
We're not writing poetry.
But if that's what you need—
Danielle is a total freak
No more excuses
Make her come. Do it again.
That's a haiku, Adam.
If it's a haiku, it must be true.
Get on it.

Danielle lets out a soft yawn. "Hey."

"Good morning."

"I like this look." She stretches her arms over her head. "The most casual I've seen you."

"In a designer robe?"

She nods. "I know. It's ridiculous. Are you going to wear a suit today?"

"What else would I wear?"

"It's Sunday."

I raise a brow.

She smiles. "Jeans and a t-shirt."

"It's January."

"Jeans and a sweater."

I motion to the closet. "Pick them out."

"Fifty bucks says there are only suits in here." She slips out of bed and pulls the closet door open. "Ha, should have waited for you to agree."

"Do you really need fifty dollars?"

"I wouldn't turn it down." She rifles through the suits hanging in the closet. "Navy. Black. Charcoal. Slate grey. More grey. You've got a lot of grey."

"It suits me."

"It does." She turns back to me. Looks me over carefully. "And the blue ties. They bring out the blue in your eyes. But not really my color. If I'm wearing them in an... unconventional way."

"Oh?"

She bites her lip. "Are there casual clothes in the dresser?"

"I can't answer that."

"No?"

"Not if it's going to keep me from wrapping that tie around your wrists."

She smiles. "You can do it anyway."

"This way is more fun."

She moves to the dresser. Checks the drawers for casual clothes. There are jeans, slacks, sweaters, even a few t-shirts. "Have you really worn this?" She pulls out a pair of jeans and a blue sweater.

"At some point."

"I can't imagine it. I think... I think you wear that suit all weekend."

"Usually."

"Why?"

"Years of boarding school uniforms. I'm used to it."

"What about the college rebellion?"

"It didn't last."

She smiles. "Okay. Wear whatever calls to you. As long as the tie is involved later." She sets the jeans and sweater on top of the dresser.

"You're not styling me for another shoot?"

Her eyes go wide. "Would you?"

"After how the last one ended? Angel, are you really not sure?"

Her cheeks blush. "I, uh... right... I... Yes. I would. But I have to show you the images first. And edit them. And I... fuck, now I don't know if I should mount you here or ask you to save the energy for later."

I raise a brow, daring her.

"I, uh… I do need to brush my teeth. And drink a lot of coffee. But after… I have to choose art."

"It's Sunday."

"Even so." She plays with the edges of her pajama top. "Did you eat?"

"Not yet."

"Well, we have to do that. And after, there might be time for art and sex."

"Might?"

She nods. "After you approve a photo." She kisses me on the cheek. "This is my only card. I have to play it at the right time."

It's not.

She can get anything she wants if she says my name in that needy, breathy tone.

But she doesn't realize it.

"I'll meet you downstairs." She runs her fingers over my chin.

I don't flinch this time.

That's progress.

Danielle notices. She smiles, runs her fingers over my chin again. Releases me and slips into the bathroom.

Still, I wait until the water is running to remove my robe.

This is an old house. There's only one mirror here, a standing floor length thing in the corner.

My eyes go there instantly.

Scars.

Only scars.

Jagged pink lines on my face.

Then darker, deeper ones on my shoulders, chest, stomach.

Would she see them as beautiful?

Would she still want me?

Or would she see every ugly deed in my heart?

I don't know.

I want to show her.

I want to trust her.

I want to feel her soft skin against mine.

But I can't. Not yet.

I finish drying, then I slip into a suit. Something familiar and comfortable.

Something that turns her on.

That isn't why.

But it feels good to believe it, at least for a second.

It feels good to believe I'm capable of loving her and accepting her love in return.

Chapter Thirty-Two

ADAM

T rish nearly doubles over when she sees me at the dining table.

"Adam, it's lovely to have you and Danielle here together." She beams as she pours coffee. Insists on making a special meal.

Coffee. An omelet with fresh herbs and goat cheese. Roasted potatoes. Bacon. Sliced strawberries.

Danielle groans over every bite.

I ask her about her plans for the photo shoot. She's still nervous about going public with her art. Especially about asking her old boss to show her photos.

But there's excitement in every word she says.

She gushes through all of breakfast and a second cup of coffee. "I have preliminary photos, if you're ready to see them."

Fuck, what a question.

Am I ready to see photos of my hand between her legs?

Of my scars on display?

A normal headshot, maybe. But it's hard to envision anything else.

I'm not ready. I don't know how I'll ever be ready. Only that I want to get there. "Yes."

Her expression brightens. It fills the entire house with light.

She's so fucking beautiful.

Warm, protective, passionate.

I need her in my life.

Not just for this ruse.

Because I need her.

The thought overwhelms me. I need her. I don't know how to keep her. I don't know if I can keep her.

Is that love?

Choosing what's best for her over what's best for me?

Or am I thinking with my cock?

I follow her to her room. She sits at her desk. Opens her laptop. Pulls up a folder of photos.

"Best to worst?" she asks. "Or worst to best?"

"Which is best?"

"The explicit photos," she says.

"Those last. Or we won't get to the others."

Her fingers curl into her thighs. She lets out a soft sigh. "Okay. Then this... these are for you. I'd love to show them, but I meant what I said. You have final approval of any image you're in." She takes the laptop to the bed. Sits next to me. Pulls up a photo.

One of the first images we took, a silhouette against the window, my back to the camera, my posture stiff.

She looks to me for approval. When I nod, she moves to the next.

My forearms, as I roll my hands up my sleeves.

My watch on the desk.

A headshot of me looking out the window.

My face is in profile. It's clearly me. Clearly Adam Pierce. But the unmarked side. The man, not the monster.

Then the next.

Me, looking at the camera, at Danielle, like I'm thinking of all the ways I'm going to fuck her.

Straight on.

My expression as revealing as my scars.

It steals my breath.

"I promised to keep you anonymous," she says. "And I will. The photos I want to show are all anonymous."

"You don't want people to know it's me?"

"Isn't that what you want?"

I did. I do. How could I walk into a gallery and see people staring at my face? I'd crumble.

"It's not just you. I'm cropping everything at the nose. People will suspect it's us. Especially me. But they won't be sure."

Of course.

"And well, there are a lot of well-built models who can wear a suit." She laughs. "People will wonder if it's you once we announce our engagement. But they won't be sure."

"Is that what you want?"

"I haven't considered anything else." Her eyes meet mine. "The final pictures are... let me show you."

"They're beautiful."

"Thank you."

"I look human."

"You look vulnerable," she says. "I don't see that side of you often."

Is that really possible? I feel exposed every minute I'm around people. I take every step carefully, so I won't shatter.

But not with her.

Not anymore.

I'm not ready to bring her hand to the markings on my chest. But I'm ready to kiss her. To feel her fingers on my neck, chin, cheek without cringing.

"It's overwhelming," she says. "To see that side of you in a photograph. Especially if it's been a long time. Or you've never seen it before. The first time I saw that vulnerability in my eyes, I was overjoyed as a photographer. I captured something real about my subject. Then it hit me; that's me, that's my face, my expression, my pain the whole world can see. It terrified me."

"You didn't show it?"

"No. I almost never show my face. You know that."

"You're naked in your photos."

She nods.

"You don't want strange men to know where to find you."

"That didn't work."

"You aren't careful," I say. "It was easy."

"I'm not trying to be careful. And after this... I'm going public, Adam. We're going public. I don't know how long it will take to find a gallery. They're booked in advance. We... we'll be public with our engagement first."

"Soon."

She nods. "Do you have a timeline?"

I did. With this image in front of me, I can barely remember my name. "Two weeks. In the city. We'll invite everyone to dinner."

"You're going to propose there?"

"No. Before."

"When?"

"It's a surprise."

"Really?"

I nod.

She smiles. "I kind of like that. A surprise proposal. I'll post the ring on my social media."

Perfect.

"That will... that will make it more obvious. People will assume it's you. They won't be able to prove it, but they'll see me, they'll see the ring, they'll see you. They'll put it together."

Fuck.

"If it's too much, I understand. I won't include you in the set."

"At all?"

"Let me show you this," she says. "If you're uncomfortable, that's okay. I won't push you. Even though I adore the photos. But I will show the images of me. Even if I have to wait until our deal expires."

"No. I don't want that." I can't speak. My mouth is too sticky. How can she capture this side of me so easily? Why am I tempted to show the world? "I want you to soar."

She looks me over, studying me for cracks. Then she moves gently, speaks softly. As if I'm made of glass.

Maybe I am.

"I do love that photo of you," she says. "But I'm selfish about it. That's my Adam, the one no one else sees. I'm not ready to show the world."

She turns to her computer. Pulls up a new folder. The first image, another image of me in silhouette. My posture still firm, but not stiff. Commanding.

How she captured that, I don't know. But she did.

Then her, in her black lingerie, looking into the mirror as she applies a coat of lipstick.

Her, in front of the mirror, picking up the camera. Holding it in front of her pelvis as she snaps a photo.

The two of us in the bedroom, her body in front of mine, her robe falling off her shoulders.

Without the camera.

Then with it, again in front of her pelvis, this time with my hand between her legs.

I'm touching her.

She's about to come.

The camera blocks the details, but the action is obvious.

The photos are all cropped at her nose. My face isn't in frame. Only the white fabric of my shirt, my forearms, my hands on her skin.

"If it's too much… I understand that," she says. "I have a set that's not quite so erotic. I might even show it somewhere else. But this… it feels right."

My eyes go to the framed photos on the wall. "You love what DeLaney does."

"Is it too obviously a riff?"

"She didn't invent artistic nudes."

"Even so."

I study the images carefully, trying to channel the art history classes I took in high school and college.

It was mostly what Bash would call stuffy. Classic works.

Bowls of fruits, vases of flowers, landscapes.

The realist movement.

And nude portraits.

Some erotic even. We passed around an oft forgotten masterwork like it was a *Penthouse* magazine.

In ways it was.

A woman reclining on her back, her legs spread, her cunt on display.

"No," I say. "I think of these photos when I think of you."

"Do you?" Her laugh eases the tension in the room. "How do you think of me?"

"I picture you as the model. Or you, alone in your room, thinking of the images as you fuck yourself."

"You aren't jealous?"

"No. I know why they turn you on."

"Because I like feeling exposed?"

I nod. "The camera placement is a riff of this set. But the images look different. I can't explain how. I don't know enough about art."

"Which do you like better?"

"You're naked in these."

"Only this last one," she says.

"Your face is in this one," I say. "With the lipstick."

"I know."

"Are you keeping it?"

"I don't know. I was planning to crop everything. Keep the suggestion of anonymity. At least for the set. But now… I like that one."

"It poses a question it doesn't answer."

"Does it?"

"You don't use your lips in this set."

"Well… There is one image. It's perfect. But it's not nearly so subtle." Her eyes meet mine. "I didn't consider including those, but I could."

Fuck. "Would you?"

"I don't know. It's crazy I'm even thinking about it." She pulls up a new folder labeled *Explicit* and scrolls past the first few images.

My hands on her skin.

Only without the camera blocking the action.

Without her silk lingerie covering.

Then her standing over me, her hand on my cheek.

She's naked.

I'm dressed.

But she's anonymous.

I'm not.

Within the context, it's obviously her.

But her face isn't in frame.

Mine is.

This—

Fuck.

I want to show the entire world. *This beautiful woman wants me. Even though I'm a monster.*

I want to destroy every copy. *After all, it's there, in beautiful soft lighting. I'm a monster.*

"This is the angle," she says. "The images are focused on you. I can crop them. I did crop some, but they don't look quite right." She scrolls through the next few images.

Her dropping to her knees.

Touching me.

Sucking me off.

Her body is blocking the action. It's clear what's happening, but the details aren't on display.

They're sexy as hell.

But she's right. They're not composed the way the others are. They're missing something.

She scrolls to the next. One that isn't cropped.

The same image, the same action, my hands in her hair, her mouth around me, all the focus on my face.

My eyes closed.

My brow soft.

My expression dripping with pleasure.

"I'll delete them if you want." Her chest heaves with her inhale. "And I'd never share them without asking. Maybe even with asking. But I hope you'll let me keep them. They're really fucking hot." She looks to me. "I-I swear I'm not trying to manipulate by saying this. I can barely say it." Her cheeks flush. "They make me wet."

"Show me."

"Adam—"

"Now."

"No." She wraps her hand around my wrist. "I need an answer first. The main set." She pulls it up. "These five photos. I need you to approve them."

"If I don't?"

"I'll still fuck you. But I'll be disappointed."

I look through the photos again.

They're beautiful, intimate, sensual.

Past sensual. Into erotic.

They put her on display.

Put us on display.

For everyone in the fucking world.

Everyone I want to hide from.

Everyone I want to hurt.

"What do you think?" She runs her fingers over my chin. "Are you ready to reveal yourself?"

Chapter Thirty-Three

DANIELLE

Adam's eyes meet mine. "Yes. I want you to show them."

"Are you sure?"

"No." He brings his hand to my cheek. "It's terrifying. But it's thrilling too."

"It is." I lean into his touch. "You can sleep on it."

"No," he says. "I don't want to lose my nerve."

"You want me to send a pitch to the gallery now?"

He nods.

"Then I have to wait to fuck you."

"How long will it take?"

"Too long."

He smiles. "Now. I might change my mind."

"You're choosing my artistic goals over sex?"

"You could put it that way."

"How would you put it?"

"I enjoy the photos while you work."

"I'm working on the laptop. How will you see them?"

He pulls his cell from his pocket. "Send one."

"No. I have a better idea." I pull up two of my semifinalists. Images of us at the window, my robe falling off my shoulders. "I'll post these."

"Now?"

"Now. Then, you can see how it feels." I show him the photos.

He stares at them for a long time, then he nods.

I load one to Instagram. Add a caption. A tease to visit my site.

Then the more explicit one.

I love a man who appreciates an artistic woman.

A little obvious maybe.

And not at all a subtle dig at the photographer ex who wouldn't pose for me.

And making it much easier for anyone and everyone to know *Broken Beauty* is Danielle Bellamy.

This is New York. There are plenty of men in suits around. But how many female photographers are bragging about dating one?

I'll have to talk to Remy.

And...

Mostly Remy.

But I can do that.

Woosh.

I post the image. Compose a formal pitch with a clock. Three days for the gallery to give me the spot or move on. I know their calendar. I know they have room. And I know how to put on a hell of an exhibition.

There. I send it.

I send my ex-boss a set of naked photos.

Photos of me and Adam.

Naked photos of me and Adam to display to the entire art world.

Holy fuck.

My body buzzes.

Then it's the entire room.

It's not a sure thing yet. I'm giving Adam the day.

I stand. Turn to him.

He's looking at his cell, at the photo on my website.

His eyes go wide. His lips part with a sigh. "Danielle." He says my name the way he does when he comes. Like I'm the only thing he's ever needed.

"Is that a yes?"

"I already said yes."

"I'm giving you an out."

He shakes his head. "Don't. I don't want the chance to do the cowardly thing."

"What if you say no later?"

"Put it in writing."

"Well, I do have a standard model release. But I... that's more time before I fuck you."

"Can I sign digitally?"

"Yes." I press my palms to my thighs. "Are you sure?"

He nods. "Now." I must pout, because he laughs. "I like you needy."

I laugh too. It's enough to ease the sexual tension in the air. It's enough I find the release, give the laptop to Adam, watch him sign.

Then it's official.

I can display the images from the shoot.

All of them.

Even the explicit ones.

Even the ones with his face.

"Thank you." I put my laptop away and turn to him. "Adam, really, I... I have no idea how to thank you."

"Yes, you do." He motions *come here*.

I take a step toward him. So my legs brush his knees. "I have lipstick in the bathroom."

"No, angel. I want to come inside you this time."

Fuck.

His hand goes to the waistband of my silk pajama bottoms. He traces the line, then he pushes them off my hips.

I kick them off my feet.

I'm standing here in my button-up pajama top and panties. He's in a full suit, shoes even.

It turns me on, undressing while he stays dressed.

He's right.

I'm an exhibitionist.

And I'm proud.

"Take off your panties," he says.

I slide them off my hips. Kick them aside.

He motions *come here* again.

I straddle him and slide into his lap.

His hands go to my hips. He pulls my body into his, so my sex is against his cock. He's hard. Even with the thick fabric of his slacks in the way, I can feel him. The length. The firmness. The heat.

God, I want my hands on his body. Every part of his body.

I bring my hand to his neck. Chin. Cheek. The left side, with the scars.

This time, he doesn't flinch.

He leans into my touch and pulls me into a soft, slow kiss.

Then harder.

Deeper.

With his hands on my hips, he pulls my body over his, my sex against his length. So close, but so fucking far.

When he breaks our kiss, he looks up at me like I'm heaven sent. "Danielle." He says my name like it's his favorite word. Like he needs it on his tongue.

My body buzzes.

Adam brings his hands to the neckline of my shirt. He undoes the top button. Then the next. The next.

The last.

He pushes the sides apart, revealing my breasts.

My eyes flit to the mirror across from the bed. The two of us, in profile. My legs around his, his hands on my breasts, his lips on my neck.

He teases my nipples with his thumbs. Slow circles, so light I can barely feel them.

Every brush winds me tighter.

His touch feels so fucking good.

Too fucking good.

I watch him toy with me until it is too much. Until I have to close my eyes.

Then he brings one hand to my back, the space between my shoulder blades, and he pulls me closer.

He takes my nipple into his mouth.

The soft, wet pressure overwhelms me. He sucks softly. Then harder.

His tongue flicks against me.

Then it's a sort of scrape of his teeth.

Harder.

Hard enough, I tug at his hair. "Fuck."

His eyes flit to the mirror. He watches as he sucks on my nipple.

My thighs squeeze his.

He lets out a low groan as he pushes my shirt open. "Watch." He brings his mouth to my nipple again.

This time, there's no warm up.

He bites me hard. Hard enough, I yelp.

Again and again.

The pain mixes with pleasure. Winds me tighter and tighter.

Until it's too much.

Until I'm not sure I can take more.

I tug at his hair.

He moves to my other nipple and tortures it just as mercilessly.

I let my gaze drift to the mirror. Watch him pull my body into his.

I'm naked in his lap.

He's fully dressed.

The contrast in our reflection—dark against light, nude against clothed—sets me on fire. I need him.

Now.

I need everything.

"Please, Adam." I rock my hips against his. "Please fuck me."

"Not yet." He wraps his hands around me and flips our bodies, so I'm flat on my back and he's on top of me.

It's the closest we've been.

I wrap my legs around his waist.

My arms around his neck.

I pull him into a slow, deep kiss.

He kisses back with steady intensity. He is claiming me. There's no doubt about that.

And I am his.

Whatever else happens, I'm his here.

I can't help it.

He scrapes his teeth against my bottom lip.

I pull back with a groan.

Then his lips are on my neck. My collarbone. My chest. He kisses a line down my body, then he pushes my legs apart and brings his mouth to my clit.

The soft brush of his lips.

Then the flick of his tongue.

He licks me up and down, then he goes to the spot

where I need him most and he works me with steady strokes.

His soft, warm tongue flat against me.

Again and again.

Pushing me closer and closer.

I reach for him.

My fingers brush his suit jacket. His neck. The back of his head.

I tug at his short hair.

He scrapes his nails into my thighs as he winds me tighter and tighter.

Closer and closer—

There.

I groan his name as I come. The tension inside me winds to a fever pitch, then everything unravels. My world goes white. The winter light, the sheer curtains, the silk sheets.

The perfect soft light of bliss.

And the warm, steady pressure of his body.

The world a perfect, soft, warm place.

He presses his lips to my thighs. Then he pulls back. Undoes his tie. Rolls his sleeves to his elbows.

My toes curl into the sheets. I still want more. I always want more from him.

"Sit up," he says.

I do.

I expect him to ask for my arms, but he doesn't. He pulls the tie over my eyes. Cinches it behind my head.

An impromptu blindfold.

There's something exhilarating about it.

I want to see him. To see us.

But not knowing where he is or what he's doing—

Fuck.

He moves off the bed. Drops something on the desk. His watch maybe. And the shoes, I think.

The weight shifts on the bed.

He moves closer.

Then he presses his lips to the top of my foot. He kisses a line up my leg, over my thigh, up my stomach, all the way to my lips.

I kiss back as hard as I can. I need him. All of him I can get.

Adam wraps his fingers around my wrist. Takes my hand and brings it to his cock.

I press my palm against him. He's so warm and hard and I need that so badly. I pump him with a steady stroke. Then harder. Harder.

Until he groans against my mouth.

He rolls me onto my back. Then he brings his body on top of mine.

For a second, I soak in the feel of him. The weight of his body, the soft cotton of his shirt, the warmth of his bare skin.

His hands go to my hips. He holds me in place as he fills me.

No warm up. No tease. He drives hard and deep.

My head falls back.

My lips part with a groan.

I reach for something. Get his neck. The tops of his shoulders. The hint of his chest.

He slows as I press my palm against his chest.

We stay frozen there for a moment. I can't see him. I can't tell what he's thinking. I only know I want to touch him.

"Please." It falls off my lips. "Please, Adam."

He lets out a low groan and drives into me again.

Harder this time.

Deeper.

A growl falls from his lips. It's feral, like the animal part of him is taking over.

Terrifying.

Thrilling.

I press my palm flat against his chest. I don't want to push him, but fuck, I want to touch him.

Again, he slows, but only for a moment. Then he drives deep into me hard and fast.

I run my fingers over his skin, exploring him, trying to soak up every inch.

My fingers brush something hard. The raised line of a scar.

His hand finds my wrists immediately.

He pulls my hand over my head.

Then the other.

He presses his palm against my wrists, holding them there, making me powerless to do anything but take him.

And he drives into me so hard and deep it hurts.

But it hurts so fucking good.

My head falls to one side.

My fingers curl into my palms.

He winds me tighter with every thrust.

Pushing me closer and closer.

Until he's there, his cock pulsing inside me, groaning my name as he fills me. He works through his orgasm, then he pulls back, turns me onto my side, lies behind me.

He undoes the blindfold and slips his hand between my legs.

"Watch." His lips brush my ear.

He runs his teeth over my neck as he rubs me to orgasm.

I come fast. It's too much, seeing him work me, seeing our bodies aligned.

His name falls from my lips again.

Pleasure rocks through my body. Knocks me senseless. I melt into the bed, into his body, into this beautiful world where he gives himself to me.

This time, he stays in bed with me, holding my body against his, melting into me as much as I melt into him.

———

ADAM RUNS A BATH FOR ME. HE HELPS ME SOAP, RINSE, DRY, dress.

At lunch—a perfect combination of lemon chicken soup and arugula Parmesan salad—Adam asks me to show him my favorite movies. We spend the afternoon in the home theater, my head on his shoulder, his arm around me, as I show him the favorites I think he'll like most.

We stay tangled together, in that state of easy intimacy through dinner, and dessert outside, in a blanket, under the stars.

I fall asleep in his arms.

Wake in his bed, rested and easy and warm.

Startled by voices downstairs.

Two I recognize.

Adam. Liam.

And a third voice asking, "What the fuck are you doing, Adam?"

Chapter Thirty-Four

DANIELLE

Liam notices me first. He nudges a tall man in a dark suit and shakes his head. "You woke her up. You're rude."

Simon. Adam's older brother. His eyes are a little deeper, his hair is a little darker, his frown is a little stronger.

The same intensity. More even.

If it weren't for Adam's scars, they'd be hard to tell apart.

"I think you finally made it happen." Liam nudges Simon again. "She's totally looking at you two like she wants a threesome."

"I'm the rude one?" Simon asks.

"Yeah, you didn't even introduce yourself." Liam nods hello to me. "We have coffee."

"I'll take coffee." I move down the stairs. Thank myself for changing out of my pajamas. I feel underdressed enough in my long-sleeved black sheath and boots.

The three of them are wearing suits.

Inside.

Yes, it's Monday morning, during business hours.

But this is a long drive from the city. Did they really make it in suits?

Does Liam really volunteer to wear a suit when he doesn't have to?

"Danielle, your muse is here." Liam touches his chest. "It's an honor to see you." He drops to his knees, takes my arm, presses his lips to the back of my hand.

"He's still doing that?" Simon asks.

Liam stands. "This is my rude older brother, Simon."

Simon looks at me as if he's assessing me on every possible level. Am I pretty enough? Smart enough? Trust-worthy enough?

Is that a protective older brother move?

Or something else?

"You didn't even shake her hand, you asshat. At least pretend you're giving her a chance." Liam nudges his brother again.

"Simon," he offers.

I shake with a firm grip.

"Coffee, Danielle?" Liam offers his arm. "I'll escort you."

"Seems like I need a lot."

Liam nods *it's true*. "I even have to talk to you."

"You do?" I take his arm.

"I'm afraid I do." He leads me to the coffee set up in the dining room. "Here, I thought I was your muse. And I see this." He pulls out his cell and shows off the photo on my Instagram.

Anonymous enough to strangers.

But to someone who knows me and Adam and his apartment?

It's obvious.

"I understand what happened." He pulls up my

website. Shows off the more explicit image. "You weren't ready for the full force of my beauty. You had to practice on someone less sexy."

"That's it," I say.

"Simon... he's got issues. Trust issues."

"Not like you," I say.

"Exactly. I have other uses for my time."

"Briar?"

"I'm not at liberty to divulge that information."

"You do like her?"

He actually blushes. "Danielle, I don't want to make you jealous with thoughts of other women. It's bad enough you can never have me."

"It is painful."

"I know." He mimes zipping his lips. "I don't want to remind you. And I'm not even mad you lied about your website."

Right.

"It's not like I bought it." He pours a mug for himself. "I searched social media the second I got home. It was easy to find you once I had a picture of your style. And then I sent it to Simon."

"You did?"

"I meant well, really. I promise. I wanted him to know Adam had a hot new girlfriend. He worries, you know. Older brother shit." He shrugs like he never worries about Adam, but there's relief all over his face.

He's glad I'm here.

Glad Adam isn't locked inside his cage.

I am too.

"You get it. You're an older sister," he says.

I fix my coffee with almond milk and extra honey. It's one of those days. "I do."

"So you know, it's not personal that he's glaring at you. He's just worried you're a corrupting influence."

"A corrupting influence?"

"Yeah. With Adam so fragile."

"Adam could snap his fingers and kill me."

"So you two are into that?"

I fight a blush.

"It's okay. I can tell from the pictures. Kinky shit. I approve."

"You don't know what it is."

"I know you got my brother to post sexy pictures. I didn't think it was possible before he developed this fixation." He motions to the left side of his face, the place where Adam has scars. "I told him Seal married Heidi Klum and had a billion little babies. But Seal's not a new wave performer, so he didn't care."

I pretend I know who he's talking about.

"You either? Kids, man. Don't appreciate the oldies."

I smile.

He raises a brow. "No, Danielle. I know that smile."

"You do?"

"Not the brother."

"Remy complains when I don't get his old references too."

He mimes being stabbed in the gut. "You're killing me, kid."

"Did you tell Briar?"

"About your pics? No. But this is gonna be hot gossip." He looks at the photo again. "You've got a nice ass."

"Thanks."

"You like her?" he asks.

"I do."

"She likes you too."

"And you…"

"Nice try." He picks up his coffee and takes a long sip. "You two done over there?" he calls to his brothers.

They look in his direction. Make that same *why is he so annoying* head shake.

"It's rude, talking about the photographer's work as if she isn't here. Also, she's a babe. And Adam is lucky people know she's fucking him," Liam says.

"You're a pig," Simon says.

"Oh yeah, I'm a pig. You have arrangements with twenty-year-olds, but I'm a pig," Liam says.

"You fuck three women a week," Simon says.

Liam motions *oh stop*.

"Does he really? Or does he only have eyes for Briar?" I ask.

"Briar? Your mentee?" Simon's outrage goes straight to him. "Really, Liam? Even by your standards…"

"Fuck you," he says.

"Clever." Simon rolls his eyes.

"Well, you're an asshole," Liam says.

Adam wraps his arms around me. Brings his lips to my ear. "They saw the picture."

"They have strong responses."

He nods into the crook of my neck.

Mmm. I want to soak up the feeling of his skin forever. "It's good, right? They think you're doing well enough—"

"To think with my cock?"

My cheeks flush. "Yes."

"It is."

"Are they dirty talking?" Liam asks. "Or talking about us?"

Simon shakes his head *you're impossible* and moves into the kitchen.

He says something to Trish. She laughs.

I can't make out the details, but it's clearly friendly.

"Did you really come all the way out here because of that photo?" I ask.

"Did you not see the photo?" Liam asks.

"Really?" I ask.

"We're overdue. Simon… he doesn't like to be here anymore. And he felt bad about skipping dinner," he says.

Simon emerges with a mug in his hand. "You didn't invite me."

"Tomatoh, tomahto." Liam shrugs. "Are you going to actually talk to Danielle? Or talk around her?"

"We introduced ourselves," he says.

"He's such an asshole, huh?" Liam shakes his head *ridiculous*.

"I understand," I say. "I'm protective of my younger brother too."

Simon eases. By about ten percent, but it's something.

Adam shoots him a look.

"They actually stayed in the city long enough to take these," Liam says. "That's progress."

"Posting pornographic photos is progress?" Simon asks.

"When it's a guy who barely leaves the house, yeah," Liam says.

"They aren't pornographic." Okay, some are, but not the ones I posted. "They're artistic. And they're none of your business."

"This a public website," Simon says. "Anyone can see it."

"And Adam gave me permission to post these photos. He signed a model release," I say. "This is what I do. If you saw my website, I'm sure you saw that too."

Simon's eyes narrow.

"Adam was gracious enough to pose with me. We took some amazing images. And I'm going to show them." I swallow hard. "I've already pitched it to a few galleries."

Liam and Simon share a look.

"Really?" Liam asks.

Simon's face fills with disbelief.

"They're always like this," Adam says. "It isn't you. They're idiots."

"You're an idiot," Liam says.

"The cleverness continues," Simon says.

"Nah, I mean, I can't even make that argument. Look at her." Liam motions to me again. "If my girlfriend was a sexy photographer who took sensual nudes and she asked me to pose with her…"

"Yes, I heard you begging her to look at your dick," Simon says.

"He's right," Adam says. "You're both being assholes."

They stop in their tracks.

"If you're here as co-owners of Pierce, and you don't approve of the CTO posing this way, we can talk. I'll refer to our contract and the lack of a morals clause. Not that either of you would survive one," Adam says. "But I'll hear your arguments."

"I think it's great," Liam says.

"Do you know what you're doing?" Simon asks.

"If you're here as my brother," Adam says. "Then stop talking around Danielle. She's an amazing artist and I won't have either of you dismissing her."

Liam nods *hell yeah*.

Simon holds his poker face. Then he nods, turns to me with the faintest sense of approval. "Your photos are beautiful."

"Super hot." Liam nods.

"If Adam trusts you… well, he's never been trusting before. But he's still a man. And men do stupid things when they want to fuck someone," Simon says.

Liam nods *true enough*.

"If you're manipulating him or using him, I'll destroy you," Simon says. "He's been through enough."

"Have you never heard of privilege, asshole? She's a broke twenty-something. You're a fucking billionaire," Liam says. "And you threaten her? You gonna destroy her career if she breaks his heart. Really? That's fair."

Simon shoots him a death glare.

"You're the asshole," Liam says.

"Thanks, Liam," I say. "But I don't need the warning. I care about Adam." I do. Deeply. But that isn't enough for this conversation. I'm his adoring girlfriend. "I love him." The words feel strange on my tongue. True. Too true. "I'd never hurt him."

Simon nods *fine*. "I don't approve of this decision. I won't pretend I do. But you're an adult."

"He's almost thirty," Liam says.

"You can make your own mistakes," Simon says.

"You are thirty. Thirty-two, actually. But still acting like a bossy teenager," Liam says.

"Are you done?" Simon asks.

"And still fucking eighteen-year-olds," Liam says.

"Oh yes, I'm the one fucking too many young women," Simon says.

"At least I'm not twice their age," Liam says.

"You are half their IQ," Simon says.

Liam just laughs. "Damn, you two." He motions to Simon and Adam. "Fucking sharpshooters." He winks at me. "Huh, Danielle?"

I have no idea what that means, but it's clearly about sex. "You're so much like Remy."

He mimes being stabbed in the gut. "Simon and I are going to help Trish in the kitchen, so you and Adam can talk. Right, Simon?"

Simon barely stops himself from rolling his eyes.

"You and Adam are going to meet us this Friday, in the city, for dinner," he says. "And Simon is going to show up with a smile. Instead of this asinine attitude."

"God forbid someone take something seriously," Simon says.

Adam looks to me. This Friday.

Soon.

Sooner than we planned to announce our engagement, but a perfect opportunity.

I nod *yes*.

"Eight o'clock. Briar will pick the restaurant," Liam says. "Wear something fierce." He blows me a kiss and leads his brother into the kitchen.

Adam laughs. Actually laughs. "I'm sorry. I can't remember the last time something in this house felt so normal." He brings his hands to my hips. "I... I'm glad you're here."

"Me too."

He leans down to kiss me. There's a hunger in it. Different than before. As emotional as it is physical.

"Are you sure?" I ask. "About the set? At the gallery? If people already know it's us..."

"Is it good for your career?" he asks.

"Very," I say.

"Then yes."

"But people——"

"People will know I'm with the most beautiful, talented woman in New York." He pulls me into a tight embrace. "What could be better?"

I melt.

———

APPARENTLY, THE OTHER PIERCE BOYS AREN'T HERE JUST TO berate Adam for his choices. They need to discuss business. Some pressing matter kept Simon from their last quarterly meeting.

They sit with me through breakfast. Mostly, Liam makes conversation and Simon picks apart my answers. He doesn't trust me with his brother. I appreciate his instinct, but his cold stare still feels, well, cold.

Liam apologizes for him being an asshole, again, then hugs me goodbye, relays the news that Briar has picked a spot for dinner, and follows his brothers upstairs, to Adam's office.

I stretch out in the theater with an extra sweet, extra creamy cup of coffee and watch an old favorite. *Raise the Red Lantern.*

The men spend the entire morning in Adam's office, only breaking for lunch, where they continue to talk business, and dinner, where, same.

I stay busy with work.

They spend the night, so they can make the long drive in the morning, and so they can spy a little more too.

I sleep in Adam's bedroom. I don't know why he wants me here. For our ruse. Because he wants to fuck me.

Because he wants to fall asleep next to me.

But when I feel his arms around me, I don't care why he's holding me. Only that he's hard and warm and close.

This is everything.

We have a lazy breakfast after his brothers leave, then he's back to work. It's different than before.

We actually talk during dinner. Spend our nights watching movies, or sitting on the balcony staring at the stars, or climbing into Adam's bed and fucking like rabbits.

He still keeps his clothes on.

Or blindfolds me.

Or both.

I want to see every inch of him, but I'm patient. I can wait.

And this—

This is really fucking good.

I spend my time working on my photography, finishing edits, curating another set from the photos of us, taking another round of pictures here.

Friday, I ride into the city with Adam.

He drives. I man the stereo. We sit in comfortable quiet. No need to fill the space with noise, to talk over the music.

Then he parks, leads me to the elevator, through the door, into his penthouse apartment.

Only it's different than last time.

The floor is covered in rose petals.

No. Not covered.

The petals spell *Will You Marry Me?*

Adam takes my hand, drops to his knee, pulls a ring box from his pocket. "Danielle, if I know anything, I know I need you by my side." He pulls the ring box open to reveal a massive princess cut diamond. "Will you marry me?"

"Yes."

He slides the ring onto my finger.

The massive rock catches all the light in the room.

And even though it's fake, I feel it.

I feel all that love and desire and promise of forever.

I'm engaged to Adam Pierce.

It's pretend.

But it feels so fucking real.

Chapter Thirty-Five

ADAM

"Pictures." Danielle's eyes stay bright. "We need pictures."

"Now?"

"It worked well last time." Her smile widens.

"Taking pictures of yourself coming?"

"Yes." She reaches for me. Runs her fingers over my neck, chin, jaw.

Her eyes flutter closed.

Her lips find mine.

She kisses me with a different kind of hunger. For my body, yes. And for something deeper, truer.

My body, my heart, my soul.

I want to give her every broken piece.

But I don't know how.

I don't know if it's possible.

My thoughts disappear as her hand knots in my hair.

I need to touch her, taste her, feel her pulsing around me.

She pulls back with a sigh. "Fuck, Adam."

"Take this off." I run my fingers over the hem of her dress.

She shakes her head. "Pictures first." She reaches for her cell. "At least a few."

We're not here to satisfy our desire.

We're on a mission.

Announcing our engagement to her brother, my family, everyone who follows her on social media.

The whole point of this.

Rubbing it in that asshole's face.

Liam already broadcast our plans. That asshole knows. He'll be there. He's as predictable as I am.

Tonight, I rub our engagement in his face.

Tonight, he frowns over the sight of my ring on her finger.

Tonight, he knows she's mine.

It still makes sense, intellectually.

But it feels far away.

Irrelevant.

I have her.

That's what matters.

Adam, we talked about this.

Less thinking.

More fucking.

She wants pictures before she takes off her clothes.

Or maybe while she takes off her clothes.

Remember how this went last time, yeah?

"Of course." I return to my surroundings. The clean, modern space of the apartment. The space I lived in for years.

It's different than before.

Still missing something. Missing Bash. But not screaming of loneliness.

"I guess these will all be me." *Click.* She snaps a photo

of the ring on her left finger. "Can I really tell Remy in a text? Maybe I'll invite him over tomorrow."

"Of course," I say.

"Your family? They follow me."

"Let them see."

"Are you sure?" She moves to me. Places her hand on my chest, on the pocket of my suit. Snaps a photo. "It will ruin the surprise."

"I'm sure."

She rises to her tiptoes to kiss me. Her fingers brush my neck, chin, cheek. "Shit. I can't get this angle. Can you?" She offers me the phone.

The ring, against my cheek.

The right side. The side that's man.

Strangers won't know.

But everyone who needs to believe this will.

It's perfect. Kismet.

How does she do it?

I take her cell. Find the angle.

"I might say I don't like the first one." She smiles. "Then the second. Third. Fourth." Her fingers brush my chin again. "So I get to keep kissing you."

"You don't need the excuse."

"I know." She cups my cheek with her palm. "But it's more fun this way."

My eyes flutter closed.

Her lips find mine.

Her kiss envelops me. Soft, sweet, tender.

Danielle.

Mine.

It echoes through my head again.

I barely find the sense to snap a photo.

Then another. Another.

She pulls back with a heady sigh. "What did I say about this dress?"

"Photos first."

Her eyes flit to the rose petals. "Maybe, during photos." She looks at her cell phone. "Can I trust you to stand there and watch?"

"No."

She smiles. "Okay. Well, I guess we'll see what happens." She checks the photos I snapped. Gives one of them a nod of approval. Then she moves toward the door, to the petals scattered over the ground.

She slips into photographer mode.

Focus consumes her. Even as she pulls off her dress, her boots, her socks.

My fiancée lies on the ground, on top of the rose petals spelling her name, and holds her cell up in the air, the camera pointed at her chest.

What the fuck happened to my life?

If Bash was here—

Adam, stop thinking about me when you're supposed to be getting laid. I'm not a cock blocker.

Don't turn me into one.

Brain off.

Dick on.

Capiche?

Danielle looks to me with a coy smile. "You must think I'm insane."

"No."

"Really?" She motions to the petals on her stomach. "I'm lying on the ground in my underwear, trying to take the perfect photo of my engagement ring."

"I've seen the results."

"You have."

"They justify themselves."

"The ends justify the means?"

"When the means include you on my floor, yes."

"Our floor."

Our floor.

"Not legally, I know. There was a prenup in those papers I signed. It's still your apartment, technically. But since we're engaged..."

Our apartment.

It steals my breath.

I've never wanted that. I've never cared about anyone enough.

But the thought of waking next to Danielle every morning? Sleeping next to her every night?

What could be better?

I push my logical thoughts aside. This is fake, yes. But we are engaged. We're going to marry.

I have a year with her.

Another eleven months.

Bash is right. No more thinking.

I watch Danielle take another dozen photos. Then she stands. Shows me the finalists.

"You don't need my approval," I say.

"You're in this one." She brandishes the photo of her hand against my cheek, the ring on display.

"I trust you."

"To post anything? Even pictures of you?"

"Yes."

"I might get carried away." Her eyes meet mine. "I do. When I'm in that trance. When I see my skin against yours."

"Even so."

"Are you sure?"

I nod.

"Fuck, Adam." She places her palm on my chest. "Let

me post these. Then…"

"Thirty seconds."

She smiles. "Okay. Thirty seconds. Then…" She motions to the bedroom. "Count me down."

I raise a brow.

"If you don't mind."

"Thirty, twenty-nine, twenty-eight." I watch her as I count down.

She takes ten seconds to pick a filter.

Another ten to add text.

Down to five.

There.

Woosh.

She posts right at the buzzer.

"One." I take her into my arms. Carry her to the bed. Lay her on the soft silk sheets.

She looks up at me expectantly. Waiting for me to bind or blindfold her.

But I don't.

I shrug off my suit jacket. Undo my tie. Roll my sleeves to my forearms.

Then I do away with her underwear. Push her legs apart. Lick her until she's groaning my name.

After she comes again, I unzip my slacks, pull her body into mine, fuck her.

No, it isn't fucking.

It's more.

A part of me pours into her. A part of her pours into me.

Our bodies tangled, our lips locked, our hearts beating together.

She tugs at my hair as she comes.

It pulls me over the edge.

For one perfect moment, the world is a place of love, bliss, light.

And this—

Our bed, our room, our apartment.

Our fuck.

This part is real.

I'm not sure about the rest, but I know this part is real.

———

AFTER, WE WASH SEPARATELY. DANIELLE TAKES THE MASTER bathroom. I use the one in the hall.

It's smaller, but it's plenty grand. Stainless steel and modern tile. A wide mirror. A marble counter.

I run the water. Step into the shower. Try to keep my eyes off my reflection.

They still go there.

The glass is fogged. I only see my outline.

The man I used to be. A tall, broad figure. A blur.

No scars.

No memories.

No emptiness.

I soap. Rinse. Let my fingers find the scars on my chest.

My doctors warned me not to touch them. Not to slow the healing. But I never listened.

I trace the lines again.

Raised, harsh, angry.

Intense and violent, but not altogether hideous.

I can't trust her with them yet.

But soon—

Soon.

I finish. Turn off the water. Dry. Step out of the shower.

Again, my eyes go straight to my reflection.

To the scars crisscrossing my torso.

There's no denying their existence.

But maybe—

Maybe they're more than the markings of a monster.

Maybe they're proof I've survived too.

But that's not any easier to swallow.

It's not fair I'm here when Bash isn't.

It doesn't make sense.

It will never make sense.

But I can't keep drowning in grief.

I have to learn to live with it.

Somehow, I have to learn to live with it.

———

I DRESS AND MEET DANIELLE IN THE MAIN ROOM.

She looks up from her phone. "We're already popular." She shows off her texts.

A message from Liam.

Briar says the ring is pretty. And you have great tits.

Briar wants me to say I added the part about the tits.

But that's bullshit. She said it. She just said it more politely.

Way to nail that down, Adam.

Even Briar agrees. Though she has "choice words" about my phrasing.

"I don't think Simon has seen it," she says. "Or maybe he doesn't like me."

"He likes you."

"Really?"

"He wouldn't bother with the interrogation if he didn't like you."

"I guess I get it. Older sibling things." She looks up at me. "I think this is my most popular post ever."

"Everyone loves a wedding."

"I told Remy too. In case he follows me. I'm going to go over there tomorrow. If that's okay with you." She presses her lips together. "We're behind on *Blood Borne*."

"I can't believe the woman who gushes over *Raise the Red Lantern* also watches a vampire soap opera called *Blood Borne*."

"*Blood Borne: Legends of the Vampire Clan*." She smiles and motions *come here*. When I do, she rises to her tiptoes to kiss me. "Do we have time to go again?"

"No."

"Can we be fashionably late?"

"Yes."

"But…"

"You hate being late."

"I do?"

"I've noticed."

She smiles. "I do. But…" Her fingers brush my tie. "Okay. Fine. And I have the hair and the dress and…" She curls her fingers around my neck. "After dinner?"

"Angel, what do you think I'm going to say to that?"

"Some bullshit that means maybe?"

I nod.

"I can't believe you treat your fiancée this way."

"Yes, you can."

She nods *yes, I can* and takes my hand.

I lead her downstairs. To the limo. Tease her on the ride to the restaurant. Up the elevator. Into the lobby.

I take her coat. Lead her to the bar.

And there he is, exactly as planned.

Cole Fitzgerald, sipping an old fashioned, staring at the ring on Danielle's finger as if it has the power to destroy him.

Chapter Thirty-Six

DANIELLE

"**M**iss Bellamy." Cole Fitzgerald rises from his seat at the bar. He forces a smile. "What a coincidence."

No. There's no way this is a coincidence.

He's here.

Somehow, Adam beckoned him.

It's strange, yes, but it's what I asked.

And it's still what I want.

I want to rub our engagement in the smug asshole's face.

Fuck him and his judgmental stare.

Adam is more handsome than Mr. Fitzgerald has ever been. He's more handsome now.

I don't care if other women disagree.

He's beautiful.

And he's mine.

My fiancé.

Our engagement isn't traditional. He didn't propose because he's madly in love with me.

But we have an agreement. An understanding.

And I care about him. I'm going to do what it takes to protect him. Whatever it takes.

"It is." I wrap my right arm around Adam's waist. Bring my left hand to my chest.

Bingo. Mr. Fitzgerald's eyes fix on the rock.

It's hard to miss. Especially when he's staring at my cleavage.

I don't blame him—my boobs look fantastic in this long-sleeved red wine dress—but I am using his leer to my advantage.

"I'm glad one of Adam's friends is here to see this." Fuck subtlety. I hold out my left hand. "We've just gotten engaged."

"I have to buy you a drink then." He stares at Adam with disdain.

"No," Adam says. "Not until I buy a round for you and your wife. To celebrate your love."

"No, baby, don't do that rich guy thing," I say.

"Rich guy thing?"

I nod. "Insisting you pay. We're engaged. He's your friend. Let him celebrate with us."

Adam turns to me with a smile. "You're right, angel." His fingertips brush my cheek. "You look beautiful today."

"You too."

"Beautiful, really?"

"Really." I lean into his touch.

He pulls me into a soft, slow kiss.

The rest of the world disappears.

It's only Adam's sweet, soft lips.

Then Mr. Fitzgerald breaks the spell. "Grapefruit martini, again?"

"Yes. Thank you." I squeeze Adam's hand. "You too, baby?"

He nods and names the same top-shelf gin.

Mr. Fitzgerald forces a smile. "I'll tell you what, Adam. Next time, we'll meet for dinner. The four of us."

"Your wife?" I ask.

"Yes. You can buy, Adam. Unless you're going to treat, Danielle," he says.

"No. I'll leave the wallet measuring contests to the men," I say. "Why is it men never want to let anyone buy them something?"

"You'll understand when you have money," Mr. Fitzgerald says. "I imagine it will happen soon. Unless you're signing a strict… prenup." His eyes go to Adam.

They trade a stare.

They're both trying and failing to hide their hostility.

Is it business? Personal? Love?

I'm missing something, but I don't need the full information now. Only enough to do my job.

"I'm new to the world of the wealthy, but I'm pretty sure it's rude discussing these things in public," I say.

"Of course. I shouldn't bring up ugly things," Mr. Fitzgerald says. "No one wants to hear about divorce on the day of their engagement. Or god, forbid, infidelity."

"Good thing we have you," I say. "Still married after all these years."

"Yes." Mr. Fitzgerald forces a smile. "I only wish Celine was here to celebrate with us. She adores you, Danielle."

"She talks about me?" I ask.

"The gallery isn't the same without you," he says.

"I might be showing there." My lips curl into a smile. "But it's a secret. So…" I mime zipping my lips.

"Really? You're a photographer?" His gaze drifts back to my chest.

Is that it?

Does he follow me online?

I'm not doing a great job hiding my identity these days. I'm not trying.

And once I do show, once I go public as Danielle Bellamy—

My stomach flutters.

People seeing my art is one thing.

People seeing my body even.

But knowing it's me?

There's a power in anonymity. However thin its veneer.

I just—

"Angel, are you all right?" Adam pulls me closer. "You look faint."

"Nervous. About the show. Even though… I don't have one yet." I turn to him. Lose myself in his blue eyes. "Did you get more handsome?"

"Since when?"

"The last time I looked at you?"

"I'm not sure. I haven't checked."

"I think you did." I kiss him hard.

He kisses back with intent. It's not the chaste kiss expected of a man of his station.

It's full-on *I need to be inside you.*

I curl my hand around his neck.

Bring the other to his cheek. My fingers brush his scars.

He doesn't flinch or still or stop.

He leans into the gesture. Kisses me harder. Pulls me closer.

When our kiss breaks, I'm dizzy.

I'm not sure where we are or what we're doing.

Only that I need him.

That I want to protect him, hold him, love him.

Maybe not love, but something close. Something way too fucking close.

"It is beautiful to see passion," Mr. Fitzgerald says. "It's powerful. Dangerous even."

"The best things are." Adam shoots him a *fuck you* smile.

I'm not imagining it. There is something between them, something I don't know.

I can almost put my finger on it.

Whatever it is, it's in their past. But how far back?

"How do the two of you know each other?" I place my left hand on Adam's chest. "You never told me."

"I'm afraid it's not a happy story," Mr. Fitzgerald says. "I knew Adam's late brother."

"Sebastian?" I ask.

"Bash, yes." Adam holds strong. "He worked closely with Celine."

"Very closely," Mr. Fitzgerald says.

Is that code for something?

Or is my mind in the gutter?

Celine is a beautiful woman. But much older than Adam's late brother. She must be in her early forties.

Bash was half her age.

It happens, but not that often.

"What did they do together?" I ask.

"He was on the board of one of her charities," he says. "You might know it." He names an organization that supports art in public schools.

"I only know of it," I say. "And, really, them supporting the gallery. I didn't realize that was Celine. Send her my regards, please."

"Mine as well," Adam says.

"Of course." Mr. Fitzgerald smiles. "She'd love to hear you're showing. Let me know when you have details."

"I will," I say.

He pulls a card from his pocket.

Adam takes it for me.

Mr. Fitzgerald tries to hide his annoyance, but he doesn't quite get there. He turns to our drinks as the bartender drops them off.

Adam takes them. Hands one to me.

"To marriage." Mr. Fitzgerald holds up his drink. "And the lengths we go to, to protect ours."

"That's very romantic," I say.

"Yes, Cole. To my future wife. And yours." Adam taps his drink against Mr. Fitzgerald's.

Then mine.

He looks to me as he wraps his lips around the glass.

I take a sip. It's a little different—we're at a different place—but it's still citrus perfection.

And all I want to do is taste gin and grapefruit on Adam's lips.

Do we have to stay here?

Can't we go back to the apartment and fuck like rabbits?

"Oh my god, Liam was telling the truth." An excited voice interrupts me. "I can't believe it. And you're so pretty."

I turn to see a young woman in a short dress and expensive shoes.

She has the same blue eyes and intense stare Adam does.

"I thought you were in London," Adam says.

"I was. Now I'm here. Rude." She smiles at me. "I'm Adam's half-sister." She turns to Adam. "Did you not tell her about me?"

"I did," he says.

"It's okay. No one talks about me. I'm the secret shame of the Pierce family. I'm not even supposed to have the last name, but what's Daddy Pierce going to do now, huh? He's six feet under." She shrugs. "You must be Danielle."

"Opal?" I extend my hand.

She nods. "You're so pretty. And your dress, oh my god." She ignores my hand in favor of a hug. Then she turns to Adam and pulls him into an even tighter hug. "I don't forgive you for not telling me you have a girlfriend."

"Adults don't talk about these things the same way," he says.

"I'm eighteen. An adult," she says. "And the 'adults' in our family are only talking about this. Do you know how many messages I have from Liam?"

"Liam isn't an adult either," Adam says.

"Do you think I'm blind? I saw that rock from across the room, Adam! It's huge. Seriously. When did you get engaged? I thought you were still chained to your office," she says.

"We talked about over-sharing," Adam says.

"Yeah, your idea of over-sharing is telling your sister you're engaged. So maybe I'm not taking your advice, huh?" she asks.

"She does have a point there," I say.

"Yes, girl power. Right?" She offers me a high five.

I take it.

Opal laughs. "I like her. And she's so pretty too. Liam told me she was pretty, but wow… look at your boobs."

"Thanks." My cheeks flush.

"Opal," Adam says. "Can you wait until we say goodbye to our friend?" He motions to Mr. Fitzgerald, who's still glaring at Adam.

"Bye, Adam's friend. It was nice to meet you." Opal turns to me. "Do you have older brothers? Do you have any idea what it's like to find out you have older brothers the same day you find out your dead father left you a bunch of money? And that bunch of money is a pittance compared to what his legitimate sons got?"

"I can't say I do," I say.

"It's a trip. Really. Now, forget Adam. Let's sit and talk about your dress. Seriously, it's amazing. Are your boobs real? They look real, but you never know," Opal says.

"Don't ask my fiancée if she's had breast augmentation," Adam says.

"Why not?" Opal blinks. "Half the girls at my school talk about doing it."

"Do you mind if we sit, Adam?" I ask.

"No. Sit." He pulls me into a quick kiss. "I have to talk to Cole."

"Oh?" I ask.

"Work. Nothing you need to worry about," he says.

I don't believe him, but I nod anyway.

"Thank you, Adam," she says. "Thank you, Adam's friend. It's great to meet you. Now, I'm stealing the woman of the hour." She nods to Mr. Fitzgerald then stage whispers to me, "Steal my brother's martini. I want some."

"Sorry. I have a younger brother."

"No. Another over-protective sibling! Danielle, I thought we were going to be best friends," she says. "But we can't if you're no fun."

"How about we bargain?"

She perks. "What kind of bargain?"

"You tell me an embarrassing story about Adam. I tell you… what do you want to know?"

"The martini is off the table?"

I motion to the host stand. She follows me to the hostess, then the hostess leads us to our seats.

"If you can sip without Adam noticing," I say. "I want to stay on his good side."

324

"Please, he's so in love with you. You're definitely on his good side," she says.

"How can you tell?"

"I've known him a long time. And, honestly, he's never looked this happy. Really, you should get used to people telling you that. Adam makes the moody guys in my poetry class look well-adjusted." She shakes her head. *He's ridiculous.* "But now… he's almost as happy as the idiots who write dirty limericks."

"He is," I say.

"Yeah. And it's all you, really. So he won't mind if you let me drink your martini."

"You're a persistent young woman."

"Thank you." She motions to the glass again.

I shake my head.

She makes an exaggerated pout, but she still launches into a story about Adam playing chaperone at her high school dance, and him awkwardly saying no thank you to ever girl that asked him to dance.

Which was pretty much every girl in the school.

I keep one eye on Adam and Mr. Fitzgerald. They don't drop their smiles, but there is something about their exchange.

Some tension.

Adam walks Mr. Fitzgerald out.

Then he joins us at the table.

Then it's Liam and Briar.

And even Simon.

After another drink, I forget about everything except how much I adore Adam and his dysfunctional family.

I don't feel like a fake fiancée.

I feel like I'm a member of the family.

Or at least, on my way.

Liam keeps me laughing all through dinner. He walks

us to the car. Whispers a request for dirty details in my ear. Winks *show Adam a good time tonight, huh?*

We don't make it to the bed.

I climb into his lap on the couch.

He keeps his suit on.

But then I keep my dress on too. I don't have the patience to strip.

I need him.

All of him.

————

THE NEXT DAY, I WAKE TIRED AND SORE AND HAPPY.

I meet Remy at the apartment with coffee. He gushes over my ring as we watch *Blood Borne* and eat takeout French toast.

Then take out Thai curry.

We talk until I fall asleep on the couch. I wake early, take the subway to Adam's apartment. Our apartment.

He's still asleep.

He looks right in his bed, in the soft glow of sunrise.

Peaceful and powerful in equal measure.

I can already see it. A life for us together. For real.

But I still haven't told him about my scars.

I still need to reveal myself to him.

Soon.

Really fucking soon.

It stays in the back of my head all day. On the ride back to his house. All night.

Through a week of lazy days and perfect nights.

Even as we set plans to return to the city for dinner with Remy and the rest of Adam's family.

All week, until the morning of our dinner, when I wake up to news on my cell phone.

The difficult artist who's supposed to show next month pulled out.

If I can be ready next week, the spot is mine.

Which means I need to tell Remy about my photos tonight.

Fuck.

Chapter Thirty-Seven

ADAM

"My brother is going to see my boobs." Danielle presses her cell phone to her chest. "Or maybe he's seen them. Maybe he knows. Do you think he knows? Is it better if he knows? Or worse?"

"What would he say, if he did?" I ask.

"Probably something about you being hot," she says. "And my pictures needing more dick."

A laugh falls from my lips.

"It's not funny."

I raise a brow.

She drops her phone on the bench seat of the limo. Brushes a stray hair behind her ear.

She looks gorgeous in her low-cut black dress, her wavy hair pulled into a loose updo, her long neck on display.

But I need those clothes gone.

I need us to be in that perfect, beautiful place where we fit together like puzzle pieces.

There, I know exactly what she needs.

Here?

I don't have a fucking clue.

"Okay. It's a little funny." She crosses her legs. Smooths her short dress. "I just… what if he thinks I'm a whore?"

"What if he does?"

She frowns. "Well, he'd probably say 'good for you, Danny.' And then something about naked pictures of women being boring."

That sounds like him.

"And then, he'd bring it back to dick. And ask if there are pictures of your dick," she says.

"There are."

She flushes. "They're private."

"Do you look at them?"

"Yes."

"What do you do?"

"Do I fuck myself?"

I nod.

"When would I do that?"

"You're working all day."

"Is that work now?"

"It's how I imagine you," I say.

She smiles. "I'm not sure if I should be offended or delighted."

I shrug as if I don't care.

"You're teasing." Her smile widens. "I like when you tease. I like getting the Adam Pierce no one knows." She brings her hand to my cheek and pulls me into a slow, deep kiss. "Do we have time?"

"No."

"Can we drive around the block?"

I kiss her with everything I have.

"Adam." She pulls back with a sigh. "Please."

"Please?"

"Don't torture me."

I shake my head. "No, angel." I bring my hand to her inner thigh. Push it higher and higher, until my palm is flat against her. That thin layer of silk in the way. Under that, all her. "I live to torture you."

"Adam."

It steals my self-control. It always does. But she doesn't realize it.

She kisses me back, digging her fingers into my neck, groaning against my mouth.

"Fuck." She settles into her seat. Finds her lipstick in her purse. Applies another coat. "You're distracting me."

"From?"

"I forgot."

The car stops.

"Are we really here?" She looks outside the tinted window.

"Are you ready?"

"No. But it's now or never."

I nod and offer my hand.

She takes it. Follows me into the Midtown hotel.

The lobby is all old-fashioned grandeur. Winding staircase, high ceiling, chandeliers.

Danielle studies the space. "This would be an interesting place to shoot. All these ornate details against the bareness of the human form. Right there." She points to the top of the stairs. "It's the place in an old movie where the poor girl steps out after her makeover." She motions to her dress. "Now, she fits into the world of the elite. And Prince Charming is standing at the base of the stairs, smiling, because he finally sees her beauty."

"Is that how you think of me?"

"A little," she says. "You want to make an impression on people."

I do.

"There's nothing wrong with that. But it is... well, you wouldn't have brought me here if I was wearing H&M."

"You'd feel out of place."

"You're aware appearances matter. It's not a criticism. It's just... the way the world works. That's what I want to do with my art. To pick at that. So this... I don't know, maybe I would include some clothes."

"Clothing on models?"

"I know. Crazy." She laughs and drifts into photographer mode, her eyes hazy, her focus on the images in her mind. "Maybe I'd reverse it. Start in designer gear. Strip everything away."

The elevator dings.

She jumps. "But I'd never be able to reserve the space. Not for nudes."

It would be difficult, expensive maybe, but... "Anything is possible."

"For the right price?" She follows me into the elevator. "Classic rich guy talk."

"You're a millionaire now."

"Not yet."

"Soon." I slide my arm around her waist. I don't want to think about the end of this. I want to keep her comfortable forever. "Your show is next week."

"I know."

"Did you set prices?"

"No. I'm still talking to Mr. Davey. He wants to price a little less than *The Voyeur*. But that's insane. She's brilliant. I'm—"

"You're brilliant."

"Not that brilliant."

"You are." I bring my hand to her cheek. "Do you need to look at the images again?"

"Maybe. No. God, Remy is going to see those." She leans into my touch. "Everyone is going to see them."

"And know you're brilliant."

"You're okay with it?" She looks up at me. "You're not scared?"

"Terrified."

"You don't show it."

"I never do."

Her fingers brush my neck. "You're sure? Even though you're terrified?"

"As sure as I've ever been."

She smiles. Eases enough to fix her dress, close her purse, check her makeup.

Then the elevator arrives and her composure falls.

"He'll be excited for you too," I say.

She nods *right*, takes a deep breath, marches to the bar, right to her brother.

"Danny and Mr. Generous Energy. My two favorite people. Plus, Mr. Rock here, my third favorite." Remy hugs her hello. Takes her left hand. "Seriously, how much does this thing weigh?" He pretends he can't lift her arm.

"You saw it all day," she says.

"Weeks ago." He looks from the ring to me. "I have to hand it to Mr. Generous Energy, here. He knows how to make a statement."

"What about me?" she asks.

"You have your tits out," he says. "Exactly what straight men like."

"Remy!"

He laughs. "You look unstoppable."

"Yeah?" Her voice lifts. She's still nervous.

"Yeah. Like the babe in *Blood Borne* who sleeps with the vampire King."

"Which one of them?"

He laughs. "The human princess."

"She's a vampire princess now."

"Well, yeah, that's the fate of all the humans. Since they're all sleeping with vampires. I bet every straight guy in here would go vampire for you," he says.

She laughs. "It's always sex with you."

"Oh yeah, it's sex with me." He motions to her low neckline. "You're not even thinking about it."

She blushes. "It's uh… you didn't say hello to Adam."

"Nice to see you again." He offers his hand.

I shake.

"Is this a bad news dinner? Or a good news dinner?" he asks.

"Can't it be an I-want-to-see-my-brother dinner?" she asks.

"Not with the look on your face." He hails the bartender. Orders their drinks. "And whatever Adam is having."

I rarely think of flavor when it comes to alcohol. Yes, I enjoy the taste of citrus and gin on Danielle's lips, but that's where my desire starts and ends.

I want to taste her lips.

The drink itself doesn't matter.

I still want to taste her lips, but I want the rest of it too. The tart citrus, the herbal gin, the hint of sweetness.

"The same for me," I say.

"Grapefruit." He sticks his tongue out. "Yuck. You're disturbed."

"You drink PBR."

"It's cheap!"

"It's disgusting." Her nose wrinkles. "Beer is disgusting."

"I'm not ordering one here. I know my settings." He

motions to his outfit, slacks and a button-up shirt and tie. "I clean up pretty good, huh?"

"Nah." She teases him. "You look better in jeans."

"Who doesn't?" he asks.

"Uh, me," she says. "I look much better in a dress."

"What about loverboy?" he asks. "Does he ever wear jeans?"

"Only the suit," I say.

"Or silk pajamas." She laughs. "Adam is like a character in an old movie. Sometimes, I expect to walk into his office and see a cigar and a glass of bourbon."

"Yeah, I see that. And then he takes the tie and..." Remy raises a brow.

"And, uh, well..." She bites her lip. "When are those drinks getting here?"

"Oh?" he asks. "So it is bad news."

"No. Not bad. Just... news." She taps her nails against the bar. Watches the bartender fix the drinks.

"Are you going to give me a hint, loverboy?" he asks.

"She already did," I say.

"Did she?" He taps his chin, turning over their last few exchanges, trying to find clues.

The bartender finishes. Drops off our drinks.

I slide her my credit card.

Remy shoots Danielle a *nice* look. "Quite the gentleman you've landed."

"Uh-huh." She takes a long sip of her grapefruit martini. Swallows hard. "Can you get started on the next?" She smiles at the bartender. "Please."

"Are you at a college party, Danny? You need some tequila slammers? Do a body shot off a hot guy's belly button." He motions to me. "Take off your boyfriend's shirt?"

"No, uh… that was too specific." Her nose wrinkles. "Why do you have so many stories about college parties?"

"Free drinks," he says. "Open-minded men."

"Way too much information." She shakes her head. "It's always way too much information."

He blows her a kiss.

She downs her drink in one gulp. "I have my first art show."

"And the pressure is driving you to drink?" he asks.

"No. Well. Maybe. It's terrifying." She watches the bartender carefully.

I wrap my arms around her.

She melts into me. "I, uh… the photos are of me. Me and an anonymous male model."

"Adam?" he asks.

"Yes," I say.

"Wait, are you saying, you're putting your fucking sexts on display?" His eyes go wide. "Straight people… you guys are crazy."

"No. They're artistic. Like Dana DeLaney."

He laughs. "Of course. You're obsessed with her."

"I'm not obsessed. I'm just…" The bartender drops off her drink and she lunges for it. "Finally. I mean, thank you."

"Already an impatient rich girl." Remy shakes his head in faux disapproval. "So rude."

"I said thank you. And Adam will tip generously," she says.

"Oh, so if you pay enough, you can be an asshole?" he asks.

"Remy!" Her cheeks flush. "You're so… omg, just look at the pictures now so I don't die of embarrassment at the show."

"What about you, Prince Charming?" He looks to me.

"I'm proud of her work," I say.

"Of course, he's nervous. This a public show," she says. "Don't be an asshole."

"You don't understand men, Danny."

She pulls out her cell. Opens a password protected page on the gallery site. One with her photos, her bio, the descriptions of the set.

"Men want the world to know where their dick has been." He looks to me. "Am I right?"

"It happens," I say.

"Of course Prince Charming wants people to know he's banging you. Look at you. With your boobs out. Straight guys love boobs." Again he looks to me the way Liam does. *Back me up here, Adam.*

"We do," I say.

"Oh my god, did you just ask my boyfriend if he likes my boobs?" she asks.

"Not yours. All. And not him. All straight men," he says.

"It's the same thing!"

"Subtle difference."

"What if I asked the last guy you fucked if he liked your dick."

"I already know the answer to that." He smiles.

"What if he said no?"

"He wouldn't."

"Maybe I should call him. Find out."

"Okay." He pulls out his cell. "I'll buy your drinks if you do it."

"Oh my god." She tries to hide behind her hands, but she's still holding her phone. She shakes her head *you're impossible* and shoves the phone in his hands. "Just don't be an asshole."

"What exactly does that entail?"

"You know what it means to not be an asshole!"

He chuckles *maybe* and takes her cell. His eyes go wide as he looks at the images. "Fuck."

"Is that a good fuck?"

"That's you?" He looks at her. "Shit, Danny… I didn't know you had this in you."

She freezes.

I pull her closer.

"You look hot. And this… it's classy. But sexy too. It is like the photographer with the stupid name. But better. Because there's a hunk in the frame. In a lot of clothes, but…" He looks to me with approval. "That's the point of it. He's in his clothes. You're not."

She just barely nods.

"It's a statement."

"It is," she says.

"They're beautiful." He hands back the phone. "But I really don't want to see that much of your body."

"I, uh… I have a website too. And social media. It's mostly my body though. So don't look," she says. "I mean, you can if you want. But I'd rather you didn't."

"I don't want to see your tits, Danny."

"I do," a loud voice volunteers. Liam.

"They are really nice," Briar says. "I wish I was as endowed."

"Baby, don't talk about your tits that way," Liam says.

She presses her palm into her forehead. "You did not just say that."

"What if I did?" he asks.

"Who is the very cute guy next to you, Danielle?" Briar asks.

"My brother, Remy," she says. "This is Liam, Adam's brother. And Briar, his—"

"Colleague." She shakes his hand.

"He likes guys," Liam says. "Not your type."

"I can appreciate a cute guy without wanting to fuck him," Briar says.

"You can?" He scratches his head. "How?"

She makes that *ugh, you're impossible* sound.

"Is this the hot brother I've heard about?" Remy asks.

"You two are so much alike," Danielle says.

They size each other up, deciding if they approve of this comparison. They must, because they shake hands, and shift the conversation back to Danielle's photos.

She eases during our second round. Even when Simon joins with his intense stare and his inability to hide his disapproval.

Between Liam's constant ribbing and Danielle's enthusiasm, the two of them knock Simon off his high horse.

We laugh, talk, drink all through dinner and dessert.

When we part, Liam offers his usual *way to nail a hottie* high five, Danielle hugs her brother goodbye, Simon nods *she's good for you*.

And I feel something I haven't felt in a long, long time: My brother's pride.

My place in this family.

The possibility the world is a big, beautiful place.

I'm on a fucking cloud on the way home.

Then Danielle steps into the elevator and slides her panties to her ankles, and I know exactly where I need to be.

Chapter Thirty-Eight

ADAM

Danielle groans as I pin her to the elevator wall. "It's been too long." Her fingers brush my neck. Chin. Jaw. "I've been thinking about this all night."

"I know."

"I know?" She shifts her hips, rocking her crotch against mine. "Should I reply that way?"

"Try it."

"You're no fun." Her lips curl into a half-smile. "I'm trying to torture you."

"Try harder."

"Okay." The elevator dings. The door opens.

She bends. Peels her panties from her feet. Slips them into my pocket.

Then she steps into the hallway. Motions *after you*.

I lead her to the door. Unlock it slowly. Hold it open for her.

"Thank you." She steps inside. Hangs her coat. Sets her purse on the end table.

Then she turns to me, with fire in her eyes.

It's already torture, waiting to touch her.

Being inches away from her.

But not because she's pushed me to the brink, made me wait an eternity to finally touch her.

Because I've made myself wait.

Because I've been locked in my cage, avoiding every hint of love and intimacy.

Because she cracked me wide open.

Does she see that?

"Close the door." She tries to copy my tone. Firm and in control. "Please."

"Yes, mistress." I do as she asks.

She fights a blush, but she holds strong. "*Can* you follow orders?"

"Can you give them?"

She half-smiles. "I should reprimand you for that."

"Oh?" I raise a brow.

She nods *yes*. "I should order you on your knees."

"Then?"

"Then you do whatever I say."

"Go on."

She places her palm against my chest. Presses lightly. Then harder. "Step back."

I do.

She turns, showing off the zipper of her dress. "Unzip me."

My fingers brush the back line of her dress.

She lets out a soft groan, but she holds strong.

I pull the zipper down her back. Trace a line back up her spine.

"Adam…"

My cock stirs. I love the way she says my name. I'm powerless to resist it.

"Take it off."

"Take what off?" I ask.

"My dress."

"How should I do that?"

"How?"

"Yes." I trace a line down her spine again. "Should I roll it off your shoulders slowly? Should I push it hard? Should I tear the fucking fabric?"

She shudders as I drag my fingers over her skin.

Higher. Higher. Higher.

They brush her neck.

"Adam." She leans into my touch.

"Yes." I let my fingers curl around her neck.

She lets out a soft groan. An *I need you* groan.

I'm not sure what she wants out of playing in control. Whatever it is, I want to give it to her.

I want to give her everything she wants.

And a million things she doesn't realize she wants.

"I…" She tries to find the words.

"Slow?"

She nods.

I curl my hand around her neck.

She lets out another soft groan. Lets her head fall into my hand.

I'm tempted to pull her close, take her into my arms, throw her on the bed.

But not yet.

This first.

I press my lips to the back of her neck as I trace a line down her spine.

Then back up.

Slower.

Softer.

Again and again.

Her breaths run together.

Her fingers curl into her dress.

Finally, when she's so wound she can't take it, I slide her dress off her shoulders.

Over her chest. Her waist. Her lush ass.

I drop to my knees to peel it off her feet.

My lips brush the small of her back.

She turns. "Adam."

"Yes." I press my lips to her stomach, the spot just above her black underwear. Then lower. Lower.

"I didn't say…"

"Didn't say what?" I place a kiss on her pelvis.

She lets out a soft sigh.

I move lower. Lower.

Closer to where she needs me.

"Adam." Her hand knots in my hair. "Not yet."

I press my lips to her stomach.

"I'm torturing you."

"I'm tortured."

"Are you?"

"Very."

"But you're so calm and in control."

"How else would I be?" I ask.

"Wound so tight you're going to break."

"I am." I slide my arms around her. Pull her to my mouth. "I'm just better at hiding it."

"Fuck."

I kiss her stomach again. Then lower. To the right. The left.

I follow her order.

She lets out another soft groan.

She tugs at my hair.

She slips her hand into my suit jacket. Reaches for my skin. "Off."

"Off?"

"The clothes." She lets out a heady sigh as she tugs at my hair. "Take off your jacket."

"Here?"

"No. Stand up."

I place one more kiss on her pelvis, then I rise. Look into her eyes as I slide my jacket off my shoulders. Drape it over the couch.

"I'm making you wait."

"You are."

"And you are tortured."

"Very."

"So, maybe…" She takes a step toward me. Taps my tie. "This off first."

I undo my tie. Toss it aside.

"Then… normal."

"Normal?"

"You're the one…"

"Are you sure?"

She nods.

Immediately, I lift her into my arms.

She squeals. "Adam. What are you doing?"

"Practice." I hold her to my chest.

"Practice?"

"Carrying my fiancée over the threshold."

Her lips curl into a goofy smile.

She's naked in my arms, in nothing but her shoes and jewelry, and I can't tear my eyes from her smile.

It's so fucking beautiful.

She's so fucking beautiful.

I want to make her smile every day for the rest of my fucking life.

Eleven months isn't enough. It's not even close to enough.

What could ever be enough?

I carry her to the bedroom, push the door open with my feet, lay her on the bed.

She sits up. Motions *come here.*

When I do, she stands, undoes the first button of my shirt.

The second.

She looks up at me, asking for permission, as she traces the third button.

I barely nod.

"Are you sure?" Her voice is soft. Patient.

I'm not sure. I'm not close to sure. But I want to be. I nod.

"Adam—"

I cut her off with a kiss. It's hard, hungry, asking for everything she can give.

She kisses back with equal parts tenderness and need. Offering everything she has. Asking only this in return.

It's nothing.

Her eyes on my body.

Her hands on my skin.

It's everything.

Her eyes on my body.

Her hands on my skin.

She undoes the fourth button.

The fifth.

The last.

She pushes my shirt off my shoulder. The right. Then the left.

Her fingers brush my shoulder. "You're shaking."

"No."

"You are." She traces my collarbone. "I can stop—"

"Don't." I swallow hard.

"Are you sure?"

"No."

She looks up at me with that same patience and tenderness.

This time, when I nod, she lets her eyes drift lower.

Over my chin.

Neck.

Shoulders.

Chest.

Stomach.

All the way to my belt buckle, then back up again.

She traces a scar on my shoulder. "Adam." Then another. Another. "They're not..." Another. Another. "They're..." Her palm goes flat against my chest. "You're beautiful."

"Beautiful?"

She nods. "Yes." She presses her lips to my neck. Shoulder. Chest. "Handsome." Her fingers dig into my skin. "Incredibly sexy."

"Because of the scars?"

"Because you're Adam." She presses her lips to my chest again. "Because they're a part of you. Because you're strong and caring and incredibly well-built."

My eyes close as she traces another scar.

"I'm fucking this up again, aren't I?"

"No."

"You're still shaking."

"I'm terrified."

"Do you want me to stop?"

"No."

"But you—"

I don't know what to say, so I kiss her.

She kisses back with hunger, need, compassion.

How the fuck can there be compassion in a kiss?

It doesn't make sense.

It's not what I want.

It's too close to places that hurt.

But, somewhere, deep down, in some place I don't want to look, I need it.

I need it too fucking badly.

She pulls back with a sigh. "Adam, please." She wraps her fingers around my wrist. Brings my hand to her upper thigh. "Fuck me, please."

That makes sense.

It's the only thing that makes sense.

I guide her onto the bed, onto her back.

She pulls me on top of her. Groans as my skin brushes her.

I wrap my arms around her. Hold her close as I join our bodies.

I should warm her up, tease her, taste her. But I'm too close to breaking.

This. Now.

She groans as I dive into her.

Slowly.

Savoring every sweet inch.

And more. The feeling of her skin against mine.

Every part of her body against every part of mine.

When was the last time I felt that?

Have I ever felt this? This overwhelming sense I'm home?

It consumes me.

From the top of my head to the bottom of my toes.

This is where I'm supposed to be.

With her.

Then her hand knots in my hair, and her lips find mine, and my body takes over.

I kiss her hard as I drive into her.

Slowly.

Softly.

Again and again.

Danielle kisses back, raising her hips to meet me, pulling me closer, deeper.

Further into her.

We stay locked like that, moving in tandem, lips locked, bodies tangled, until she's there.

She groans against my lips as she comes.

Her nails dig into my back.

Her pulsing pulls me over the edge.

I rock through my orgasm, spilling inside her, groaning her name as I come.

After, I collapse next to her, pull her body into mine, hold her close.

Every inch of her against every inch of me.

Every part of her mine.

And every part of me hers.

I ALMOST JOIN HER IN THE SHOWER.

I almost give into my desire to be in that tiny space with her.

But I'm not ready for the harsh fluorescent lights. Not yet.

I wash in the bathroom in the hall, dry, dress in silk pajamas, find her sitting on the couch, staring at the skyline.

"What's wrong?" I ask.

"Nothing. Just… I have to tell you something."

"Right now?"

She nods. "Before I lose my nerve." She turns to me. "Sit. Please."

I do.

"I need you to make me a promise."

"What kind?"

"Promise you'll wait until I'm finished to respond."

"What are you talking about, angel?"

"Can you promise, Adam? Yes or no?"

I nod. "Of course."

Then she takes a deep breath, and she starts.

Chapter Thirty-Nine

DANIELLE

I take a deep breath. Let out a slow exhale.

I'm sitting here, in Adam's penthouse apartment, in the fancy silk pajamas he bought me.

I'm ready to say this.

Okay, that's not true. I'm not ready. I'm not ever going to be ready.

But I'm capable.

I've imagined this conversation a thousand times. With my photographer ex-boyfriend. With a theoretical man. Someone kind and strong and understanding.

Even then, even with my sweet, hypothetical boyfriend, the conversation went poorly.

He was hurt for me. Hurt I didn't tell him sooner.

Too scared.

Or not scared enough.

He understood too well.

Or he had no clue what it meant.

This is different.

Adam isn't theoretical.

He's flesh and blood, here, in front of me.

Warm and hard and safe.

He cares about me.

He supports me.

He sees me.

Is that enough? I don't know. But it's what I have.

And this is what I have to do.

"Danielle?" His voice is soft. Slow. Careful. "Are you okay?"

"I just…" I take a deep breath. "I am. Just. Nervous."

He nods.

It comforts me. I don't know why, but it does.

Okay. Here goes nothing. "Have you noticed?"

"Noticed what?"

"In my photographs? Or maybe when you looped your tie around my wrists." I suck a breath through my teeth. "Have you noticed?"

"I'm not sure what you mean."

"I…" Fuck, I have to do this. I can do this. "You really haven't?"

"Angel, you're scaring me."

"It's not…" Maybe it is bad. I don't know anymore. "It's just something I have to tell you."

Adam's deep blue eyes fix on me.

He studies me intently. Like I'm a subject he's photographing. Like I'm his favorite painting.

No. It isn't that. It's something much scarier.

He studies me the way a man studies a woman.

The way a person studies someone they love.

With all this concern and affection.

It's overwhelming.

Terrifying.

I want to touch him again. I want to disappear into that space where everything makes sense and nothing else matters.

But I have to say this.

I have to get it off my chest.

I take a deep breath. Push my exhale through my nostrils.

The lights are off. The space is dark. Lit only by the soft blue of the city and the silver glow of the moon.

In the dark, my scars are faint. Barely there.

In the dark, he can't see the fear in my eyes.

How the fuck can I do this?

"Are you ever overwhelmed by your feelings?" I run my fingers over the edge of my watch. "By your life going out of control? And you need to do something, anything to take control?"

"What do you think I'm doing with my tie?"

"It's not just your scars?"

He shakes his head.

"But that's a lot of it."

"Yes. But it's the same. The need for control."

"Is that the only thing you've tried?"

"Alcohol."

"Did it work?"

"No."

"Anything else?"

"What's wrong, angel?"

"I guess it's a stupid question. With everything you went through with Bash and the accident. Of course, you felt lost. Of course, you wanted control. I'm sorry. I don't want to speak for you. I just—"

"Slow down." His fingers brush mine.

It brings me back to Earth. "I used to feel like that all the time. Overwhelmed. With nowhere to put my feelings. Even before Mom died. There was always so much going on. There was always so much in my head. And then she died, and I couldn't pull myself together enough to keep us afloat… that's when it got really bad."

"When what got bad?"

"I used to cut." I swallow hard. "I was hurt. Angry. Disappointed. And I knew the only person who could take it was me. So I… I did the only thing I could. To punish myself. To make sense of it. To feel something else, something I could control for one fucking minute. I knew I shouldn't. I knew it was dangerous. But it was addicting."

His eyes stay glued to me.

"For a while I did it all the time. Then Remy caught me. And I told him I'd stop. I went to therapy and started exercising. And I did for a while. But then things got hard again, and I didn't know any other way to handle it. I didn't have anywhere else to put my pain." I turn my arm over. "Most of the scars have faded. They're light. Barely there. Most people don't notice."

Adam runs his thumb over my wrist.

"Did you?"

"No."

"There are so many."

"You wear long sleeves."

"But we were… I was naked."

"Yes. You were naked."

A laugh spills from my lips. "So you wouldn't be looking here?"

He nods.

"I-I didn't know when to tell you. If I should tell you. It doesn't feel fair, to know everything about your scars when you know nothing about mine."

"Did you stop?"

"Mostly."

"Mostly?"

"When I started taking self-portraits. They helped me channel my feelings. Take control."

"But only mostly?"

"A few times. When things were too hard and I was too tired to fight the temptation." I push my watch aside. Run my fingers over the raised marks on my inner wrist. They're harsher, deeper, fresher.

Adam wraps his fingers around my wrist.

Not the way he did before. All softness.

He runs his thumb over a faded scar. Then a fresh one. "This is deep."

"I know."

"You can hurt yourself."

"That's the point."

"Danielle—"

"I know. I'm careful."

His eyes turn down.

"I was careful. I haven't... I haven't since Christmas."

"That was six weeks ago."

"I know," I admit. "I'm not making excuses. I just..."

"No. Don't apologize for explaining yourself."

"You look terrified."

"I am." He intertwines his fingers with mine. "I can't bear the thought of losing you."

"I... me either."

"Are you okay?"

"Am I okay?"

"It's a simple question."

Is it? It feels hopelessly complicated. "I don't know."

He nods. Runs his thumb over the raised scar on my wrist. "Christmas?"

"It was too much. Without Mom. With the mounting bills. With Remy worried about school."

"Danielle—"

"Don't. I appreciate the impulse, Adam. I do. I want to protect you too." I bring my hand to his cheek. Run my fingers over the scar on his cheek.

He doesn't flinch. He leans into the gesture.

"But this is my issue. My burden to carry."

"No."

"No?"

"You asked me not to lock you out," he says. "I'm asking the same."

Fuck. I can't really argue with my own request.

"What did you say? You can tell me to fuck off. You can tell me if I'm overstepping. But don't hide from me. Don't lock yourself away. Don't try to shoulder everything on your own."

I blink and a tear catches on my lashes.

"Angel—" He wipes my tear with his thumb.

"You're not mad?"

"Why would I be mad?"

"I don't know. Remy was mad. And I... I will try. But this is mine, Adam. My problem to solve. Not yours. You can be there, you can listen, you can even step in and tell me I need to get help. But you aren't my shrink. And you can't play my shrink."

"Are you seeing someone?"

"For a little while. But it was too hard. The timing, the fee. I..."

"Will you start?"

"Your house is in the middle of nowhere."

"And I have three cars."

"That's true." I blink, and another tear catches on my lashes. "I... I don't know what to say."

"We can make a deal."

"Sex for therapy? That doesn't sound healthy."

"No." He cups my cheek with his palm. "I'll go if you go."

"Therapy for therapy?"

He nods.

"You're not already?"

"I was. For the first few months. But I wasn't interested in feeling better."

"Only in drowning in self-loathing?"

"Yes." He states it so plainly. And without shame too.

How does he do that?

He keeps proving it again and again.

Adam Pierce is the strongest person I've ever met.

"But you want to get past it now?" I ask.

He nods.

"This a very strange romantic gesture."

He pulls me into his lap.

"But it's perfect too."

"It is." He presses his lips to mine.

I dissolve into him. Body, heart, soul.

Every broken piece of me claiming every broken piece of him.

Love.

It's obvious.

I love him.

I don't know what that means or where to put it.

But I don't want to run from it.

I want to feel every fucking second.

Even if it kills me.

Chapter Forty

ADAM

Sunday night, Danielle asks me to stay in the apartment. She needs to finish preparing for the show and it's easier, here, sixty blocks away.

She wants me to stay with her.

At first, I say no. I'm not sure how I'll survive a week here. It's one thing when she's next to me, filling the space with her laugh, her smile, her groan.

When it's me and the memories threatening to consume me?

That's harder.

But when I wake next to her, I can't bear the thought of leaving. I'd rather face the emptiness here than the ache I feel without her.

Is that love?

I don't know. I only know that I need her. I need her in a way I've never needed anyone.

THE WEEK PASSES MORE QUICKLY THAN I EXPECT. PIERCE IS launching our new privacy suite. I'm busy. And Danielle is working morning to night.

The night before the show, she takes me to the studio after closing.

She puts her hands over my eyes, guides me to the right spot, says, "Okay, now," and pulls her hands away.

There it is.

A story in five images.

Anticipation. Tease. Release.

Sensual photos, erotica even, but not explicit.

Sexy enough, every man in the city will want her.

Every person who sees them will wonder.

Is that really Adam Pierce?

Will they say it with surprise? Disgust? Envy?

I don't know.

Right now, I don't care. I don't care if strangers see me as a monster or a man.

I don't care about anyone but Danielle.

"Do you like them?" she asks.

Like isn't a strong enough word. "They're perfect."

"Really?"

"Yes."

She turns to me with a smile. "Are you nervous?"

"Are you?"

"Very. But I know you… I know it's different for you."

"I'm proud of you."

"Yeah?"

"Very." I bring my hand to her cheek.

She leans into the gesture. "Adam, I… I can't tell you how much it means to me. Your support. Your bravery. Really. I'm so happy we're together. Even if it's not a conventional situation."

I love you. The word forms on my tongue. But my

mouth is too sticky. I've never said it before. Not to a woman.

It's the kind of thing you can't take back.

Like the truth.

She deserves to know why I found her.

She deserves to know every ugly detail.

I can't say it yet.

Not until she knows.

But I can't tell her today. I can't steal her moment.

She's worked hard for this. She deserves it.

She deserves the entire fucking universe.

"It's my honor," I say.

She smiles. "You're like a prince in a fairy tale."

"Am I?"

"Yeah. Formal and chivalrous. And handsome." She runs her fingers over the scar on my cheek. "If you're Prince Charming, what does that make me?"

"You have it wrong, angel. You're the one saving me."

"Broken beauty and the beast?"

I nod.

She smiles. "It's a little wordy. But I like it." Her fingers go to my tie. "You know, Remy is always asking if I blew someone in the backroom."

"Remy? No?"

"I know. Hard to believe he'd ask such an inappropriate question." She laughs. "I never really saw the appeal until now."

"Is that a request?"

"If it is?"

"I have a better idea." I lift her into my arms.

She squeals as I carry her to the backroom.

I set her on her ex-boss's desk, drop to my knees, dive between her legs.

Then I hold her close as I fuck her.

She comes twice.

The second time, with me.

I help her into her clothes, onto her feet, into the limo.

"Better?" I ask.

"Much better." She rests her head on my shoulder. Falls into an easy sleep. Comfortable. Quiet. At peace.

After the busy week, she needs it.

Tomorrow is her day.

After that, I tell her the truth.

That's one more day with her.

I need to savor every minute.

Chapter Forty-One

ADAM

The gallery is buzzing. There are two dozen people in the small space. All in chic clothes, with an air of sophistication, sipping wine and staring at photographs of Danielle.

Me and Danielle.

My stomach flip-flops.

My limbs go light.

Technically, I'm anonymous, but I'm her fiancé. The second people see me with her, they'll put the pieces together.

It's one thing to imagine it.

To actually face a room full of people staring at photos of my hands on her skin?

I force my breath through my nose. I can do this. I will do this. For her.

I take another deep breath, force another slow exhale, then I step into the gallery.

Noise fills my ears. Soft music. Laughter. Snippets of conversation.

Can you believe these photos?

So much like DeLaney.

Self-portraits. How can she show her face?

How can she not? If I looked like that, I'd want everyone to know it was me.

And the man.

Isn't that him?

He's familiar.

The rich guy with the scandal.

"Hey, Adam!" Liam waves like we're a thousand feet away at a theme park.

Everyone in the room looks at him—he's alone today—then at me.

At once, a dozen people add two and two.

The room fills with the energy of the epiphany.

Holy shit, that's Adam Pierce.

The rich guy who killed his brother.

Is he seriously showing off like this?

"You drinking red or white?" He motions to the bar behind him. A dozen bottles of wine next to a row of clean glasses.

I shrug off the attention in the room. Yes, everyone is staring. Half with wonder. Half with a more familiar response—the need to see the freak in great detail.

I'm not here to enjoy the spotlight.

I'm here for Danielle.

And besides, this is what I want. It's what I wanted.

This was the whole fucking idea behind this ridiculous plan.

Make Fitzgerald writhe with envy.

I know he's seen these pictures. I know he's coming—he RSVP'd. But the thought does nothing to soothe me.

I don't care if he sees me with her.

I don't care if he's jealous.

I don't want these strangers to see me, know me, talk about me.

Only Danielle.

"The artist is preoccupied." Liam pats me on the back. "She went all out this time. Best wine under thirty dollars a bottle. It's not bad." He turns to the table, as if no one is watching, pours two glasses, hands one to me. "To you coming out of your cage."

I tap glasses. "To you being an asshole."

"I'll drink to that." He laughs and takes a long sip. "Still tastes like wine. But… not bad, for wine."

It's good wine. Not fancy, maybe, but plenty rich, bold, fruity. I swallow half my glass in one sip. The rest in a second.

Liam laughs *one of those nights* and refills me. He turns to the room, to the people shooting us curious glances. "They're not staring 'cause you're a freakshow."

"Thanks for stating it in such beautiful terms."

"My pleasure. You are a freakshow. But not because of this situation." He motions to my face. "Girls like guys with scars. Shows character."

"Does it?"

"Yeah. You need the photographic evidence?" He motions to the photo in the middle. Me and Danielle. Her naked body against my clothed one. "It's right in front of your beautiful face."

"Don't."

"Don't speak the truth? You know I'm not capable of that." He finishes his glass and refills it. "I haven't said anything, because I know you. I know it won't help. But you're gonna fuck up a good thing here. And I don't want to see that."

"How is that?"

"Maybe you're not ready to step into a room full of

pretentious art assholes staring at you," he says. "But you need to be ready with her. Or you're gonna lose her. And nobody wants to see that."

He's right.

He's often right. But he always expresses his points in the most offensive way possible.

People miss the insight.

Liam nods hello to someone.

Danielle steps between a couple. She smiles at Liam, then her attention turns to me. Every molecule of it.

She bites her lip. Lets out a schoolgirl giggle. One that can only mean *I really, really like you.*

It brings me back to Earth.

I can feel my feet on the ground.

She crosses the room to us, wraps her arms around my waist, brings her lips to mine.

She tastes so fucking good, like red wine and Danielle.

Need overwhelms my senses. Nothing else matters. Nothing else has ever mattered.

She pulls back with a heady sigh. "Mmm. I'm glad you're here." Her palm curls around my neck. "I'm not used to this much staring. Are you okay? It's a lot."

"It is."

"You don't have to stay if it's—"

"You'll have to tear me away," I say.

"Are you sure?" she asks.

For once, I am. "Positive." I don't care how much this hurts. I need to be here for her moment.

"Liam." She turns to him and nods *hello.* "Where's Briar?"

"She isn't my shadow," he says.

"Couldn't bear to let her see photos of a more attractive man?" she teases.

"Danielle, you gotta know you're daring me with that," he says.

"Am I?" she asks.

He nods and tugs at his tie. "One more word and this is coming off."

"What will that do?" she asks.

"Then the buttons," he says.

"You're just going to unbutton your shirt?" she asks.

"*Just* unbutton my shirt?" He feigns insult. "And you're *just* wearing a dress." He motions to her low neckline. "And you're *just* showing off photographs."

She smiles.

"What is that? Danielle! You're killing me here," he says.

She kisses him on the cheek. "Thanks for coming."

"She's learning your tricks," I say.

"I have new tricks," he says. "I never run out."

She laughs. "Thanks for distracting me. I need it. You're sweet."

"Sweet? No, that's not the image I'm curating here," he says.

She mimes pulling a zipper over her lips. "Our secret."

He mimes wiping the sweat from his brow. "You need to mingle more?"

She nods. "People always want to talk to the photographer."

"Especially when they can see her tits," he says.

She flushes. "Especially then."

"Any sales?" he asks.

"A few interested parties," she says. "If you want to put in a bid, I'd do it now."

"No, I'd never get anything done with those on my wall," he says. "Besides, Adam would kill me."

"Is he going to kill whoever buys them?" she asks.

"Just me," he stage whispers. "He's been waiting for an excuse for, oh, twenty-seven years now."

She laughs. "I really like you, Liam."

He has no idea what to do with the sincerity. He freezes.

"You're so much like Remy."

"Danielle!" He mimes being stabbed in the gut again. "Is he here?"

"He was. He's grabbing more wine for me." She beams. "It's busier than I expected. We're almost finished with our supply."

"You're popular," he says.

"Yeah. We are." Her eyes meet mine. She moves closer. Pulls me into another slow, deep kiss.

The rest of the world disappears. It's only the two of us, melting together, in some perfect place where everything makes sense.

Then she pulls back and we're still here, in this busy gallery, all eyes on the two of us.

It's strange.

But it's like the apartment. It's not as hard with her next to me.

"I do need to mingle." Her fingers brush my wrist. "Take care of him for me, okay, Liam?"

"He needs some sex tips. I get it." He winks at her.

She smiles, squeezes my hand one more time, returns to the crowd.

He watches her talk with an older couple in designer clothes. "She's in her element, huh?"

She is. Bright, animated, vibrant. Her passion fills the entire room.

"And damn, everyone looking at these pictures all night. I bet she's fucking soaked already."

"Fuck off."

He chuckles *too easy*. "You are planning on fucking her senseless after this?"

"What do you think?"

"You're different with her."

"Different how?"

"Happy."

"I am."

He teases me as she mingles. People lose interest in us. Turn their attention to Danielle.

She's as luminous as the sun. It's impossible to look away.

I finish another glass. Settle into the space.

Simon joins the three of us.

At nine, Danielle raises her glass, taps it with a fork.

Everyone turns to her.

"Hi, if you don't know, I'm the artist. Danielle Bellamy. This set is called *The Promise*. I made a promise to my model, that I wouldn't expose his identity. Some of you might guess, but he wanted to stay anonymous, and I wanted to honor that."

Half the room turns to me.

She presses on. "That was the seed of my inspiration, this promise I made to honor my model's wishes. Then it became more. The promises we make to ourselves. The promises we make to each other. The trust and vulnerability we share when we take off our clothes, invite someone to truly see us." Her eyes flit to me, then they're back on the room. "I asked a lot of my model. I asked him to trust me with pictures that... well, pictures that didn't make the set, pictures that most people would want to keep private."

A collective gasp fills the space.

"And more than that, I asked him to trust me with his fears, his hopes, his secrets. And he did. Even though it was hard. I want to thank him for that. For being so open and giving. And I want to thank all of you for coming. Enjoy. Drink wine. Eat cheese. Spend a lot of money." She takes a bow.

The room claps.

My stomach twists.

And right on cue, that asshole steps into the room.

Cole Fitzgerald. His jealousy is written all over his face.

It doesn't fill me the way it's supposed to.

Yes, his envy is killing him.

Who fucking cares?

He crosses the room to us. "Mr. Pierce." He extends his hand.

Liam shoots me a *who the fuck is this asshole* look, but he shakes.

"And Mr. Pierce." Fitzgerald looks at me like he's contemplating how he's going to destroy me. "Lovely to see you."

"Always, Cole." I shake.

Simon doesn't hide his disdain either. He ignores Fitzgerald's hand.

Fitzgerald tries to shrug it off, but everyone around us notices.

"Where's your wife?" Simon asks.

Fitzgerald's eyes fill with surprise.

Simon continues, "She's an art lover. Is there a reason you didn't bring her? Besides the obvious?"

Liam looks to me for a clue, but I stay quiet.

Simon knows something.

Does he know everything?

"Should we talk outside?" Simon asks. "Or do you want everyone to hear what I'm about to say?"

Fitzgerald plays along. "I could use some air."

"Of course." Simon motions *after you.*

Fitzgerald moves toward the door.

Then Simon.

Liam starts to follow.

I stop him. "Don't."

"What the fuck, Adam?" he asks.

"I'll explain later," I say. "Make sure Danielle is okay."

"Adam."

"Later." I follow them outside.

The crisp air hits me immediately. It's a cold night. With the tall buildings making wind tunnels, the entire city is howling.

Simon turns to me. For the first time in years, I read him like a book.

He knows. Maybe not everything, but he knows about Bash and Fitzgerald's wife.

He knows I know.

And this, Danielle, the setting, our agreement, Fitzgerald's obsession—

He knows that too.

"I don't like to waste time," Simon says. "So I'll skip the pleasantries. I know who you are. I know who your wife is," Simon says. "And I know what you do when you lose your toys."

Fitzgerald holds a poker face.

"You weren't all that careful, Cole. Foolish, really. You should have known better. This isn't the first time you've fucked with one of your wife's boyfriends," he says. "But it is the first time you went this far."

"I don't have the faintest—"

"Save it for someone who buys it. Bash wasn't like you. He wasn't restrained, jealous, angry. When he was happy, everyone knew. He couldn't stop talking about Celine. At first, he tried to be discreet. He'd refer to her as the married woman. But, well, you don't know Bash, but if you did, you would know he couldn't hold out for long. Fuck, Cole, the way he talked about your wife. You'd probably deck me if I repeated it."

Fitzgerald scowls.

"No. You wouldn't, would you? You're a coward. You need someone else to do your dirty work. But I'm not. I'm happy to repeat a few choice phrases about the low, deep groan she made when she came. The secrets she shared with Bash. That her husband ignored her. That he had no fucking idea how to please her. That she was desperate to leave him. But afraid she didn't know where to land."

"That isn't true," Fitzgerald says.

"That's why you went this far," Simon says. "She was going to leave you. And you wouldn't have that. Better to leave her a broken shell then let her be with someone else. Not because you love her. Not because you need her. Because you can't let anyone else take what's yours."

The door swings open. A couple steps through. Looks at us strangely.

Simon moves away from the door.

I follow.

Fitzgerald too.

We're no longer in view of the show.

Fitzgerald can hurt Simon without witnesses.

Or Simon could hurt him.

I should stop them. Do something. But I can barely move.

Simon knows.

How the fuck does he know?

"I don't have my brother's restraint," Simon says. "I'm willing to stoop as low as you did."

"Simon—"

"Don't bother, Adam. I know what you're doing. I appreciate the ingenuity. But it's too complicated for me."

He looks to Fitzgerald. "Better to keep things simple. Better to destroy the person who hurt you the old-fashioned way. Don't you think, Cole?"

"I don't—"

"You were smart. The evidence I have isn't the type that's admissible in court."

The door swings open again.

Cole looks to it, steps backward, runs off.

I watch him race around the corner.

"Don't worry," Simon says. "I have eyes on him."

"Eyes?" I ask.

"Don't play dumb, Adam. You hired someone to dig into this. That's how you found Danielle, isn't it?"

"Yes," I admit.

"You're using her to make him jealous? Is that supposed to satisfy you somehow?"

"Yes."

"Did it?"

I don't know.

"It would be cheaper to have him killed," Simon says.

"Then why haven't you done it?" I ask.

Simon starts to respond. Then he turns to the door.

To Danielle, standing in the cold, in her low-cut dress, holding a glass of wine.

She stares at me, dumbstruck. "I thought… you might need another glass."

"Danielle—"

"Do you want me to take you home?" Simon volunteers.

"No." Her voice is soft. "I…" Her eyes go to me. "This was about him?"

"Yes," I admit.

"The engagement, the photos, the secrets we shared… it was all about him?"

"No—"

"You told me this was for your brothers," she says. "Because they worry. Not because... because you wanted to use me for revenge." She blinks and a tear catches on her lashes. "You could have told me, you know? I would have agreed. But I... you should go."

"Danielle."

"Please, Adam. Go." She stares at me for a minute, then she turns and disappears into the room.

And, just like before, I'm powerless to resist any request she makes in that voice.

Chapter Forty-Two

DANIELLE

I hold it together for another round of mingling, then I fail to fake a smile. I slip to the backroom. Sink to the cold, hard concrete, pull my knees into my chest, bury my face in the fabric of my dress.

Adam didn't want me because he was worried about his brothers.

He didn't want me because I'm beautiful and passionate.

He wanted me because someone else did.

Was anything he said true?

Did he pick me knowing I'd want to take these photos?

Did he fuck me so I'd want to capture the two of us on film?

Does he care about me at all?

It doesn't make sense.

How can a lie feel so real?

I stay in the backroom, alone, until the show clears. The voices fade, then drop. The lights turn off. The space cools.

Liam steps into the backroom. "Danielle, I should have

told you. I don't like when girls cry. I'm not like Adam that way."

I don't say anything.

He offers his hand. "I promised your brother I'd take you home."

"Is he okay?"

"He's making a sale for you, kid." He waves his hand again. "Or do you no longer want a career?"

"Adam—"

"Yeah, Simon filled me in."

"He did?"

"Not the whole story. But enough." He peels my hand from my knees. "I'm not going to leave you here on the cold concrete. So you might as well come with me now."

"I don't want to hear about Adam."

"I promised him I'd get you home."

"I thought you promised Remy."

"I can't promise multiple people?"

"It's not really the intent."

"Two birds, one stone. Come on. You don't have to go home, but you can't stay here."

"You don't work here," I say.

"Neither do you." He peels my other hand from my dress. "I'll take you to a bar, take you dancing, fill you with coffee. Wherever you want. But not here."

"What if I want here?"

"All right, let's try this. You look me in the eye and tell me you want to sit on the cold concrete floor. You really make me believe. And I will."

"You're annoying."

"Very true." He bends next to me. "Annoying. And not willing to leave you here."

"So you'll keep being annoying?"

"Oh yeah."

"Fine." I take his hand.

He helps me to my feet. Leads me to the main room. Slides my coat over my shoulders. "I called a car."

"I don't have to go home, but I do need to get into it?"

"Exactly."

I follow him into the stupid car. It's a stupid limo, actually, with bench seats and obnoxious mood lighting.

Who wants purple lights?

I'm not going to prom.

I'm a fucking adult.

I cross my legs. Fold my arms over my chest.

"Adam is an asshole." Liam sits next to me. "I am too. That's how I know." He looks to me. "Home?"

"My apartment, yeah."

He relays the information to the driver. When I shoot him a curious look, he says, "Your brother."

"He gave you our address?"

"Is it 'cause he thinks he can turn me?"

"No." A laugh spills from my lips. "Do you think everyone wants you?"

"They do."

Another laugh. Fuck. "I don't want to laugh."

"I know. I'm trying hard, here."

The limo pulls from the curb. I rest my head against the window. Close my eyes. "I've spent more time in a car the last month than the rest of my life combined."

"The mansion is too fucking far from the city," he says. "I thought that when I was fifteen. I know it now."

"You don't stay there?" I ask.

"Fuck no. Moved out the second I could. I have places to go."

"It's just Adam?"

He nods. "He moved back after the accident. At first, because we could fit an entire medical suite in the place.

Then because he couldn't face people. The way they stared. The whispers."

It is horrible, people thinking he killed his brother.

And this thing with Fitzgerald.

It was to make him jealous.

But why?

Why would Adam do that? Unless—

"He's still so handsome," I say. "I can't believe he doesn't see it."

"But he does, Danielle. He's different now."

He is?

"I've known Adam a long time. Twenty-seven years now. And the guy I've seen the last year... that's not Adam. That's a shell of Adam. With you, he's awake and alive and... happy."

God, I want him to be happy.

I shouldn't. He lied to me. He used me. He treated me like a fucking pawn.

How can I still want his happiness this much?

"He cares about you," Liam says. "If I know anything, I know that."

"How?"

"It's fucking obvious. To anyone who looks at him. He spent an hour in a crowded room, full of people staring, for you."

"To make Fitzgerald jealous."

"Was Fitzgerald there?"

"No," I admit.

"So how was he making him jealous?"

"But the photos—"

"Maybe he had some idiotic plan. I don't know the details. But I know he cares about you. And you care about him."

I do.

"Whatever this is, is it really bigger than that?"
I don't know.
I can understand why he did this.
Hell, my heart breaks for him.
But can I forgive him?
Can I ever trust him again?
Can I believe he isn't using me?
That, I can't answer.

Chapter Forty-Three

ADAM

All night, my phone buzzes.

All night, I ignore it.

I can't answer to my brothers.

I can't offer Danielle enough to fix this.

She's right.

I used her.

I hid the truth.

I lied.

Yes, I had my reasons, but they're excuses. She deserved the truth, and I was too cowardly to give it to her.

All night, sleep eludes me.

In the morning, I rise, dress, fall into my routine. Two laps around the grounds. An hour of weight training. Stretching. A shower.

Usually, the workout feels like penance. The ache of cold air against my cheeks in the winter. The pain of the humid sun in the summer. This physical discomfort channeled into something productive.

Today, it feels normal.

Difficult, yes, but routine.

This is how I trained Bash for varsity soccer. We spent more time running and less on weight training, but it was this same routine.

Early mornings, before the rest of the house was awake, no matter what he'd done the night before.

Usually, brutal exercise is a way to make sense of the pain in my heart. Make it physical. Hold it close, since it's all I have left of him.

It doesn't hurt today. Not the way it usually does.

I'm honoring him.

Maybe not the way he'd ask—no doubt, that would involve naked women—but it is something of his. Of ours.

It hits me in the shower. The tension in my jaw releases. Then my shoulders. Relief spreads through my body.

An overwhelming ease.

I barely manage to stay upright.

I love Bash.

I failed him.

I have to let it go.

Holding on to this pain isn't fair to him. It isn't honoring him.

It's selfish.

I close my eyes.

Let his voice fill my head again.

Did you really have to think of me in the shower, Adam? Could you have invited a babe first? You are going to fix shit with Danielle, aren't you? She's gorgeous AND she's a total freak. Perfect for you.

Fix that.

That's how you honor me.

The best revenge is living well.

You know what that means, don't you Mr. Broodypants? Erm. Mr. Put on those Broodypants?

It means getting laid.

Go.

Fuck her.

Love her.

Let her love you.

For me.

I love you, kid.

I'll see you in the next one.

And then I open my eyes and he's gone.

No longer a voice in my head.

No longer haunting me.

No longer protecting my heart.

The walls are down.

And if I want to make this right with Danielle, I have to keep it that way.

Chapter Forty-Four

DANIELLE

For two days, I hide in my room. I leave only to shower, eat, use the bathroom.

Finally, I go to the main room. Accept Remy's offer of homemade French toast and coffee and vampire soaps.

He doesn't ask about Adam. He doesn't push me to talk. He sits next to me, gushing over the hot vampire king, complaining about the lack of full-frontal male nudity, discussing the merits of going vampire for someone.

I almost feel normal.

After a full day of binge-watching, Remy convinces me to leave the house. We get dinner at our favorite Thai restaurant.

I stuff my face with red curry and jasmine rice. Arrive home full, worn, ready for bed.

To a sealed letter and a bouquet of roses at our door.

Of course.

"New secret admirer?" Remy picks up the bouquet. After he opens the door for me, he sets them on the dining table and runs his fingers over the card. "It's addressed to Danielle Bellamy, but if she's not going to open it…"

"Will you not?"

"No. I will not, uh, not. I will." He holds up the card. "You've moped for two days."

"Why can't I mope for once?"

"Mope all you want, Danny. But read the card from the sexy billionaire, huh?"

"But he—"

"He hurt you, yes. Was it unforgivable?"

"Maybe."

"Maybe means no."

"Sometimes it means yes."

"Usually no," he says. "The guy who hides at his mansion let you take pictures of him naked."

"He isn't naked—"

"Whatever. He's fucking you. They're sexy. That's a big deal."

It is.

"Maybe he had an ulterior motive, but he did trust you."

Maybe.

"And he cares about you."

"Are you seriously taking his side?"

"I haven't seen you this bright since Mom died. Even before that… he made you happy. And I'm on the side of happy Danny. If that's his side, then yes, I'm on his side."

Ugh. Why is he using reason?

That's so annoying.

"Fine." I take the card. Break the red seal. Pull out a stack of papers.

A folded note.

And our contract for the year.

Voided.

He has the option to void it at any time, so long as he pays me in full.

"What is it?" Remy asks.

I don't answer. I unfold the note.

Dear Danielle,

I'm sorry I wasn't forthright with you. I should have been honest from the start.

I did hire you because Fitzgerald wanted you. I wanted him to suffer the way I did.

It was a foolish plan. Deep down, I knew that. Deep down, I knew it was an excuse. A way to give myself permission to find you.

I wanted you the second I saw you.

That was true. Not the full truth—my PI is the one who sent me your photos—but most of it.

Your pictures consumed me.

I wanted to touch you, taste you, fuck you.

Because you're an artist.

And because you're gorgeous.

I've never lied about my feelings for you. Or the way you've changed me.

You did convince me to push aside my self-loathing and give in to desire.

Deep down, I knew that.

Deep down, I sought you out because I wanted to fuck you.

At first that was it. I did like you, but, more, I wanted you.

The more I had you, the more I fell for you.

I did.

That's the truth. All of it, completely unadorned.

I love you, Danielle.

I should have told you.

I should have told you everything.

I'm sorry.

I understand if you never want to see me again, but I hope you'll give me another chance.

Even if I don't deserve it.

I promise, I'll do everything I can to make this up to you.

I'm staying at the apartment for the next few weeks. Come by anytime.

Please, even if it's to throw this note in my face, I want to see you.

Love,

Adam

"IT'S GOOD," REMY SAYS. "I CAN TELL IT'S GOOD."

"No." Maybe.

"What does it say?"

"Personal things."

"He apologized?"

"Yes," I admit.

"And…"

"And what?"

"There's an and on your face…"

"He loves me."

Remy's eyes go wide. "Do you love him?"

"I do." It fills the space. A bright light I can't ignore. I love Adam.

"Then what are you doing here! Go get him! What could be more important than that, Danny?"

Chapter Forty-Five

ADAM

A knock on the door rouses my attention.

The jingle of keys.

Footsteps.

"Adam?" A soft voice calls. "Are you here?"

I step out of the office. Through the hallway. To the main room.

To Danielle, standing in front of the door in a short black dress and tall boots, the card I left in her hands.

The seal is broken.

She read it.

She might be here to tell me to fuck off, but she did read it.

"Hey, uh." She runs her fingers over the card. "The transfer went through. I'm not sure if you checked. But it's all there. I'm a millionaire."

"How does it feel?"

"Weird." Her eyes meet mine. "And the photos sold. Not to anyone in the Pierce family, I checked. We're going to be on someone's wall."

"Bedroom wall, maybe."

She half-smiles. "Probably. Do you think they're in it for the art or the eroticism?"

"Isn't that the point?"

"That is what I said."

It is.

"And with what they paid... There are plenty of free pictures of naked people out there. And I... uh, I did mean what I said at the gallery, about the trust. I just—"

"I'm sorry. I know there's nothing I can say to make it right, but I want you to know I'm sorry."

"Thank you."

"I should have been honest."

"I wouldn't have said yes."

"Even so." My eyes meet hers. "It wasn't right to use you."

"Even for a million dollars?"

"I should have told you everything. Maybe not at the beginning. But at some point. Before I fucked you."

"Before you posed for me."

I nod. "I was scared to lose you. More every day. I couldn't bear that thought. I know it's not an excuse, but I want you to know I wasn't pretending to care. I did. I do. I love you, Danielle."

Her eyes go wide.

"You're bright and vibrant and you make me feel bright and vibrant. You turn the world into a beautiful place. A place full of possibilities."

"I love you too."

My limbs go light.

"I... You should have told me, but I understand why you didn't. I understand your impulse. If something happened to Remy... I... I understand." She takes another step toward me. "You meant everything you said?"

"I did."

"And the pictures? Was that for him?"

"I knew it would make him jealous. That was part of it, but it wasn't just him. I wanted the whole fucking world to know someone like you wanted someone like me."

"That's petty, isn't it?"

"Yes."

"I felt the same way." She blushes. "I wanted people to know I was with someone so strong and powerful and handsome."

My cheeks flush.

"It wasn't pretend?"

"No. Never."

"You really want me that badly?"

"More."

"You promise?"

"Is a promise from me worth anything?"

She motions *a little*.

"I promise."

She closes the distance between us. Places her hand on my chest. "I love you, Adam Pierce. There's a lot to figure out, but that... it's so big and bright it takes up all the space in the room. I love you." Her eyes meet mine. "And I really, really need you to fuck me. Please. Adam."

Once again, I'm powerless to resist her request.

Epilogue

DANIELLE

"**A**re you sure?" I check the frame again. Soft glow. White cotton. The perfect blue of the New York City sky. The steel and glass skyline.

And Adam, sitting on the bed, waiting for me.

He's already halfway out of his suit. No jacket. No tie. Top two buttons undone. Sleeves rolled to his forearms.

The scars on his chest visible.

Light and faint, but there.

The signs of what he's been through.

Proof he's survived.

"Adam?" I straighten. Look to him without the camera in the way.

His deep blue eyes fix on me.

My body buzzes. Two years and I still buzz when he shoots me that *I'm going to fuck you senseless* look.

There's no maybe today.

Only the promise he made last night.

We agreed. We try it. On film.

On video.

No cold feet. No last minute no.

393

The two of us, out of our clothes, in front of the camera. For as long as the, ahem, action lasts.

Then, we watch. And we can say *delete it forever* or *replay it every night*.

It's not like this is for public consumption.

Though—

The look on his face right now. The intensity in his eyes, the slight curl of his lips, the light scars on his cheek—

This is my Adam.

I want to take this picture and hold it close forever.

I want to keep it mine.

I want to share it with the world and shout it from the mountaintops.

This beautiful, powerful, vulnerable man is mine.

All mine.

Always.

"I could say anything I want, angel. You're not listening." His voice is light. He's teasing.

"I am too."

"What did I say?"

"You said I'm not listening."

"Before that."

"You didn't say anything."

"Before you asked if I'm sure?" He motions *come here*.

"It's not on yet."

"Then turn it on."

"You didn't answer the question."

He shakes his head. "I did."

"Okay, yes, before I asked if you're sure—"

"For the fifth time."

"You did say yes."

"Do you think my answer will change?"

"No, I just…" My cheeks flush. My chest too. How is it

I'm more nervous than he is? I've been taking naked self-portraits for years. Almost half a decade. And since I met Adam, I've leaned into the eroticism.

But then I'm not in the self-portrait business these days. Not exclusively, at least.

I still post an image as Broken Beauty, of Broken Beauty, once a week.

An explicit one on my website.

A tame one on my social media.

Now, I sell prints. A lot of prints. Liam helped me set it up (after a lecture about how I should have monetized sooner. Under the *I don't give a shit* veneer, he's a helpful guy. And more practical than he lets on).

Those images make up half my earnings. But I'm behind the camera the rest of the time.

After Adam and I made up, I spent a lot of time photographing him. Myself. The two of us together.

I spent a lot of time in his bed.

Or watching soaps with Remy.

I even dragged Adam on vacation. Yes, we went to a secluded island, not a busy city, but I got him in a swimsuit in public.

Well, a private beach.

Adam Pierce in blue trunks on a sunny beach. The mental image is absurd. And absurdly hot.

For the first time in my life, I had room for myself. Room to play. For six months, I didn't worry about money or food or preparing for my future.

I took the pictures I wanted to take. I watched the movies I wanted to watch. I fucked my boyfriend the way I wanted to fuck him.

Okay, it's more accurate to say he fucked me.

But that's a minor technicality.

After six months of playing, and taking self-portraits in

increasingly exotic locations, I started looking for actual photography work.

Small campaigns at first.

A new lingerie company. An aspiring model who needed images for her portfolio. A bride and groom whose photographer bailed on them last minute.

Then a friend of a friend asked a favor. She wanted pictures for her wife. To surprise her on their one year anniversary.

She wasn't a model. She was a normal woman, with no experience posing, and a lifetime of being told she wasn't perfect.

I had to coax her out of her shell. Make her comfortable in front of the camera.

It wasn't like working with a professional model. It was different. More intimate. More honest.

It took a while to get great images, but we got there, then I selected, edited, showed her the final pictures.

The second she looked at me, I knew. That was what I wanted to do.

Danielle Bellamy, boudoir photographer.

Yes, I shoot a lot of fine art in my free time. I hire models, take beautiful black-and-white images of them, pose questions about the line between art and pornography.

And then I go and work with women who've only posed for selfies, who want images for themselves or their partners, who want to feel glamorous and beautiful.

And I give that to them.

It's an amazing feeling.

"Angel, you're already off somewhere." Adam chuckles. "Do I need to lose another layer?"

"You sound like Liam."

"No. Liam would say, 'do I need to whip it out to get

your attention, Danielle? Well, I better try and see how it goes.'" He raises his voice an octave to imitate his brother.

It's dead on.

It's scary.

"Don't do that again," I say. "It's terrifying."

"What are you thinking about?"

"You. Us. The last two years. It's almost our anniversary."

He nods. "Next week."

"We met two years ago. Can you believe that?"

"It's gone fast."

"And we've been through so much. You've been through so much." After we made up, Adam gave me the details about his brother's accident. The foul play he couldn't prove. Not legally.

It made more sense, why he needed to take such drastic measures.

He wanted revenge.

But he knew he had to let go of that to move on.

And he did.

Simon… not so much. I still don't know the aloof older brother that well. He's, well, aloof.

I don't know the details, but I know Simon got his revenge. He's satisfied. The Pierce family is safe.

The other details are his. Maybe the family's.

They're not mine. I don't want them.

I get too protective. If I knew someone wanted to hurt Adam, if I knew every detail of how Fitzgerald hurt Adam—

I'd kill the asshole myself.

I'd do anything to protect him.

And he'd do anything to protect me. Even stupid, reckless things. Especially stupid, reckless things.

"Do I need to whip it out?" he asks.

"Did you just say 'whip it out'?"

"I did."

"Adam Pierce just said 'do I need to whip it out'?"

"You have a problem with that?"

"No." A laugh spills from my lips. "It's just… not very Adam Pierce."

"No." He motions *come here* again.

"You didn't answer."

"I did."

"Say it again."

He shoots me that *really* look. The one the entire Pierce family shares. Even Opal, somehow. Even though she didn't know her brothers until she was a teenager.

"Please."

"I'm sure."

"Thank you." I turn the camera on.

"If I have to say it again, I'm not fucking you."

"Now, I want to call your bluff."

"Then do it."

I shake my head. "I can't risk it." I take another step toward him. "You look too yummy like this."

"Like this?"

I nod.

"Which part?"

"Every part."

He taps his bare chest.

I nod.

The forearms.

Again, I nod.

The tie on the bed next to him.

My cheeks flush. "All of it. I told you." My knees brush his. "I love you." I bring my hand to his chin. "So much it hurts sometimes."

"I know."

"You know?"

He nods.

"What happened to 'I love you, too'?"

"Angel, you're too easy."

"Too easy how?"

"To tease."

"This is how you tease me now?"

He pulls me into his lap.

I gasp as I straddle him. "Adam."

"I love you too."

"Yeah?"

"Have you ever doubted it?"

"Never." It's in everything he does. The coffee he fixes me every morning. The look he gives me when I climb out of bed. The way he holds me. The attention he pays as I describe the events of my latest soap. The way he teases.

How can the woman who loves obscure foreign films also love such trashy television?

I feel it more every day.

I love him more every day.

It's scary sometimes. It hurts sometimes. But in a good way. In a really good way.

"Do you?" I ask.

"Do I what, angel?"

"Ever doubt I love you?"

"Love me? Or love me as much as you love photography?"

"Don't be ridiculous."

He laughs. "I know where I rank."

"Adam—"

"I'll never compete with your camera."

"Is that what this is?" I ask.

"You didn't realize?"

"So this is kind of... a weird threesome," I say.

He nods. "Me, you, camera."

"It's a good combination."

"I know." He pulls me into a slow, deep kiss. His tongue slips into my mouth. Dances with mine.

My body melts into his.

My thoughts drift away.

There's so much I want to say to him. There's always so much I want to say to him. But this is everything.

This is bliss.

I bring my hand to his cheek. Run my thumb over his temple. The soft skin. The raised scars.

All the pieces of him.

Broken. Mended. Everything in between.

He doesn't flinch or freeze. He leans into the gesture.

Then he undoes the sash holding my robe together.

The sides fall open.

I groan as he cups my breasts.

He teases me with his thumbs. Slow circles. Feather light. So light I can barely feel them.

But fuck, how I feel them.

My eyes close.

My hips buck against his.

He's already hard.

I rock my hips against him, savoring the feel of his cock against my sex. His slacks and boxers are in the way. The soft wool of his suit is so different than his smooth skin.

But I can still feel him.

He presses his palm to the space between my shoulder blades. Pulls my chest to his mouth. Wraps his lips around my nipple.

Fuck.

He sucks softly.

Then harder.

The soft scrape of his teeth.

Then harder.

Enough it hurts.

But fuck, it hurts so good.

"Adam." I reach for him. Get his shoulder.

He tortures me with soft scrapes of his teeth. Winds me tighter with every brush. Again and again.

Until it's too much to take.

Then again.

Again.

I rock my hips against him.

My fingers brush his neck. Collarbones. Chest.

The soft skin under his shirt.

The raised scars.

He slows as I trace one. Pulls back. Looks up at me like I'm the only thing he's ever wanted.

He's not shy about his scars. Not exactly.

But he's still careful. This is a lot for him. I'm pushing him.

We push each other. That's what we do.

We trust each other enough.

"Danielle." He presses his lips to my collarbone.

I run my fingers over his chest. Not tracing his scars, but not avoiding them either.

Lower and lower. Until I have to shift back to make room.

"Stand," he whispers.

I do.

He stands with me. Takes my hand. Brings it to his collar. "Take it off."

I push his shirt off his right shoulder. Then the left.

I take my time running my fingers over his shoulders, chest, stomach. The soft skin. The ridges of muscles. The rough scars.

The raised lines of ink. The tattoo on his side. The one he got to remember his brother last year.

And the other.

The one he got with me.

A rose wrapped around a key.

To match the one on my side. A lock, sitting on a bed of petals.

He leans into my touch. His eyes close. His lips part with a groan.

But he stays patient.

Even as I undo his belt, unbutton his slacks, push them off his hips.

Then the boxers.

My robe.

I take it in for a moment. Adam and I, completely naked, in front of the camera, in his modern penthouse apartment.

Our modern penthouse apartment.

And we're about to fuck on film.

It's perfect.

I rise to my tiptoes to kiss him.

The kiss he returns is hard, hungry, completely without patience.

He pulls me onto the bed. Lays me on my back. Pushes my thighs apart.

Then he climbs on top of me.

I wrap my legs around his waist as he brings our bodies together.

His tip strains against me.

Then it's one sweet inch at a time.

Fuck.

He feels so good. Hard and warm and mine.

He feels like home. There's no other way to say it.

For a second, I savor the feel of his body against mine.

The two of us, in our bed, completely without pretenses.

As intimate as anything has ever been.

I wrap my arms around him.

Then he kisses me like he's claiming me. Like he knows I'm his as much as I know he's mine.

I rock my hips to meet him.

He drives into me.

We move together, in perfect rhythm, every thrust pushing me closer and closer.

Until I'm so close I can taste it.

Then he flips me onto my stomach, slides his hand between my legs, rubs me as he drives into me again.

The tension in my sex winds tighter and tighter.

Until I'm so taut I can't take it.

With the next brush of his fingers, everything inside me releases. I groan his name as I come, my sex pulsing around his cock, pulling him closer, deeper.

It pushes him over the edge.

He scrapes his teeth against my neck as he comes, rocking into me, spilling every drop.

When he's finished, he collapses next to me, pulls my body into his, holds me like he'll never let go.

We linger there for ages. Until the camera beeps with a low battery warning.

"Fuck." A laugh spills from my lips. "I forgot."

He smiles. "Should we watch it now?"

"Later. I need to shower before dinner." I slide out of bed. Stretch my arms.

Then he says the last thing I expect. "I'll join you."

He's never done that before. We've never been in that small space together.

Something about the lights. Or his memories. I don't know.

"I can't promise I won't try to fuck you again," I say.

He cups my cheek with his palm. "I wouldn't want you to."

I lead him into the shower, run the water, climb into the small space with him.

He helps me soap, rinse, condition.

Then I do the same for him.

We stay there for a long time. Until we're prunes.

He helps me dry. Dresses as I finish my hair and makeup.

I see it when I step into the bedroom.

Adam, at the modern dresser, his back to me, his eyes on something in his hands.

A tiny blue box.

A real engagement ring.

He runs his finger over the metal. The rock. Takes a deep breath.

Then he closes the box. Hides it under his black boxers.

I jump into the bathroom. Force my eyes to the mirror.

He's going to ask.

For real this time.

Adam Pierce is going to ask me to marry him.

Two years ago, the request was terrifying.

Now, it's everything.

I adjust my hair again. Add one more coat of lipstick.

When I step into the bedroom, he looks at me like he's considering the question.

"You ready, angel?" He offers his hand.

I take it. "I am."

"You're thinking something?"

I'm going to blow the surprise. And I know Adam. He's planning something special. "That I want to go again."

"Already?"

"What do you mean already?"

"You're insatiable."

"You love it."

"I do." He cups my cheek with his palm. Pulls me into a soft, slow kiss. "I love everything about you."

When I pull back, I'm shaking. "Is that a yes?"

"What do you think?"

"After dinner?"

He nods. "After dinner. Trust me. It will be worth the wait."

Want More?

What are Danielle and Adam up to in a few years? Read the Broken Beast extended epilogue to find out.

Playboy Prince, Liam's story, is coming soon. (Keep scrolling for a sample. Sign up for my mailing list for exclusive updates, details, and excerpts).

In the meantime, check out *Dirty Deal*, a sexy Cinderella story. Kat is broke and out of options. Billionaire Blake Sterling is willing to dig her out of debt... if she submits to his demands.

Playboy Prince - Special Preview

LIAM

"You're like a son to me."

No.

That's a bad beginning.

No one follows *you're like a son to me* with *and this party is going to be off the chain.*

Or *I'm sending you to the Caribbean for two weeks, on me.*

Or *have this fine scotch I've been saving.*

Not that I want the scotch.

I know, I know. I'm a spoiled rich kid. I'm supposed to wear designer suits, smoke cigars, sip scotch.

I've got the suit down—according to Briar, the navy tie brings out my blue eyes—but the rest?

Cigars are nasty.

Scotch is bitter.

I'll take a mixed drink any day. The more embarrassing the better. I love the look I get when I sip a Cosmo or an Appletini.

Men roll their eyes.

Women giggle. Ask for a sip. Fall into my fucking arms.

Easy peasy.

"Sit," Preston continues. "Have a drink with me." He motions to the leather arm chair across from him. Pulls out a decanter filled with brown liquor. Two brandy glasses.

Bad news.

I'm being indicted. It's been nice knowing you, kid news.

"Let me get that." I pick up the bottle. Fill both glasses. Sit in the burgundy arm chair across from Preston.

The same way I have a hundred times.

Dad died when I was a kid. Preston was there. Every Thanksgiving. Every Christmas. All fucking summer.

Every break, he called me into his study, sat me down, told me how much he appreciated me.

Then...

I got into a lot of trouble as a kid. I get into trouble now, but I'm smart enough to get myself out of it.

I don't need him calling the principal. Or the parents of a fellow student. Or every person on the school spirit team.

Preston Charles doesn't bail me out of jams anymore, but he still looks out for me. He's the only father figure I have left. And he's sitting there, reminding me I'm like a son to him, with a mournful look on his face, and a bottle of expensive booze on the table.

Bad. Fucking. News.

I feel twelve again.

The way I did when he sat me here to explain my dad died of surgery complications.

It's the office. The stupid shelf full of economic theory.

The oak walls.

The hardwood floors.

The leather chairs.

It's too familiar.

"You're supposed to pour two ounces." He waits for me to settle. "But you've always marched to the beat of your own drum, Liam." He stares into the middle distance with a soft smile. One of those *I'm lost in a memory* smiles.

I appreciate the look on a former fuck. When it's *oh God, do you remember that night in Paris, up against the wall? I've never come that many times before.*

This?

I can't fucking do this.

Sincerity isn't in my wheelhouse.

Uh-uh. No way. Absolutely not.

"Give it a chance." Preston raises his glass. "Cheers."

"Cheers." I raise. Force a smile. Swallow a mouthful.

A little sweet, fruity, the distinct taste of expensive alcohol.

Not my preference. But if I'm having this fucking conversation?

I down half my glass.

Preston sets his on the side table. "How is it?"

"Fucking fantastic." I finish the rest. Refill. Settle into my seat.

Preston holds his gaze. The parental one I know. Only mixed with something I can't place.

Usually, I read people well. It's the key to fucking with them properly.

Right now—

It's bad. I know it's bad.

"Harrison's wedding is going to be great." I swallow another sip. Try to find some other change in subject. Harrison is Preston's son. His only son. This is prime celebration time.

Not prime sitting in the study wistfully time.

But, hey, there's booze. That's the common denominator. Drink to celebrate. Drink to mourn. Drink to numb.

Doesn't matter as long as it's good.

"It will be quite the spectacle." Preston nods. "He's over the moon. He adores her."

"It's good to see him in love." It would be. If his fiancee wasn't as awful as she is gorgeous.

"It is. He's over the moon." His eyes go to his cup of brandy. "I said that didn't, I?"

"Good to hear it twice." My next sip is sweeter. Fruitier. The alcohol is working. Thank fuck.

"I want him to enjoy the festivities without worrying about me."

"We've got a boss bachelor party planned."

"I'm afraid I'm losing my ability to keep up appearances."

Fuck.

"Liam, I mean it. You're like a son to me. Simon and Adam too." He mentions my older brothers. "And Bash... I still feel that loss. I can't imagine how much you miss him."

No, we're not going there. This conversation is torture enough. We're not adding my kid brother's death to it. "He was unstoppable."

"You've always been my most difficult son." He offers a soft laugh. "The best liar."

I don't like where this is going.

"I need your help now."

"Anything."

"I'm dying."

All the air leaves my lungs at once.

The room stills.

I can hear the hum of the air conditioner, taste the apricot in the brandy, smell the leather and oak.

He just—

I—

Fuck.

"I hate to tell you this way, son. I do." His words are practiced. Sure. "I hate to ask this of you."

What the fuck am I supposed to say to that?

"This is Harrison's time. The happiest in his life. I want him to enjoy his wedding without this specter hanging over his head."

"He'd want to spend time with you."

"He will. After the honeymoon. We're setting up the London office together. For six months. That's longer than... I'll tell him once we're settled."

That sounds like bullshit, but I can't exactly argue. *Hey, dying father figure, take my advice on how to handle your relationship with your son. Cause I'm the expert.*

"I know how much I'm asking, Liam. But I need your help."

"How?"

"The symptoms are starting to show. He's going to notice."

"And you need me to cover for you?"

"Like you did for Harrison, when he snuck out to meet his girlfriend."

"You knew about that?"

"Harrison's footsteps woke me up."

He does clomp like a Clydesdale. "Simon? Adam? Your colleagues?"

"You're the only person I've told."

Fuck.

"I know what I'm asking. And I know you're capable."

He's right. I can cover for him. Say we spent the night partying. At the clubs late. Drinking too much apricot brandy. Watching the opera.

If anyone doubts me, I'll distract them with a ridiculous claim about dancing on the bar or buying a six thousand dollar bottle or bedding a soprano.

It's not hard to deceive people. Not practically speaking.

But the blow back from lying to my friends and family?

My co-workers?

My oldest brother Simon is already the most distrustful person on the planet. Now that he has a year of digging into a suspicious accident…

That's not an easy feat.

"I know it's a lot to ask. Especially with your fiancee here."

My what?

"Briar. She's perfect for you. I never thought I'd see the day. Liam Pierce finally settling down. My son marrying the woman of his dreams. And Adam's found someone too. This isn't easy. But it's easier, knowing my boys are happy."

"I'm—"

"I know. Simon is still closed to love. It's not perfect. But I can see it coming for him. He isn't like you. He wants to love and be loved. He just can't admit it."

"But—"

"I never worry about him. I didn't worry about Adam until the accident. But you, Liam…" He lets out a joyful laugh. It fills the air. Brings color to the room. "I worry about you. You and Harrison. Knowing you've found someone… it's a wish come true."

Fuck.

"If you can't lie to your fiancee, I understand. It's no way to start a marriage. But I can't have anyone looking at me like I'm falling apart. Please. Do me this kindness." He presses his palm into the arm of the chair. Uses it for leverage to push himself up.

All at once, I see it.

The lack of color in his cheeks, the thinning brows, the loose suit.

The man who sees me as a son is dying.

He's disappearing, one piece at a time.

First, the flesh around his middle, the hair, the complexion.

Then the movement, the energy, the spirit.

I've seen it before.

I don't want to see it again.

But he's right.

It's his call.

And I owe him more than this.

"Will you help me, Liam." He offers his hand. "Please?"

"Of course." I shake. Promise to lie to my friends. My family.

And to my father figure too.

Briar isn't my fiancee.

She isn't my girlfriend.

She's not even a fuck buddy.

And, somehow, I've got to convince her to play my paramour for the next two weeks.

Author's Note

Do you want to hear something funny?

I started *Broken Beast* because I didn't want to write about grief.

I know. I fucked that one up.

When I finished my previous series, Dirty Rich, I wasn't sure what I wanted to do. I wasn't sure if I wanted to officially end the series. After all, I had so many exciting Dirty titles left. Dirty Letters, Dirty Promise, Dirty Demands… the list goes on. But the series was reaching a natural conclusion and I was itching to do something new.

Something like my other books--the close-knit California bad boys in found families--but still new to me. So I thought, well, what if I take what I liked about this Dirty Rich series (boys in suits, luxe settings, the problems of the rich) and married it to what I like about my other series (banter, humor, family dynamics, secrets, main characters who march to the beat of their own drum). It was a perfect plan. I even veered away from a grief heavy start--a dying patriarch and his wish to see his son married. That was too close, too painful. I needed something else.

My subconscious didn't agree. (That idea eventually became the starting point for Liam's book). That's the funny thing about writing. At least, the way I write. It's intuitive. My subconscious gives me away before I consciously realize what I'm doing. When I catch quotes from my old books, I always think, "of course, I said that."

I didn't go in with an intentional message or theme, but it was there, built into the characters, waiting to spring from the back of my mind.

I tried to start this story a bunch of ways, but this was the one that worked. The one centered on grief. And it was hard to watch Adam let go. It was hard to say goodbye to the Bash voice in his head. By the time I finished the book, Bash was my favorite character! And he was already gone.

But that's life. We love, we lose, we struggle to move on. If we're lucky, we don't lose too many people. But we all face loss. Family, friends, colleagues. People we love, people we hate, people we barely know. We all have to ask ourselves: what the fuck does my life look like without this person?

I'm not sure I have any insights. If I do, they're in these books. I've pitched this series, to my husband, as being about death, sex, and secrets. And that *really* comes to a head in Liam's book.

I can't wait to share it with you, to show you a new angle on the same characters and events. That's the fun of romance series. Looking at something from multiple angles, moving the story along in different ways. This is my first time writing an actual series arc--at least, a specific one. (The guys in Sinful Serenade do have a trajectory of some kind). An actual villain. Right now, I don't know what's going to happen with the Pierce family and their struggles with closure, revenge, love. And that's an exciting place to be.

I can't wait to finish this series and I can't wait to share it with you.

I hope you loved Adam & Danielle as much as I did.

And I know you'll love Liam and Briar as much as I do. Liam is my favorite kind of guy: a troublemaker with a heart of gold.

I hope to see you then.

As always, thanks for reading. Thanks for going on this journey with me. I hope you loved the book. But, more than that, I hope it made you think or feel something.

Love,

Crystal

Acknowledgments

My first thanks goes to my husband, for his support when I'm lost in bookland and for generally being the sun in my sky. Sweetheart, you're better than all the broken bad boys in the world.

The second goes to my father, for insisting I go to the best film school in the country, everything else be damned. I wouldn't love movies, writing, or storytelling half as much if not for all our afternoon trips to the bookstore and weekends at the movies. You've always been supportive of my goals, and that means the world to me.

A big shout out to all my beta readers. And also to my ARC readers for helping spread the word to everyone else in the world.

To all my writer friends who talk me down from the ledge, hold my hand, and tell me when my ideas are terrible and when they're brilliant, thank you.

Thanks so much to my editor Marla, and to Angela Haddon for the cover design.

As always, my biggest thanks goes to my readers.

Thank you for picking up *Broken Beast*. I hope you'll be back for *Playboy Prince*, Liam and Briar's story.

Made in the USA
Monee, IL
27 February 2022

91969459R00249